SAINTS + SINNERS
2013

NEW FICTION
FROM THE FESTIVAL

SAINTS + SINNERS 2013

NEW FICTION
FROM THE FESTIVAL

edited by

Amie M. Evans and Paul J. Willis

SAINTS+SINNERS

2013

SAINTS + SINNERS 2013:
NEW FICTION FROM THE FESTIVAL
© 2013 BY SAINTS & SINNERS LITERARY FESTIVAL. ALL RIGHTS RESERVED.

ISBN 13: 978-1-62639-030-0

THIS TRADE PAPERBACK ORIGINAL IS PUBLISHED BY
BOLD STROKES BOOKS, INC.
P.O. BOX 249
VALLEY FALLS, NY 12185

FIRST EDITION: MAY 2013

CREDITS
EDITORS: AMIE M. EVANS AND PAUL J. WILLIS
PRODUCTION DESIGN: SUSAN RAMUNDO
COVER DESIGN: SANDY BARTEL

Acknowledgments

We'd like to thank:

The John Burton Harter Charitable Trust for their continued support of the contest and anthology as well as the Festival.

Radclyffe & Bold Strokes Books for their continued support of the Festival.

Sandy Bartel for her fabulous cover design.

Felice Picano for serving as this year's final judge.

Everyone who has entered the contest and/or attended the festival over the last 10 years for their help in keeping the written LGBT word alive.

Greg Herren and Wendy Stone for supporting us in countless ways during our endless projects.

CONTENTS

INTRODUCTION
Felice Picano   1

WHAT TOOK YOU SO LONG?
Vince Sgambati   5

IT ONLY OCCURRED TO ME LATER
Anne Laughlin   23

BRUNO'S LAST SUPPER
Jeff Lindemann   39

THE FAVOR OF A REPLY
Joe Landrum   59

THOU SHALT NOT LIE
N.S. Beranek   73

IN A CHAMBER OF MY HEART
Sandra Gail Lambert   91

MOUNTAINVIEW
James Russell   109

LOOKING FOR PHILIP
George E. Jordan   129

BUCKY AND THE WOODS COP
Jim Stewart   141

SILVER PUMPS AND A LOOSE NUT
    J.R. Greenwell   155

STAINED GLASS
    Karis Walsh   173

SKY BLUE
    'Nathan Burgoine   187

CONTRIBUTOR BIOS   201

ABOUT THE EDITORS   205

INTRODUCTION

Ten years isn't a great deal of time in a human life. We consider a person of ten a child. But in terms of an annual arts event, ten years is a golden decade of achievement to be celebrated. In a rapidly changing landscape, that long a span of time signifies endurance, as well as the fulfillment of a need, and, on top of that, it signifies that a certain high level of quality is perceived by those attending and wishing to attend.

When it first came around, the Saints and Sinners Literary Festival for writers and readers was seen as an outgrowth of the successful Tennessee Williams Festival, held a few months earlier in the year. It was also viewed as a replacement for those previous LGBT conferences such as OutWrite which had been around for a while, moving from city to city—year by year.

Unlike OutWrite and other forebears, Saints and Sinners had several real advantages that I believe are responsible for its continuation and improvement. First, it is set in New Orleans and who doesn't want to visit the Crescent City? It is one of the oldest, one of the most vulnerable, and certainly one of the most unique cities on our continent. If you like books, food, poetry, music, and good living, or any combination thereof, you must visit The Big Easy.

Then there's the question of size, and while most Americans and certainly most gay male Americans believe that bigger is better, Saints and Sinners handily disproves that axiom. Unlike the huge earlier conferences, this one is manageable, and at times even intimate. Take for example the 2010 Saints and Sinners Festival that I attended. I was lodged in the nearby Faubourg Marigny, a good fifteen to twenty minute walk to most of the S&S venues, which means little to me as I'm an inveterate walker. Yet I spent most of my time from morning until sometimes quite late at night either attending readings or panels, or having meals with people I knew or had just met who were also attending.

There were enough writers whose work I admired or whose topics interested me that I'd often go from one lecture or panel to another, from one reading to another. And yet there was also enough time in between in the common room spaces to relax and plan out the next literary treat to come. The atmosphere was so conducive to conversation, discussion, and just getting to know one another that I and all the writers I met were hesitant to be out of each others presence except to get some much needed sleep late at night.

Clearly that means that there is an ongoing need for Saints and Sinners. As writers we are separated by large spaces that are certainly bridgeable by our phones and tablets and e-mail, but nothing can replace five authors talking around a table for two hours over crayfish etouffe and jamabalya and a pitcher of beer. Amazing what gets said, what is revealed. And it's good for networking too.

The Saints & Sinners Festival's annual short fiction contest and, in the past, the playwriting contest are reason to be in New Orleans in May. I'm pretty choosy where I decide to send in new fiction or dramatic writing. One reason is because I've luckily reached the point where I don't have to: people ask me. Despite that, I have anonymously entered both contests, and trusting in the integrity of the S&S Festival staff and judges, I've come out pretty well. So, when I was asked to judge the short stories this year, I felt honored. I knew that I would be given free rein to read and evaluate some interesting new short fiction—if past anthologies were any indication.

Nor was I wrong. When the batch of finalists were sent my way, I cleared my reading table, and sat down. Every day for some time I read two of them, thought about them, let them roll around my mind like a good brandy rolls around your mouth and tongue for its individual flavor and weight.

What I most liked about the stories as a group was that they were so—improper. Not salacious, or pornographic—although one is ribald, delightfully so. No, they were improper because they were not the standard, typical urban tales I'm so used to reading from various academically acceptable literary Queer collections. Instead, like the city of New Orleans, like the Saints and Sinners Festival itself, the stories were wildly individual, a little gamey, some deeply introspective, others wildly anti-religious, others simply laugh out loud funny, while others were shocking, painful to read, and eloquent: all of them stand apart. They really did need to be read separately: there is not a cookie-cutter patterned tale in the bunch of them.

So I really enjoyed the variety. For example I think that "Bruno's Last Supper" is a hoot—Flannery O'Connor on Angel Dust—and a must-read for anyone who had been subjected to religious training of any kind. "Bucky and the Woods-Cop" is a lot of fun, in terms of its inventive and sexy plotting, its one of a kind characters, and its surprising pro-ecology finale.

By contrast, "In a Chamber of My Heart" has absolutely superb writing. I was inside this woman's life in one page, and when the story was over, even though I felt that her life and her one love were completed, I was sorry to leave.

"What Took You So Long" again has evocative writing, and I loved the unique angle of this story, this new perspective by which we see successful LGBT lives from another other's sudden and final understanding. I also loved the lesbian couple's old friend Merrill: I feel I know him.

"Sky Blue" is a family story of intolerance and contrariwise acceptance that is painful, and yet resolved, and it is told just right. "Mountainview" is also surprising in how a fairly ordinary tale of teen bullying suddenly becomes upstaged and put in its place by a major world event.

In "Stained Glass" we meet two of the more wounded of contemporary lives, those who have become damaged and wary of any kind of relationship, but are forging something together. These women and their tenuous, so oddly connecting relationship. are new in American fiction. This story felt like the first chapter of a novel. I hope it is.

"Silver Pumps and a Loose Nut" reminded me of when I met my partner. Although the butchest of young men, he lived in a Greenwich Village building the police called 'Love American Style'. Needless to say, the Trans tenants accounted for a lot of NYPD visits because of the drama, drama, drama—which as pals we got to see close up. The author does a lovely job here of relaying that overly dramatic life and nails it all exactly: including the last image of high heels as victory symbols.

But all of the stories are worthwhile. I urge you to read them and savor them.

Hope to see you at the S&S Festival next year in New Orleans!

Felice Picano, 2013

Runner up

What Took You So Long?
Vince Sgambati

Nick said that the will granted Ida lifetime rights to the house and its surrounding eight acres. Nothing would be sold before she died unless she agreed to it. Nick had mentioned that he was the sole heir to assuage her concerns—he was quite comfortable with his Aunt Winifred's wishes. Ida asked him if he wanted a drink.

"Beer or something stronger?" Ida said. A lit cigarette hung from her frown, and behind blue smoke her face was a grille of February frost.

Nick wondered if Ida had always been sharp edges and abrupt angles or had age stolen some hint of softness. Most likely she was never pretty. He had seen pictures of her, but she was well into her forties when the photos were taken. Handsome was the most you could have said about Ida and that was being kind. Before her, there were photos of Millie, but Nick had never met Millie, nor Ida for that matter, not until that day when he told her the details of his aunt's will, as if she hadn't already known them. They sat beside the creek, beneath hemlocks, and she used gardening shears to cut open the plastic bag of powdered ash and chips of bone.

"Here, you do the rest," Ida said and handed him the open bag then lit another cigarette.

"Isn't there something we should say?" Nick asked. "Maybe read a favorite poem or prayer?"

"I've already said goodbye," Ida muttered. "This isn't Freddie. No way she'd be sealed in a bag. How's that for a prayer?" Maybe it was the cigarette smoke that caused Ida's eyes to tear.

Nick whispered Amen.

He thinks of that day and tastes the shock of Ida's Bloody Marys, more vodka and hot sauce than tomato juice, as he unfolds a letter signed by Jonathan Wheaton, Esq., Skaneateles, New York, and then reads Ida's enclosed obituary. They had exchanged empty words—he and Ida—as empty as her obituary, which says nothing of his Aunt Winifred, just as Winifred's obituary had said nothing of Ida.

The house is now Nick's to do with as he pleases. Only his. No kids to consider, and as of four months ago, no wife either. An amicable divorce, little fuss over money. She made more than him anyway; Nick could keep his teacher's salary. No pets. She was allergic to dander, cats and dogs, or so she said. Plants? Who had time to water them? However, she had found time for affairs. He pretended not to notice, like he pretended not to notice the birth control pills she said she had stopped taking after he suggested children, only a suggestion. Nick wasn't one to make demands. Ultimately, his wife's indiscretion with a delivery boy, one of Nick's high school students, would be his final humiliation. When he asked her for a divorce, she simply smiled and said, "What took you so long?"

He folds Ida's empty obituary. Selling his aunt's house might be just the distraction he needs. He remembers little of the house except that like many tired, old farmhouses it was in a state of quaint decline and its furnishings were flea market, circa 1950. No heirlooms would be discovered among the laminate and Naugahyde, but the surrounding trees were magnificent and it's only four hours from the George Washington Bridge. He can use a change of scenery before starting his new teaching position.

❖

The crushed stone driveway announces Nick's arrival. A forest of conifers and deciduous trees give way to threesomes and couples and solitary specimens framing the driveway and house. Did he inherit his love of trees from his aunt? Except for random facts, Nick knows little of his Aunt Winifred: she was his father's only sibling and ten years his father's senior, served as a WAC in World

War II, graduated from Wells College, worked as a school social worker, hated the name Winifred, owned a house upstate, and had a *friend*, Ida, whose very name caused Nick's mother to roll her eyes. He had been in Winifred's company at family gatherings—holidays, graduations, weddings, funerals, etc...—but like his paternal grandparents, Nick found her to be aloof, or, as his mother said, cold.

Nick's father was from white, protestant stock dating back to Mayflower times, but his mother was second-generation Sicilian, and Nick grew up mostly among Sicilians and other Italians, a stark contrast to his father's family. Plus, there were bad feelings. Nick's paternal grandparents and aunt felt that his father was marrying down; in fact, they didn't attend his parents' wedding. Nick's mother was not one to forgive—ever—even after Nick was born and his grandparents spent their remaining years making amends, especially after his father died prematurely. "A curse," his mother said, "from your father's heartless parents."

Nick's mother had often complained to his father, "You know damn well that if Winifred had found a husband and given your parents grandchildren, we'd never hear from them." But there was no discussion about why Winifred hadn't found a husband, just rolling eyes and snide remarks. And Nick's grandparents, already tightlipped, were mute about Winifred. The only hint that Winifred was more than a list of random facts were the few photographs circling the mirror in her childhood bedroom in her parents' house where she slept when she visited and moved back into during her parents' declining years.

"Who's that, Aunt Winifred?" Nick had asked as he pointed to the photo.

"Ida," she answered.

"And that, Aunt Winifred?"

"Millie," she answered.

But no matter.how many times Nick asked her, she offered the same terse response. He learned early not to ask her questions.

From the front porch he looks out across Willowdale Road where acres of hayed land slope away to hedgerows of willows, sugar maples, and ash trees. He views glimmers of Otisco Lake through breaks in the hedgerows, and beyond the lake are more hills, mostly wooded, but with patches of farmland. Above the hills, blue-white clouds, like immense vaporous circus animals, lumber across the sky and draw giant shadows along the landscape.

Inside the house smells of shut windows and loneliness. Less faded patches of wood flooring, carpet, and wallpaper speak of missing furniture. The lawyer assured Nick that Ida's nieces had removed only *their* aunt's belongings. Maybe a great niece or great nephew was furnishing a college apartment. Who else would want such junk? One room is empty, except for a photograph of his aunt— probably Ida's bedroom or a study. Another bedroom, most likely Winifred's, has numerous framed photographs hanging on walls or perched on a dresser. Like in her childhood bedroom pictures are taped around a mirror. He recognizes his grandparents and Ida and maybe Millie. But there are others, not familiar. Snapshots of Winifred's life: picnics, boating, fishing, and cross-country skiing. On a desk is a studio portrait of Winifred and Ida resembling each other the way old couples do. There's also a small picture Winifred must have taken of Nick at his college graduation.

Nick unpacks the few things he has brought with him and places in the dresser—shirts, underwear, and socks atop of his aunt's clothes then hangs a pair of jeans and a rain jacket in the closet. He hears:

"Hello! Anyone here? Hello!"

Nick closes the closet door, steps from Winifred's bedroom, and down the steep creaking steps back to the living room. The front door is ajar, and a man leans into the house while his feet remain planted on the porch.

"You, Nick? Freddie's nephew?" The man asks.

"Yes," Nick answers. He remembers that Ida had called his aunt Freddie.

"I'm Merrill. Been keepin' an eye on this place since Ida went to the hospital. I figured you'd show up sooner or later."

Merrill's about the same age as Nick (50ish), and though his tanned skin is lined around his smile and his hair thinning at the crown, Merrill reminds Nick of his students. Maybe it's Merrill's wiry build, or the way his T-shirt is half tucked into his grass-stained jeans, or the way he looks Nick right in the eyes as if he hasn't yet learned not to trust.

"I received a letter and the obituary from the lawyer," Nick says.

Merrill shakes his head, "Yea', lung cancer. Ida smoked like a chimney. Lousy way to go. She stayed here almost to the end. She was a tough one. Mind if I come in? Holdin' this door open, I'm invitin' flies."

"No...I mean sure I don't mind. I just got here myself."

Merrill kicks off his shoes and lets the screen door slam behind him. The big toe of his right foot peeks through a hole in his sock and there's black under his fingernails. Nick wonders if Merrill works one of the local farms.

"Sorry I can't offer you a beer or something, but please sit down." Nick looks around the room. "Guess that's easier said than done. Not much to sit on."

"You sit there," Merrill says. He points to a well-worn recliner and raises his voice as he disappears through an open door. "I'll get a chair from the kitchen. Yea', I saw one of Ida's nieces an' some kid load up a U-Haul. A couple of her nieces used to visit once in a while, more so as Ida got sicker." Merrill walks back into the living room carrying a chrome kitchen chair with a gray and red vinyl back and seat. Much of the vinyl is cracked. "Guess they just about emptied the place."

The men sit facing each other. Nick's jeans and T-shirt speak of Manhattan, a stroll through Central Park and a beer at Tavern on the Green; Merrill's jeans and T-shirt speak of jeans and a T-shirt.

"You're lucky they left that," Merrill points to a painting—oil, sharp contrasts between dark and light, an arc of boughs, a bracken of ferns, rocks, and fallen trees interrupt the rush of water, splashes of light against dark browns and greens, a spring representation of the November creek where Nick and Ida had left Winifred's ashes.

Nick examines the painting, "I recognize that spot."

"Their favorite," Merrill says.

"Their?"

"Freddie an' Ida. They loved it. The creek runs along the west side of the land, borderin' what used to be the Sharp's place. In summer Freddie an Ida sat there before dinner an' had their drinks. Cocktails, they called them. We had plenty of picnics by that creek. Freddie an' Ida, the Sharps, an' me, an' Victor an' sometimes musician friends come visit for most of the summer. I don't know how they managed in this little house, but they did. Those were good times. Once, one of your aunt's dogs…you know she always had those corgis, looked like God forgot to give them legs…well it came nose-to-nose with a tiny fawn that was all curled up in the tall weeds. There they were, just starin' at each other tryin' to figure things out while we was drinkin' our cocktails. Freddie grabbed the dog's collar an' the fawn stood up on its skinny legs an' wobbled up into the woods callin' its mama. Freddie loved nature. She knew the name of every kind of tree an' wildflower. Like one of those guide books."

"Sounds like you knew my aunt well."

"'Bout as well as a person could know another. Real nice lady. Funny. Ida wasn't so funny, but still nice. Anyways, it's a good thing Ida's niece left that painting. Victor's stuff always sold pretty good, but got pricier after he died. I'd say you could get a couple of thousand bucks for that one. Funny how what folks do is better appreciated after they're gone. Anyways, I just stopped by to introduce myself. You know, in case you need somethin'. You're probably gonna sell, but you should do a little paintin' or fixin' first, so you get a better price. The house ain't much, but the land's pretty. I helped plant a lot of the trees." Merrill stands and extends his right hand. "Real nice meetin' you. You need anythin'; I'm pretty good at fixin' things. I live right down the road. The old Victorian at the four corners, across from the schoolhouse. Just turn right, out of your driveway. Less than a mile."

Victorian, Nick thinks. *Guess I had that wrong.*

At some point during his teen years Nick had assumed that his aunt was a lesbian, but he didn't give it much thought. His father's family was always reclusive; Winifred just a little more so. But as he sits on the front porch listening to the trill of tree frogs and the drum of a bull frog, he imagines his aunt's life here with Ida—a full life that could never have flourished under rolling eyes and snide remarks. He wonders if Winifred and Ida were in fact lovers or if the weight of oppressive times had confined them to their separate bedrooms. Regardless, they were a couple and from the little Merrill had said it appears as if they were happy—happier than Nick had been in his marriage.

Above dark undulating hills the sky is awash of pink and orange. Nick picks at macaroni and cheese, a box mix he found in the cupboard. What might it be like to live here? Merrill mentioned that across from his house is a school, though Nick can't imagine a school located in such a remote area, although he also can't imagine Merrill living in a Victorian house. Soon Nick would begin teaching at a new school—why not make a big change? Like his aunt, he could build a life away from rolling eyes and snide remarks. It's not too late. He leans against the porch railing taking in the silhouettes of trees and of bats feasting on insects. Not Manhattan, but is that so bad?

Later, through his open bedroom window, an owl's mantra lulls him. Wasn't Merrill too young and, considering Winifred's attitude, too illiterate to have been her friend, and what was the artist's name? Victor. Nick's glad that Ida's niece left the painting and glad that Merrill visited. Friendly enough guy. It's been years since Nick's felt glad about anything. He draws a frayed quilt up over his shoulder.

Morning fog obscures Otisco Lake, but by the time Nick showers, shaves and slips on his jeans and a fresh T-shirt, then drives his car left onto Willowdale, the fog has lifted or burned off or whatever fog does when it dissipates. He retraces yesterday's drive past farmhouses, some in the same disrepair as his aunt's or worse, some restored. He also passes trailers and an eclectic mix of new homes, modest doublewides and large contemporaries with expansive windows. A dairy farm to Nick's right on the downhill side of the road appears abandoned except for cows grazing in a pasture, peeking out of dilapidated barns, or standing alongside the road as if they're waiting for a bus. The farmhouse is overgrown with sumac and grapevine and the skeletal barns lean precariously. Feral cats vanish like wizards into clumps of chicory and Queen Anne's lace.

The GPS advises Nick to turn left, up a road he hasn't traveled where rows of corn soak up the morning sun. A flock of wild turkeys awkwardly take flight. Nick meanders upwards through the cornfields until he reaches Route 41, where he turns right onto the crest of the hill between Otisco and Skaneateles Lakes towards the village of Skaneateles. To his left is a pull-off overlooking the expanse of Skaneateles Lake, more elegant than Otisco, and it glitters under the morning sun as if boasting of its splendor. It's a ten-minute drive to the village where stately homes lounge on expansive lawns accessorized with hydrangea and hibiscus and framed with ornate wrought iron. Gradually these mini-estates morph into commercial buildings—on the lakeside is a stretch of attached two-story brick buildings with first floor shops and second floor condos.

After parking his car and buying a coffee and scone in one of the village shops, Nick finds a bench in the lakeside park where the view of sailboats and Gatsbian estates is stunning, and he savors the taste and texture of his coffee splashed scone. Folks stroll the promenade along the lake. Nick watches an elderly couple, returning arm-in-arm from their walk on the pier. Had Winifred and Ida enjoyed this lakeside paradise, exchanging greetings with the locals, nodding at tourists? He can't imagine Merrill in this village, but then Merrill is an enigma. With his grimy fingernails, holey socks and homey vernacular, but with stories of sipping cocktails and...again Nick wonders about the artist—Victor?—Merrill had mentioned '...me and Victor.' Did he mean as a couple? Nick shrugs and tosses the last few crumbs of his scone to some rather tenacious ducks.

Across the street is a real estate office, and Nick's impressed by the hefty prices of the listings in the window, not just lakeside mansions, but also smaller more modest homes throughout the village. From a conversation with the realtor, he learns that Skaneateles prices are an anomaly and that homes in the Otisco Lake area sell for less. She tells him that buyers from New York City and Long Island are amazed by the bargains they find here in Central New York.

"Of course that's good news for the buyer, not the seller," she chuckles. She hands Nick her card, "But I'm sure that I could get you a good price. You said the house has a view of the lake? Otisco is one of the Finger Lakes' best-kept secrets. Just lovely."

He pockets the agent's card, thanks her, asks where the closest supermarket is, then makes his way back to his car. After grocery shopping he tours the village side streets, admiring the modest but well-kept homes with the hefty price tags. He passes Skaneateles High School and remembers that before last year he had loved teaching.

❖

To the right of Nick's house the roadsides are more heavily wooded. A mangy white dog bounds up to Nick, tail wagging. "Hey, boy!" Nick bends to pet the dog then they walk together as if they are long-time buddies. Nick spots a school under a canopy of sugar maples, an old one-room schoolhouse with a belfry and a fresh coat of white paint. A sign stands close to the road—Side-Hill School—but Nick can't read the smaller print.

Beyond the trees, to Nick's right, is a Victorian house, high gabled and draped in gingerbread. Like the schoolhouse it's freshly painted, but with multiple colors. Resplendent gardens border the foundation, and the lawn looks more like carpet than grass. This can't be Merrill's house. The white dog barks as if announcing Nick and Merrill appears from out of a small barn, which is nearly as impeccable as the house.

"Hey, Hobo, you brought a visitor." Merrill holds a wrench. He runs his right forearm across his face, smearing grease or soil on his left cheek and smiles. "Just let me clean up," Merrill says then disappears back into the barn.

Nick walks up to the house. No caked or chipped paint, every detail is perfect, as if it were built yesterday.

"You like these kinds of houses?" Merrill startles Nick. His hair is wet and freshly combed, and he smells of soap.

"There's a place, a short ferry ride from Sag Harbor…Long Island," Nick says. "We used to vacation there when we were first…I mean I used to go there years ago. There were a lot of houses like this, some not much bigger than a doll's house."

"This one's Queen Anne," Merrill folds his calloused hands behind his back and nods his scruffy chin as if lecturing, "but all that fancy stuff is called Eastlake after Charles Eastlake."

Nick stares at him incredulously. Who is this man? Again, Merrill reminds Nick of his students, attempting to impress the teacher, but unguarded, innocent. Though innocent might not be the right word for high school boys considering that a twelfth grader in Nick's American Literature class copulated with Nick's wife, then boasted of his conquest to every student in the small private high school.

"It was built by a Methodist minister, hoping to build more an' turn his land into some kind of religious camp. Not sure why it didn't work out, but there's all kinds of stories. Mostly idle gossip. You know how small minded folks can be." Merrill punctuates his commentary with a nod and a broad smile. "Wanna' go inside?"

Before Nick has a chance to answer, Merrill's on the porch, removing his shoes and holding the screen door open for Nick. Nick follows him then bends to remove his own shoes. "No need. Mine's always dirty, but you look like you just stepped out of a magazine." Nick blushes, something he has no recollection of ever doing.

The interior accents are even more pristine than the exterior gingerbread—high-gloss, hardwood floors and wainscoting, coving arches at the juncture of walls and ceilings, an entry hall staircase with ornate, fluted newel posts and balusters. The two parlors and dining room are replete with European antiques, intricately carved, and heavily lacquered, the upholstery is plush and of warm subdued golds, greens, and burgundies, as are the drapes which hang from heavy rods trimmed with gilded finials. On the walls are tapestries and oils, similar to the lone painting in Nick's sparse living room. "Yes, Victor did those," Merrill says as Nick observes the paintings.

"This place is amazing," Nick doesn't add—Are you sure that you live here?

"An' a bear to clean, just ask Violet," Merrill says.

"Violet?"

"Yea', she's the one who keeps this place so spotless. I take care of the outside an' Violet takes care of the inside. Used to be my Granma who done the cleaning an' most of the cooking." Merrill lifts a silver framed photograph from off of a fringed scarf covering a baby grand piano and hands it to Nick. "That's Granma an' me."

A sepia Merrill, about twelve years old, folds himself into the pleats of an old woman's apron. They stand next to lilacs in full bloom. As Nick returns the photo to the piano, he eyes other photos of Merrill at various ages and one of Merrill with an older man. The man is tall and slender and formal in his dress and posture.

"That's me an' Victor," Merrill says. "He'd fasten the camera to a tripod, have us pose, then he'd run back and set something on the camera, then run back next to me an' the camera would shoot the picture. I was never much of a photographer. Victor always took the pictures. Guess it was the artist in him. I'll show you upstairs, then we'll get somethin' to drink."

The second floor furnishings are as opulent as the first floor's. Beyond the master bedroom is what Merrill calls a 'tea porch'. There is also a smaller bedroom, and as they pass a closed door, Merrill mentions that it's Victor's studio.

The kitchen is bright and more functional than decorative. An old farmer drives a honey wagon down Willowdale Road, and a whiff of aged manure drifts through the screen door and open kitchen windows. Hobo sniffs at the air as Merrill points to a room off the kitchen. "That's my room." There are books stacked on a nightstand, which surprises Nick.

"Lemonade?" Merrill asks.

They sit at a small kitchen table and Nick speaks of his conversation with the Skaneateles realtor.

Merrill chuckles, "Yea', some maps of the Finger Lakes don't even show Otisco…like it's a bastard kid. May be one of the runts, but if you ask me it's the prettiest, especially the southwest part, right below us. Tomorrow we'll drive down to the lake in the gator."

"I'd like that," Nick says, though he has no idea what a gator is.

The worst part of Nick's wife having had an affair with his student was how people changed after it. Students averted their eyes and giggled, and faculty avoided conversations that went beyond discussing the weather. Nick's mother summed it up perfectly when she said, "Well, it's late, but finally you're rid of that bitch." Merrill doesn't know about any of this, instead he rambles on about how his family has lived in this area forever, and his great grandfather then his grandfather owned a boat livery on the east side of Otisco, until his grandfather drowned when he got tangled up in his fishing line and after the family lost the livery his grandma went to work for Victor. And all the while Merrill talks, he looks right at Nick with no pity in his eyes and Nick can't help but enjoy the refreshing company of this unassuming man.

After a deep breath and a swallow of lemonade, Merrill asks, "So when do you think you'll sell?"

"I don't know. Maybe I won't sell. Maybe they can use an English teacher in Skaneateles."

Merrill laughs. "Now wouldn't that be somethin'."

"I'm just thinking aloud."

"Well you keep thinkin' that way. With Ida gone, seems like all folks do is leave here."

"Do you miss her?" Nick's surprised by his own words. He's not one to question. "Sorry, I didn't mean to pry."

"That's okay. I miss all of them. Guess that's the problem with havin' friends that are old. They up an' die on you or they move to Florida. That's what the Sharps did...the couple that lived on the other side of the creek from Freddie an Ida. It's like I'm also old, but I'm not near dyin' and I don't think I'd like Florida." Merrill chuckles.

Nick doesn't think of Merrill as old. If anything, he seems to Nick like one of Peter Pan's lost boys, and earlier when Nick viewed the photograph of a young Merrill with the tall, slender and much older Victor, he got a queasy feeling. But Nick is a pro at dismissing feelings, queasy or otherwise.

Early the next day while the sun still shines on the west side of Otisco Lake, before it disappears behind the heavily treed shoreline, they drive the gator, which resembles a heavy-duty golf cart, down the steep, rutted, winding road past ravines and abrupt drop-offs, which Merrill says are waterfalls in the spring, but now they're barely trickles. After Merrill parks the gator, they traverse the many steps down past a wall of ferns, myrtle and bare tree roots, like corroding anchors that might give way to a sylvan landslide. They pass the remnants of a stone fireplace and chimney, beyond this is a shed, then along the shale shoreline is a rowboat with a small outboard motor and two kayaks.

"Been a dry summer," Merrill says, "Lake hasn't been this low since '96."

The lake mirrors the blue sky and the shadows of gulls and a great blue heron. Merrill opens the shed door and removes two life jackets and paddles. He slips one of the jackets over his T-shirt with the image of a folksy trio and the words Happiness is an Otisco

Firehouse Pancake, then hands Nick the other jacket and a pair of water shoes. "Zebra mussels. You'll cut up your feet."

"Those were Freddie an' Ida's." Merrill points to two wooden kayaks leaning into each other. "Ida gave them to me after Freddie died, but I was just watchin' them. Kind of like I was watchin' the house. They're yours now. Do you like kayaking?"

"Never tried it," Nick says.

"Well it's a good day to learn."

After a brief lesson on getting in and paddling, Nick's kayak glides easily, not far behind Merrill's. They hug the west shore of the lake, craggy and dense with hemlock, hornbeam, beech, basswood, ash, and aspen whose leaves flutter like the wings of 1000 silver butterflies. A regal sycamore dwarfs the other trees.

"Another plus for Otisco over Skaneateles," Merrill shouts.

"What's that?"

"Weekdays there isn't much traffic on the lake. Come fall, it's even quieter."

Nick scans the lake. Merrill is right; there are more gulls and ducks than people. A largemouth bass breaks the water's surface.

Merrill waits for Nick to catch up. "On Skaneateles, all those folks with the fancy houses have to show off their fancy boats. It's like a damn pissin' contest. Sometimes Freddie an' Ida would drive their kayaks over the hill to Skaneateles, an' after they come back from fighting the wakes of those big, fancy power boats, Ida would complain about wastin' the day, an' Freddie would say somethin' about the grass being greener. They liked bickerin'. Seemed like they just liked talkin' to each other." Nick finds it difficult to imagine his aunt being a talker, considering how quiet it was in his grandparents' house, even when his aunt was there.

"Unfortunately, I didn't know my aunt very well," Nick says.

Both men stop paddling. Merrill holds onto the rim of Nick's kayak and they drift into a bog of milfoil. Nick looks into the weeds and thinks of the books on Merrill's nightstand and asks a question that's not really about his aunt, "How long did you know Freddie?" This is the first time he calls his aunt Freddie and the first time he observes Merrill's eyes look inward.

"When Granma's cancer got bad we moved in with Victor, he was already good friends with Freddie an Ida. I was about twelve.

They helped me an' Victor take care of Granma, especially the personal stuff."

"I'm sorry," Nick says.

"'Bout what? Old folks die. It's only natural."

Before the school year begins, Nick resigns from his position at the new charter school in Manhattan and sublets his studio apartment. Skaneateles and other surrounding high-schools are not hiring. His best offer is a tentative yes as a long-term sub to replace a teacher going on maternity leave in Homer, about twenty miles south, but the teacher's baby is not due until January. Violet, Merrill's housekeeper and as it turns out his cousin, had suggested that Nick apply at Homer High School—her daughter being the pregnant English teacher.

September is exceptionally warm and dry, and Merrill and Nick spend their days scraping and painting the outside of Nick's house. Victor may have been a master with oils on canvas, but Merrill is a master with latex on clapboards and he's just as skilled at carpentry. The men share an easy rapport and, without asking, Nick learns more about Freddie and Ida. Stories about Freddie's job as a school social worker and Ida teaching music at a small college, and that they vacationed in the Adirondacks and on Cape Cod, and had many friends and loved to entertain. Again, Merrill speaks of musician friends, some staying all summer. He speaks of summer nights filled with music, laughter, fireflies, and, of course, cocktails and Nick misses this aunt that he never really knew. Merrill doesn't say any more about his grandmother being sick or about when they moved in with Victor, and Nick doesn't ask—not that he doesn't have questions. Like why had Merrill come to live with his grandmother? Or why had he stayed with Victor after his grandmother died? And who was this Victor anyway? Nick left these questions in the bog of milfoil.

By the time evenings turned too cool for paint to set, Nick and Merrill had already begun working inside, and the refurbished farm house, cottage red with forest green trim, complements the changing leaves.

It's too beautiful a day to be inside and Merrill suggests a drive to the apple orchards. He'll show Nick where he's worked on-and-off since he was a kid—pruning trees and harvesting apples and pressing cider. Merrill has pieced together odd jobs his whole life. "When you're ready, give a call." Merrill says. "We'll go in my pickup."

Instead of calling, Nick walks to Merrill's house. The truck is in the driveway, but there's no sign of Merrill or of Hobo. During the past month and a half, Nick's visited Merrill enough times to feel comfortable entering the house unannounced. He opens the kitchen door and calls Merrill's name, but there's no answer. He passes an empty coffee cup on the kitchen table and calls into the living room, then stands at the foot of the staircase to the second floor and calls again.

Nick barely hears Merrill's response, "In the attic. Come on up."

Nick climbs to the second floor. "Which way?" he shouts at the ceiling.

"Through the closet in the master bedroom," Merrill answers.

The first door Nick opens is to the bathroom, the second is to a room he doesn't recognize—Victor's studio. And Nick remembers his first time in the house and that he thought it was curious that this was the only room they didn't enter. The drapes are drawn, but despite the darkness, Nick observes outlines of large canvases, probably on easels, and more canvases propped against walls. The canvases on easels are covered with fabric, maybe tapestries. Soon his eyes would adjust to the dark.

"Did you find the stairs?" Nick hears Merrill's voice as if it comes from beneath a tapestry. He leaves the studio and closes the door behind him. A closet door in the master bedroom is ajar, and Nick enters then climbs the stairs up to the attic.

"There you are," Merrill says. "I thought you got lost." With the steep pitch of the roof there's limited space for an adult to stand. A naked light bulb barely illuminates Merrill's back. He's hunched over in a corner, holding a flashlight. "From outside, I noticed a few holes in the eaves. Carpenter bees. With the heavy frosts, they're gone now. Just checkin' under this insulation to see if they drilled their way into the attic."

Nick hears the words *bees* and *insulation*, but his thoughts are in Victor's studio, and they linger there in the dark while he and Merrill drive to the orchards, pick apples and buy cider. Several times Merrill asks if something is bothering Nick and each time Nick answers no. After all, why should Nick care so much about those veiled canvases or Victor for that matter? For someone who has long made a practice of not asking questions, now all Nick has are questions.

Before leaving the orchard, one of the owners complains to Merrill about being short staffed. Merrill agrees to work for a few days and asks Nick to join him. "We can use a break from painting."

Come Monday, Nick feigns feeling ill. He knows that Merrill's house will be unlocked, but he hadn't expected Victor's studio to be locked. He searches the kitchen and Merrill's bedroom for a key. Aside from books stacked on the nightstand, there's also a wall of bookshelves, and among how-to books are works of fiction, maybe Victor's, including classics by Wilde, Forster and Mann. A newspaper article spills out from a copy of *Death In Venice*.

Local Artist Dies In Fire

Victor Carpenter succumbs to smoke inhalation. Upon seeing smoke, boaters came ashore to find Carpenter facedown outside of his burning camp. By the time fireboats arrived, the Otisco Lake camp was engulfed. Arson suspected…

Nick sits at the edge of Merrill's bed and skims the article. At the time of the fire, Merrill, referred to as Carpenter's handyman, was repairing a barn on Willowdale Road. Nick sighs, returns the article to the book, slides open the drawer to the nightstand and discovers a key ring with a single key.

After opening the drapes, light pours onto dust-covered tubes of dry paint, brushes, palettes and canvases leaning against walls and onto tapestries covering four canvases propped on easels. Through the dust he glimpses unfinished paintings of scenery, cursory portraits and sketches of nudes. He removes one tapestry and another and another. Three paintings of the young Merrill, nude and in classic poses—Pan, the God of the wild with the hindquarters, legs and horns of a goat; Ganymede being abducted by Zeus in the form of an eagle; Narcissus mesmerized by his own reflection. Nick recalls a trip to his maternal grandparents' hometown of Taormina, Sicily, where photographs by Baron Wilhelm von Gloeden were on exhibit. Von Gloeden's most famous pictures were of nude Sicilian boys—peasant youth with dirty fingernails and dirty feet—in classic poses before the backdrop of ancient ruins and Sicily's unforgiving landscape. Nick remembers his mother rolling her eyes the way she did when speaking of Winifred. And he thinks of the first day he met Merrill and of Merrill's dirty fingernails and his toe peeking through a hole in his sock. But Merrill is a man. Not always. Not when he posed for the paintings. *Arson suspected.* That's what the article said. Nick's mind spins with thoughts of Merrill being the victim of the pedophile Victor and Merrill taking his revenge. But hadn't Nick's high school student bragged of fucking Nick's wife? Maybe Merrill at eighteen, twenty or twenty-five was the seducer, for attention or money or as a joke. Not Merrill. And Nick is weary of rolling eyes, smirks and secrets and regrets the years he wasted in an empty marriage.

One last canvas remains covered. But while Nick removes the tapestry, he already knows why he cares so much about the other paintings and why he is concerned about their implications. He knows why he gave up his job, sublet his apartment and moved into a house that was all but falling down. And when Nick views the painting of the adult Merrill wearing a T-shirt, jeans and sneakers and staring back at him, Nick knows the answer to the question he feared most. For the past month and a half he's been happier than he's ever been. "What took you so long?" Isn't that the question his wife had asked him? Nick hears the front door close. He doesn't cover the paintings or draw the drapes, nor does he lock the studio door. In the living room Violet untangles the vacuum cleaner cord. Nick startles her.

"I thought you boys were working at the orchards," she says. Violet is at most ten years older than Nick, but to her all men are boys.

Nick sits on the steps. He's at eye level with Violet. "May I ask you a question, Violet?" Just planning to ask a question feels liberating to Nick. He's been in Violet's company a half dozen times and likes her no-nonsense ways, but doesn't know if he can trust her.

It doesn't matter. Later, he plans to ask Merrill the same question anyway.

"Sure," Violet says. She plugs in the vacuum.

"Did Victor hurt Merrill?"

Violet looks at the key ring and key dangling from Nick's finger, then looks Nick in the eyes. She reminds Nick of Merrill. "Honey, that boy was hurt long before he ever met Victor. If anything, Victor saved him."

Nick tries to object, but Violet holds up her long fingers as if she were stopping traffic. "I don't know what you think you just seen, but when Merrill came to live with our grandma, he had stopped talking. Who knows which one of his mama's no-good boyfriends had stolen his voice or what else they took from him." Violet purses her lips as if she's about to spit. "When Grandma got sick, Victor took them both in. No one else would have done that. My mama was working fulltime, and I was also working and pregnant with my first baby and my uncles lived far away and Merrill's mama wasn't worth the time of day. After Grandma died, you couldn't pry Merrill away from Victor. Why would you want to? Even after Victor was gone, he took care of that boy. He left enough money to keep Merrill in this house and to keep me cleaning it. Didn't your aunt ever tell you how Victor helped that boy? Now I got to start vacuuming or I'll never get my work done." Violet presses the toe of her shoe against the vacuum switch and Nick walks back upstairs. He draws the drapes and covers the paintings, then locks the door to Victor's studio. As he passes Violet on his way to Merrill's bedroom, she turns off the vacuum. "I take it you know where that key belongs," she says.

That evening, Nick sits on his porch. The air smells of wood smoke, and the moon is so bright Nick can barely see the stars. Hobo barks and Nick spots Merrill and Hobo approaching. Nick wonders if their glow comes from the moon or from something within them. Merrill waves a half-gallon jug, "Fresh cider!" In his other hand there appears to be a fiddle. "Time for cocktails!" Merrill shouts.

Who is this man? Nick thinks, and he can't help but smile.

It Only Occurred to Me Later
Anne Laughlin

When my boss told me we were heading to Cheyenne, Wyoming, for a four-month federal trial, my first thought was how nice the hotel room was going to be. Not nice as in fancy. The place was called Little Sister Hotel, so my expectations weren't high in that regard. But the room would be all mine. I could clomp around as loud as I wanted. I could go a whole day without saying I'm sorry. And when I returned home, Jane and I would both remember what it was that brought us together in the first place. As it was, I had no fucking idea.

We worked twelve to sixteen hours a day in Cheyenne, so I didn't see much of that hotel room. We were preparing the evidence needed to bore an unsuspecting jury into a catatonic state. The case issues were so astonishingly tedious that I never did wrap my head around them. It didn't matter. I managed case logistics. I'm not a lawyer, thank God.

The weeks started to roll by. It was summertime and the air in Cheyenne was gloriously warm, clean, and dry. Back home in Chicago people were keeling over from a horrendous heat wave, while the only discomfort I felt was during my daily phone calls with Jane. They were growing increasingly strained.

"I don't think you understand what this heat is like," she complained one day.

"I'm sorry. It sounds bad." I made it sound like it was my fault.

"It's horrible. You can't even breathe outside. Megan picked me up last night and we drove around to stay cool."

Hmm. That was the second or third time she'd mentioned Megan, who was a friend of mine from college. When did they become buddies?

"Isn't the air conditioner working?" I said.

"It's good to get out. She took me for ice cream."

Little flares lit up in my chest. Even if the city was under a state of siege from the heat wave, there was something off about Jane and Megan suddenly hanging out together. It only occurred to me later that it might have been a good idea to ask Jane about it. Honestly, that kind of communication wasn't natural to either of us.

❖

During the few hours I had off from trial work, I'd drive around in my rental car. I was astonished to find that the second you crossed the Cheyenne city limits you were in wild country. It seemed wild to me, anyway. Huge, empty expanses of land kept appearing around every bend in the highway, one after another. From Chicago, you couldn't drive far enough in a day to reach that kind of emptiness. It opened me up and at the same time made me nervous. I was used to feeling nervous. I've been nervous since the day Jane and I got together. But the opening up sensation was new and I didn't understand it. I suppose it was like a flower turning toward the sun, though that would seem an unlikely direction for me. I tended more toward the shadows.

One Sunday afternoon, I drove toward Laramie, just over a mountain pass from Cheyenne. It was a university town and from the pass it looked like it had been placed on top of the landscape by a giant hand. I was hoping for a good bookstore, maybe a shop or two to poke around in. After two months in Cheyenne, I needed new things to look at.

My phone rang as I parked near campus.

"You're birthday present's all done," Jane said without pre-amble.

"What are you talking about?"

"The new driveway. The one I bought you for your birthday. The asphalt guys just left, though I don't know how smart it was to lay an asphalt drive when it's a hundred degrees out."

How is it possible that I forgot Jane was giving me an asphalt driveway for my birthday? I must have filed it in the things-that-aren't-quite-right, drawer of my brain. That drawer was close to bursting.

Jane and I had just moved into a new house when I was sent off to Cheyenne. I don't suppose she was too happy being left to supervise all the work that needed to be done on the place, hence the unusual birthday present. It was a grand passive-aggressive move on her part. Driveways aren't cheap, but it's not like I could brag about the expensive birthday gift my girlfriend gave me. Nothing says 'I Love You' like an asphalt driveway.

"I can't talk now," I said. I couldn't stand to, really.

"Me neither. Megan's picking me up. We're going to the Navy Pier Ferris Wheel."

There were those little flares again. There were enough of them now that I could see them lighting up the car wreck of our relationship from five hundred yards.

"Well, have a fabulous time," I said grumpily and hung up. I hoped they got stuck at the top of the wheel and roasted. Who goes on a Ferris wheel in that kind of heat? People who are about to become lovers, that's who. They do dumb things like that and then giggle about them in that private-joke kind of way that's so annoying.

I got out of my car and peered around. I'd forgotten my sunglasses, which is practically dangerous around here. All that Big Sky and piercing sunlight that Chicago can never prepare you for. The UW campus was on my right, the town on my left, and I wondered how well they fit together. There were sure to be queers on the campus. Could they cross the street and walk into the Silver Saddle Saloon for a drink? I decided to head over there myself for a beer, figuring if they pegged me for a dyke—and they'd have several reasons to do just that—I'd find out soon enough how friendly the town had become since Matthew Shepherd was killed. I was just in the mood to rattle a hornets nest.

First I stopped at the kiosk that held scores of flyers for campus events and other goings on in Laramie. It looked like the town wasn't as sleepy as I'd presumed. It also became clear that the Silver Saddle wasn't the place to go if I wanted to spend some time with my people. The most colorful flyer on the kiosk (naturally) was for a gay bar advertising a traveling drag show that had taken place a few weeks earlier. I checked my map of Laramie and headed over two blocks to the Fancy Man wondering if the place would have any women hanging around on a Sunday afternoon. The name wasn't all that promising.

Cheyenne had a gay bar, but I hadn't yet been to it. I wasn't much of a drinker. Going into a gay bar was usually for one reason only—to find a woman for the night, or possibly longer. I'd met every girlfriend and one-night-stand I'd ever had in a bar, which is saying something for someone who doesn't drink very much. So what was I doing going into a bar with a five-year relationship hanging around my neck like a yoke? Good question.

The Fancy Man wasn't all that fancy. Wooden bar and shiny bottles, postage stamp dance floor, and, reassuringly, the obligatory pool table decorated with lesbians standing around its perimeter. The guys were hanging out at the bar, most of them wearing softball uniforms with Fancy Man written on the back. I wondered what kind of league they were in out here, and tried to imagine a tense play-off game between the Fancy Man and a team of ranch hands.

I ordered a beer from the bartender, who looked like the woman who ran the divorce ranch in the movie *Desert Hearts*—handsome and warm, sort of rakish with a red bandana tied around her neck. She swiped at the bar before putting down my bottle and flashed a smile at me. Within ten minutes she had my whole story—the long stay in Cheyenne, the girlfriend going astray. She stood there with her arms across her button down shirt, shaking her head when she heard about the Ferris wheel.

"That's no good," she said. "Sounds like she's stepping out on you."

I drank from the bottle and it tasted good. Maybe it was the dry air out here that helped it along for me. It was the best tasting beer I'd ever had.

"Maybe I shouldn't jump to conclusions," I said, as if that would stop me from jumping to conclusions.

"But you will anyway," the bartender said. "My name's Deirdre, by the way." She reached over to shake my hand with a solid pump and then pulled her arms back across her chest. "What are you going to do about the situation?"

"I haven't the slightest idea." I took another drink from the bottle. Delicious.

"Here's what I think you should do," Deirdre said. "All the girls from around here are about five miles down the road at Pam and Molly's ranch for their annual roast and I'm going to send you over." She started reaching for her phone.

"Wait! I can't do that. I don't know a single person there."

"What does that matter? Do you know a single person here?"

I looked around and my eyes settled on the group of butches around the pool table.

"Forget about them. They'll be out at the ranch soon enough," Deirdre said. "And I'll be there tonight, after this damn shift ends."

"Really, I can't do this. I can't just show up somewhere uninvited." Deirdre ignored me. pulled out her phone and called someone on speed dial, then turned her back to me.

A guy a few stools down leaned my way. "Don't bother trying to reason your way out of this with D. Anyway, you should go. We all would go in a heartbeat if they'd let us. It's the only time of the year that the women go separatist on us. No boys allowed."

A vision of a hundred dusty cowgirls came floating into my brain. Deirdre got off the phone and I let her convince me I'd be a fool not to go to the party. She jotted down directions and shooed me out of the bar. From the Fancy Man to the Double Circle Ranch was five miles of sere land that by now was getting under my skin in unexpected ways. I wondered about the women who lived here, tried to imagine how different they must be from my city friends. I realized that I didn't have many friends left in Chicago, my social circle having shrunk considerably since I got together with Jane.

The Double Circle would have been impossible to miss. Rainbow streamers decorated the two uprights that framed the entrance to the property, and a tall woman wearing a cowboy hat was leaning against one of them, a radio dangling from one hand and a cigarette from another. She raised her hand as I pulled up to her, dropped her cig and ground it out with the heel of her boot. I rolled down my window and looked up at her. She had a big smile on her face like she'd just stumbled upon a rare specimen of some kind.

"You must be the Chicago gal Deirdre called us about. Angie, right?" She was peering through the window, trying to check out as much of me as she could. She was at least fifteen years younger than me, so I chose to be flattered.

"That's me. She said it would be okay to come, but I still don't feel quite right just showing up like this."

"Oh, hell. As soon as you get back there you'll see there's nothing to it. There're always new women here. I'll find you after my shift here and make sure you're getting on alright."

She pointed me to the two mile road into the ranch house. Two miles seemed like an excessively long driveway. I suppose I could brag about a birthday driveway that impressive. But there was no asphalt here, just gravel and dry earth kicking up dust. The first thing I saw after the long, bumpy ride was a big jumble of cars and trucks parked off the road, just below what looked like a corral, if that's what they called it. I found a spot to tuck my rental and trudged up the road, dust filtering through the webbing on my Keen sandals.

The corral was surrounded by women leaning against the fence, watching two stupendously aggressive women barrel race their horses up and down its length. I knew about barrel racing from spending five minutes on the wrong TV channel one afternoon at home with a head cold. The cameras had failed to capture the way these women's thighs gripped their horses as they flew around the barrels. I'm sure they could have squeezed the life out of a sumo wrestler in no time flat. My mind, however, skipped right to how those legs would look stripped of their blue jeans.

The race was over before I could make much sense of it. The riders pulled up their horses and jumped off in tandem, like a circus act. Apparently the show was now over. All the women began to move away from the corral, just as I'd snugged my way into a spot and hitched my sandal onto the lower fence rung.

"You've got the look of someone who's never been to one of these roasts before."

I looked to my right and saw that another woman was still leaning on the fence. She didn't look like she was from the area anymore than I did. She wore linen capris and a silk T-shirt and she was tall and graying and really smart looking, as in brainy smart. I don't know what it is that makes a woman look intelligent, but when my pheromone factory detects it, it goes into overtime.

"You're right, I'm a roast virgin," I said. "I'm not even sure how I ended up here."

She turned fully toward me and smiled. "Did you stop in at the Fancy Man?"

"I did."

"That's what happened to me last year. I'd just arrived in town that week and was checking out the bar. Before I knew it, Deirdre had me out here. It was fun."

"Yeah?" I must have looked skeptical. She stepped toward me and gently spun me around toward the ranch house.

"Come on. I'll show you around and you won't feel so awkward. My name's Carol, by the way."

"Angie," I said.

"There's a big yard between the ranch house and the barn. That's where everyone's gone."

Carol had a long stride and a determined pace. She seemed like a blend of friendly and all business, which somehow worked for her. I was a little intimidated.

"You live in Laramie?" I asked. I looked at her profile and saw that the gray hair was probably premature. The lines around her eyes were there, but still etched only lightly into the skin. I put her in her early forties, about the same as me. She turned to me as we walked.

"I teach in the English department at the university. I live in the faculty housing there."

Oh, crap. I had a bit of a thing for academics and it had been my undoing in the past. I'd been an undisciplined college student who then made indifferent career choices, so I put on a pedestal anyone who had the wherewithal to get a Ph.D., especially if female and attractive. This reverence diminished somewhat after I became lovers with a professor some years ago. She regularly toppled off the pedestal in her all too human way, so I'm a bit more realistic now. But still, it's a thing.

"What are you doing in Wyoming?" she asked.

I could feel her looking at me, but I kept my eyes forward. I was afraid I was about to lie and say I was something I'm not, like a writer or painter, something I could fake pretty well. Telling her I was here to put numbers on exhibits and black tape on redacted documents felt humiliating. I had to give myself the pep talk about it being okay to be me—the talk I regularly failed to listen to if I even remembered to recite it.

I turned to her. She looked interested in what I was going to say.

"I'm working a trial in Cheyenne. I'm the lead paralegal and it's insanely boring. We've been at it for two months already."

"How much longer will it last?"

"Probably a couple months," I said. "Or we could settle at anytime."

"I hope it lasts the two months. Maybe we can get to know each other a bit."

What does that mean? My brain started spinning. We reached the edge of the lawn between the ranch house and an enormous white barn. Women were spread out and it was hard to tell how many were there. Maybe fifty? Certainly it had to be every lesbian in a hundred mile radius.

A four woman string band played country music. They seemed to be pretty good. They were just finishing a song as we approached and the singer announced that the next tune would be the Something Something Valley Yodel, which made Carol and I look at each other in alarm. The mandolin player stepped to the microphone and went right at it, her yodel piercing my brain in an instant. Honestly, you could record that and play it on continuous loop at Guantanamo Bay.

Carol took me by the elbow, which seemed rather courtly, and steered me around the edge of the lawn toward the barn. To the right of it was a team of women setting up food. As we passed the tables, Carol nodded to the women who were moving casseroles around like carnies working a shell game. There was an unbelievable amount of food, and when we finally got past the tables I saw a pit dug into the earth, over which an enormous pig, head and all, was hanging from a spit. Its feet were pointed skyward, feet that would perhaps one day be pickled and kept in a jar at the Silver Saddle Saloon.

Carol stopped in front of the pit, where two sweaty women were keeping watch. She took her hand from my arm and I felt the loss.

"Hey there, Carol. Glad you could make it," said one. She looked to be about sixty, but that was a complete guess. Her face was weathered while her body was strong and slender.

"I wanted you to meet Angie, who's a newcomer here," Carol said. "This is Molly, and that's Pam, overseeing Molly, as usual."

Molly took off her asbestos gloves and shook my hand. "Welcome, Angie. Deirdre called to let us know she was sending you over."

The communications network these women had was impressive. They would've been an asset in the French Resistance.

"Thanks for having me," I said.

Pam walked over to shake my hand and give Carol a quick hug. "You're just in time for food, the most important part of the day. I'd say this pig is about perfect, wouldn't you?"

I grimaced. "Don't ask me. I'm from Chicago. The pork I see doesn't look anything like that, I'm somewhat relieved to say."

"Give us another hour and we'll have her cut up and more familiar to your city eyes." Pam looked me over with a smile on her face, but I realized I might have sounded like I thought they were crude, which I suppose I kind of did. Maybe if they'd taken the head off that poor pig I wouldn't feel so disturbed. But I wanted them to like me.

"I'm sure it's delicious," I said.

Carol intervened. "This party is to celebrate Pam and Molly's anniversary. How many years is it now?"

"Twenty-seven," Molly said. She looked proud. Pam moved next to her and gave her a kiss. She was a little on the rotund side, but when Molly wrapped an arm around her you could see how well they fit. You could almost hear a *snick* as their bodies came together.

"Congratulations," I said. "I don't know anyone who's made it that long."

Molly laughed. "You make it sound like an endurance test. Every year with Pam has been a joy."

"And every year it gets even better," Pam said.

I didn't want Pam or Molly to ask me if I was in a relationship, which is what people in happy relationships seemed to feel compelled to do. From their perspective, there was no other road to happiness and they wanted to be sure to give you directions if you weren't already well along that road yourself. I wanted to tell Carol about my relationship, but not in front of others. Anyway, I wasn't even sure I was still in a relationship.

We left Pam and Molly and Carol led me around the back of the barn to look at the ranch land. I could see pastures and cattle and a burbling brook, all stretching out toward the mountains. It was hard to imagine owning property like this.

"I feel like I made a lousy impression on Pam and Molly," I said.

"Why?"

I shrugged. "Everything came out negative. I didn't mean to sound that way."

We stopped at some boulders that seemed to have settled into the clearing for no reason at all, as if they'd rolled off a foothill that had long ago been erased from the earth. She sat on one and patted the one next to her. I felt the warmth of the rock when I sat.

"You're pretty hard on yourself," she said.

"There's no one else to be." I couldn't understand why I'd just said that. Jane was certainly hard on me, but worse, I was implying that I was on my own.

Carol was watching me carefully. I imagine she sensed my nervousness. "You're single?"

"Why do you say that?"

"Only because it sounds that way, that there's no one close enough to be truthful with you."

That was accurate enough. At the moment I didn't feel close to Jane, nor did I believe she was truthful with me. How long had I thought that way?

"I don't know how to answer you," I said.

"Really? That's intriguing. Usually a person knows if they're single or not." Carol looked genuinely curious.

"Why don't we join the party?" I said. "You can give me the gossip on who's sleeping with who."

Carol stood and reached out to pull me up. "I understand. You don't want to talk about your girlfriend. But I won't promise to not bring it up again."

"I didn't say I have a girlfriend," I said.

"Please. You don't know me, but you should give me a little credit. Now, let's join the others."

"What about you. Are you in a relationship?"

"Not since I've been in Wyoming," Carol said. "And yes, it feels like a long time."

I wondered if she meant it had been that long since she had sex. Surely with all these energetic women around she could indulge whenever she wanted. She led me back to the lawn where we settled in near a group of women Carol knew. Our awkward dance around relationship status faded quickly. We talked and laughed and ate an enormous amount of food. We drank a fair amount. As the day turned to evening, Carol was still by my side, apparently disinclined to spend time with anyone else. I found myself at ease, but with a strangely elevated heart rate.

The band started their after dinner set with "The Anniversary Waltz," and everyone watched happily as Molly spun Pam around the lawn. I was a bit in awe of them. They looked so damn happy together. And for twenty-seven years! My parents and all their friends fell far short of that mark. None of my Chicago friends had been together longer than my rather impressive, or so I thought, five years with Jane. If Pam and Molly were the model for a happy relationship, then Jane and I were clearly in big trouble.

"I'm sure I've never been that in love before," Carol said. Her eyes were tracking Pam and Molly. Other women were starting to pair up, forming a ring around the star couple as if it were their wedding dance. I was hugging my knees to my chest, rattled by confusing relationship thoughts. I'd been living in fear for a long time that Jane would dump me, while at the same time I never believed we would have a long-lasting relationship. Either scenario meant we would break-up. How could I have been so unaware of that?

"What about you? Have you ever been that in love?" Carol nodded her head toward Pam and Molly. The song was coming to an end and Molly dipped Pam and gave her a nice long kiss, which was romantic and also pretty impressive, given Pam's extra padding and Molly's wiry build. Carol kept looking at me as everyone clapped. The band switched gears and moved into a sort of country rap sound that quickly had everyone on their feet.

"I should tell you that I don't dance," I said.

"Okay. I guess you were thinking I was going to ask you to dance," Carol said. She was stretched out on her side, holding her head up with her bent elbow, and plucking at the grass.

"Were you?"

I was still hugging my knees. She made it hard for me to concentrate on what an idiot I'd been to stay with Jane for five years when I'd only been happy for six months. The sex months. Carol and I were the only two not dancing, but she was concentrating on me and not the dancers. I could see Pam looking our way and whispering in Molly's ear. Whatever she said, it would be all through the ranch and back to the Fancy Man in short order.

"I'm not sure I had anything in mind," Carol said. "I'm trying to figure you out. I'm not sure if you know this or not, but your face changes expression like a slide show. You might want to take a pass if anyone invites you to play poker."

"What are you talking about?"

"I can tell what you're thinking from your expression. It moves from reserved to vulnerable to annoyed to flirtatious. You get the idea."

"Flirtatious! I do not have a flirtatious expression. I wouldn't even know how to imitate one."

"You have one, and it's quite original. But just as I get up the nerve to take advantage of it the expression changes to defensive or embarrassed."

Carol was smiling, but I felt stripped bare. "It makes me sound like an imbecile."

"I think it's adorable," she said. Her hand reached over and rested on mine, still clasped at my knees, the knuckles gone white. "Isn't now about the time you should tell me about your girlfriend?"

In the swirl of confusion dusting my brain, I considered the fact that to tell Carol about Jane might mean the end of Carol's apparent interest in me, and I wasn't ready to cut that loose. On the other hand, I didn't want to bed Carol now and tell her about Jane later, thereby killing what may be something special. I was feeling something from her that was different than other women I'd been with, and way different than the almost business like way that Jane and I had got together. Maybe I could navigate a middle path and tell her I was living with someone, but it seemed like it was falling apart. That would be honest. And she still might sleep with me.

"See, your face is doing that thing again," Carol said. "I wish you could see it." Now she sat up so that we were knee to knee, facing each other. "Why don't you just tell me? Maybe it's not such a big deal."

How humiliating. There Carol sat, composed as can be, while I apparently looked like I was doing warm-ups for a clown parade.

"I have a girlfriend," I said. I looked off to the side, not able to look her in the eye. The party didn't seem to be slacking off at all, from what I could see. From the corner of my eye I could see Carol lower her head, and then she removed her hand from mine.

"How long have you been together?" she said.

"About five years. But since I'm being honest, I have to say that since I've been here in Wyoming, the relationship seems to be rockier than when I left, and it was rocky enough then." I turned to look at her, to see if she believed me.

"Rocky how?"

I took a deep breath. The idea of Jane having an affair was supposed to be deeply painful, but truthfully, it didn't feel that way now. "I'm almost certain that she's having an affair with a friend of mine, or about to have one. They've gotten very chummy since I've been away."

Carol took this in quietly. I heard a truck pull up somewhere behind me and Carol started to rise. "That'll be the first of the shuttles back to Laramie," she said. "I think I'll grab it."

"Oh. I have my car here. I could drive you back to town."

"Nope. It's against the rules. Unless you're a pre-registered designated driver, Pam and Molly won't let anyone leave the ranch behind the wheel."

"But what about my car?"

Carol grinned. "This whole thing is run like a huge military campaign. You can bivouac in Laramie and then a shuttle in the morning will bring you back to your car. There's no point arguing."

There must have been some choice expressions racing across my face over this news, because Carol started laughing so hard she had to bend over. This caused me to see down the top of her V-neck shirt and the rather intellectual desire I'd been feeling for Carol all evening suddenly flared into something more elemental. It was the first physical desire I'd felt for a long time. Maybe I'd share with Carol the news that Jane and I hadn't had sex for over a year. That couldn't be any more embarrassing than my freakishly mobile face.

"And where do I stay in Laramie? My hotel's back in Cheyenne."

The woman driving the pickup had moved to the truck bed and was unloading a big pile of pup tents and tarps. Other women gathered round and started helping.

"You could pitch a tent and stay here; lots of women do that," Carol said. "Or you could spend the night at my place and we'll take the shuttle together back to the ranch in the morning."

Christ. I had no idea what the right thing to do was. I clamped my jaw shut and fixed my eyes on the pickup truck, determined to not let Carol see what I was thinking. But I knew what I wanted to do—had probably known since she said hello to me at the barrel races. I turned from the truck and found Carol standing right in front of me.

"Just so we're clear," she said. "I'm not going to try to seduce you. So if you just want a place to sleep, that's fine. I have a second bedroom and I also have boundaries. I'm not into one-night stands, even though I live in the middle of fucking nowhere and should learn to take it when I can."

That was a little earthy sounding for the professor. She shouldn't be hurting for company. She was gorgeous, and there were all those gorgeous cowgirls.

"There's opportunity with the women here," she continued, "but it's just not sexy for me if we don't have something in common. Sadly, I just don't with most of them. Don't get me wrong; I do respect them a great deal. Now here you come, the first woman I feel some connection with, and you're involved in a crumbling relationship and only here for two months, maybe not even that, and despite those very good reasons to suggest you stay at the Travelodge in town, all I can think about is having you in my little house and hoping you'll break down and make love to me."

"I thought you just said you're not into one-night stands."

She sighed. "I'm afraid I'm not making much sense. That's part of what tells me this is something a little more complex."

The driver called out that the first shuttle would leave in five minutes. I had to run to say my good-byes to Pam and Molly and then run to my car to get my backpack. When I made it back to the pickup, Carol was sitting in the bed of the truck with a few other women. She'd saved a place for me and I lowered myself down next to her. The other women were much drunker than we were and as we took off with a roar they fell all over each other and couldn't stop laughing. It was contagious. Carol and I started in, and when we hit a bump in the gravel road that made us all nearly bounce out of the truck, I thought we'd pee our pants. Carol and I held on to each other, and we didn't stop when the truck moved onto the smooth pavement of the interstate.

Our backs were to the sidewall of the truck bed and I found myself leaning into Carol, maximizing our area of contact. I was giving her my answer, even if I couldn't yet say I was ready to cheat on my girlfriend.

"Let me see a picture of her," Carol said.

"Why?"

"It might remind you of what you have at home and how you want to try to fix it. I'd rather you know that before you decide what you're going to do in Laramie. Surely you have a photo in your phone."

I pulled my phone out of my pack. I hadn't taken a picture of Jane since I'd gotten the phone, which was quite a long time ago. I guess that said something right there. I pulled up Facebook, because she had a ton of photos of herself there. Carol was looking over my shoulder as I clicked my way to Jane's page. After a few seconds the first photo on her page appeared. I gasped. There were Jane and Megan on the fucking Navy Pier Ferris Wheel, lip locked as they were being let out of their chair. It wasn't a peck-on-the-lips kind of kiss. It was a how-far-can-my-tongue-go-down-your-throat kind of kiss. The caption below said "Megan and Jane after a hot ride." Who knows who took it? Probably some friend of Megan's not clued into the fact that Jane had a girlfriend. Or maybe Jane had given the okay to post the damning shot, figuring it was a much easier way to break up with me than actually telling me herself.

"So that's Jane, is it?" Carol said.

I nodded. "She's on the right. It's odd to see what she looks like being kissed. Normally I'd be too close."

"Because it would be you kissing her," Carol said.

"Yeah. Though I haven't kissed her like that in a long time. It looks like she's enjoying it."

"And that shot was taken when?"

"Today."

Carol leaned back against the truck bed and pulled me against her. "Do you feel awful?"

"I'm not sure. What does my face say?" I turned to her and tried to not have any expression at all.

"Your face says you've had a lot going on tonight."

The five-mile trip to Laramie didn't take long. Not long enough for me to decide if the absence of feeling about Jane and Megan was true disinterest or just numbness. But there was no denying the sense of freedom and liberation that was making its way from my toes up. We climbed out of the truck in front of the campus and stood there as the truck pulled away with its raucous passengers.

"What would you like to do?" Carol asked.

I looked around me and found the street largely disserted. Then I pulled Carol toward me and leaned in for a kiss. She seemed surprised, but recovered quickly. Her arms came up around my neck and she opened her mouth to mine. She was lovely.

"I don't think this has to be a one-night stand, do you?" I asked.

"It can be a two-month stand," she said. "At the very least."

That seemed like so much more than I'd had over the past five years.

She led me toward the faculty housing, just a few steps from our drop off point.

"Caution would have me suggest we take it slow and see how you digest this news," Carol said.

I loved how she talked—a bit formal, even when speaking of very personal matters. It was sexy, a challenge, an invitation to get behind the precise diction, and undo her a little. We stopped in front of her door and faced each other, her keys dangling from one finger.

"Maybe caution would be the worst thing for us. Who knows how long I'll be here," I said.

"That's something to consider. We can talk about it."

Talk about it? Hadn't we talked all day? Hadn't there been enough talk already?

"That doesn't mean we're going to talk all night, does it?"

"I doubt it," Carol said. Then she unlocked her door.

BRUNO'S LAST SUPPER
JEFF LINDEMANN

Can anything good come from Nazareth? Come an' see,
Nathaniel. *John 1:45-46*

Vienna," she said out loud. "Brace yourself! You can do this!
Dear Jesus, help me!"

After a spirited Sunday morning revival, Mrs. Vienna Pierce, gripping the wheel of her 1976 diaper-brown Chevrolet Chevette, drove alone down the hot, rocky dead-end East Texas farm road outside Lufkin and stopped before the daunting sign with large bruised purple letters: "Welcome to the Reverend Jediah Madcock Psychiatric Institute for Penal Offenders. Erecting Vibrant, Long Lives Out of Your Hardened Juvenile Delinquents."

Exactly two years earlier, a judge allowed her to admit her sixteen year-old son Bruno into an expensive, private, religious, reformatory school after a jury found him guilty of robbing—while intoxicated and at gunpoint—Daddy Dan, owner of Dark Side Men's Leather Clothing, Painful Pleasures, and X-Rated Videos on lower Westheimer in Houston.

The armed security guard admitted her through the gate of the heavy, electrified chain-link fence topped with razor wire. She drove past the large statue of suffering Jesus with his arms outstretched and parked in front of the entrance to the stark stone and rusty iron edifice built at the turn of the century as an asylum for the hopelessly insane.

Vienna reached for the make-up mirror in her large purse and began to primp her hair. She had worn the same style dyed jet black since the day in 1954 when she saw her favorite actress, Joan Crawford, wearing the short bob in *Johnny Guitar.*

"All right," she said, looking heavenward and closing her purse with a definitive snap. "Let's go!"

❖

"Follow me, Mrs. Pierce," directed Dr. Brachman, a cross between Liberace and the Pillsbury Doughboy swathed in a green and blue physician's jacket. He ushered Vienna into the lobby decorated with a gaudy mural depicting the destruction of Sodom and Gomorrah. "Bruno's finishin' his lunch in the dinin' hall."

"Doctor, tell me," she pleaded, "Bruno? Is he...is he... *repaired?*"

"Yes, Ma'am! He's been tot'ly rehabil'tated thanks t' these two years you've had him enrolled in 'Straight t' Jesus,' our repar'tive conversion ther'py program."

They sat at the table under the full-sized portrait of craggy-faced, tense-necked, clenched-lipped Reverend Jediah Madcock, founder of the Madcock Institute, who was holding a Bible in one hand and a tennis racket in the other.

"Usin' the 'No Pain, No Gain' techniques taught t' me person'ly by Dr. Jediah Madcock, God rest his soul—he done hanged himself— Bruno has experienced ev'rything from day-t'-day psych'atric couns'lin' 'long with Bible lessons t' sensory deprivation, nausea-inducin' per-scription drugs, sol'tary confinement, an' 'lectric shock treatments t' his gen'tiles."

"Dr. Brachman! I had no idea 'till now Bruno was receivin' these treatments! An' fer two years! Can anything good come from this?"

"You'll soon see the results! Believe me, I know whut I'm doin'," he added with a confident smile and a wink. "I bring years of experience t' the table. Rest assured that Bruno has repented an' promised *repeatedly* he'll never again touch a rum an' coke or, fer that matter, another man. Yer thirty thousand dollars has been well spent perm'nantly curin' him of whut I call 'Gender Identity Deficit Disorder in the Young', also known as 'G.I.D.D.Y.'."

"Bless you! But I hope Bruno won't hold it 'gainst me fer these—ugh—treatments."

"When you first brought Bruno in handcuffs t' me, he was a young barbarian who needed t' be educated an' disc'plined. T'day he's a God-fearin', het-ra-sexual, sober, young man who now knows right from wrong. His release t'day is an important moment in yer lives. Ya'll oughta cel'brate!"

"I got surprises waitin' fer him! Now, whut should I do fer Bruno at home?"

"Practice 'reward therapy.' Encourage him t' date respect'ble young ladies he meets at church an' in Sunday school, an' when he does reward him with a bowl of vanilla ice cream, a bag of pork rinds, or a manly baseball cap."

"I'll do it."

"I advise you *never* serve him any food that is phallic shaped or requires sucking. I recommend no bananas, Hostess Twinkies, pickles, lollipops, popsicles, an' 'specially *no* hot dogs. These damagin' foods can encourage sinful behavior. Do *not* serve him any rainbow-colored food comb'nations on the same plate such as green beans, t'matoes, an' eggplant. An' fin'ly, by all means, *no* fruit salad."

Bruno appeared.

At eighteen, he looked the remnant of a brawny lumberjack who could have graced a package of paper towels. With a glazed-over pale face pocked by two sad, deep-sunken dark brown eyes and topped by a mop of thick, unruly black hair, the stocky, slump-shouldered inmate wearing a dirty T-shirt that read "Spent Chicken" shuffled into the lobby carrying a tattered suitcase, a well-worn pillow, and a tennis racket.

"Dr. Brachman, I never seen no tennis courts at the Madcock Institute."

"Ain't none. We use tennis rackets in all our per-vention ther'py programs. In Bruno's case, when he felt—ugh—naughty pref'rences, I forced him t' beat that pillow with the racket an' shout repeatedly, 'Romans One: Twenty-Six an' Twenty-Seven. Ain't no homos gonna make it t' heaven.' I use different Bible verses dependin' on the partic'lar mental disorder. Now, go on, say 'hello' t' him. No doubt he's eager t' see you."

"Sweet Bruno! Sugar dumplin'! Come over here an' hug yer Mama!"

He kept his distance. In a low, dull monotone, he mumbled, "Hello, Muther."

❖

As soon as they arrived at her small, ramshackle 1950s house on twenty acres right off the 59 Freeway on the northern fringe of Lufkin, Vienna, began practicing "reward therapy."

"Bruno, sit with me here at the dinin' room table. I'd like t' talk t' you."

"Yes, Muther."

"Please know I've fergiven you fer yer past perversions an' am ready t' start brand new. But I'm worried you might be unhappy with me fer commitin' you t' the Madcock Institute. I had no idea 'till t'day 'bout Dr. Brachman's—ugh—treatments."

"I am unhappy," he spoke in a flattened voice. "You shoulda asked two years ago 'bout his treatments. Ain't no joy in life no more—nuthin' but sufferin'."

"Bruno, please fergive me. But I'm convinced that any sufferin' you done was worthwhile. Dr. Brachman says ye're tot'ly cured of that...sinful illness."

"You an' Dr. Brachman done worse than my wrong. Ya'll tortured me. Ain't right t' make people suffer. I feel like a zombie— dead t' life. Jus' a lot you don't understand. Ya'll betrayed me. Whut ya'll done is unfergiv'ble."

Vienna reached deep into her purse. "Bruno, here—take this thirty dollars, borrow m' car, drive t' the Wonderland strip mall, an' treat yerself t' a cup of vanilla ice cream. Then buy a nice shirt an' pair of pants at St. Judy's Thrift Shop. Git a good bargain! Next, stop in fer a sporty haircut at Dottie's Clip Joint, an' you can keep whut's left over all fer yerself."

"Yes, Muther."

"An' I got another surprise! T'night we're havin' Frito pie an' creamed corn cas'role fer supper with a nice young girl I met at church—Bitsy Mae Duckworth. She's 'bout your age an' sweeter than molasses on a Hostess Twinkie—I mean cupcake. An' after supper, the four of us are drivin' t' the Red Bluff Drive-In t' see a re-run of Bette Davis in *All 'Bout Eve*. You know how much I love an ol' movie with a happy endin'."

"The four of us?"

"Yes, you see Bitsy Mae's father, Donald, is divorced. I've decided t' start datin' again—an' eventually re-marry. Imagine that! After all these years! So, me an' you are sorta havin' a double date t'night. I'm hopin' that maybe this time, ev'rything's gonna work out jus' right fer once."

"Yes, Muther."

"I want me an honest, hard workin', God-fearin', church-goin' man fer m' next husband. You know I'm only thirty-eight."

"Forty."

"Yes, forty. But I'm still young an'…rather attractive…don't you think?" Vienna primped her hair, smiled, and batted her long lashes.

"Ye're all right."

"You'll have t' fergive me; I was fishin' fer a compliment. Don't seem t' git 'em these days. Ain't no gentlemen left in East Texas any more. But when I was a young gal, people used t' tell me I looked jus' like Joan Crawford."

"I know in *Johnny Guitar.*"

"I'm still young. I could even have me another baby—or adopt one—of course with the right man this time. I always wanted a sweet, pious daughter. I prayed an' prayed you'd be born a little girl. Don't know whut happened. Guess it jus' wasn't in the cards. Now don't you think fer a minute I'm blamin' you fer bein' born a baby boy."

"Sure, Muther."

"Oh, if only I had married that nice, young Rev'rend Bunion when I had the chance. He adored me! Such a fine gentleman, too! He once gave me a romantic card sayin', 'Vienna, ye're the purtiest wildflower on the roadside!' But no. I fell fer yer father—a shiftless, smooth-talkin' travellin' shoe salesman with a big grin from ear t' ear."

"Yes, Muther, I know the story. He hit the road…"

"He hit the road right after we tied the knot an' then run off with some jus' married two-bit tramp from Nac'doches who already done had yer father's baby. He betrayed me! Then you was born nine months later."

"Five months."

"Yes, five months later," Vienna sighed. "One day when I see Jesus face t' face, I want t' sit down an' ask him direc'ly why ev'rything in m' life done…"

". . . done turned out all wrong—includin' me."

"Oh no, sweet Bruno! You were born a bit—ugh—broken, but Dr. Brachman repaired you at the Madcock Institute, an' now ye're ready t' start yer life as a respect'ble law-'bidin' citizen an' a sober, God-fearin', church-goin' young man—who likes ladies. An' one day you'll open yer heart an' fall in love with a good Christian woman—like me or Bitsy Mae Duckworth."

"M' heart ain't nuthin' but a locked box."

"Oh, Bruno. Give me a smile. You ain't smiled all afte'noon. The one good feature you inher'ted from yer father was that big grin from ear t' ear. That sinner could smile like a saint."

"I ain't got nuthin' t' smile 'bout."

"Well, I bet you'll be smilin' by the end of t'night. Oh, the preparations! Gotta bathe in a hot tub, wash m' hair, do m' nails, cook dinner, set the table—an' wait 'till you see m' new bargain dress from the thrift shop. Now remember t' be back home by six so's you can git all spruced up fer yer date. The Duckworths will arrive at six thirty."

"Yes, Muther."

"An' Bruno, ugh—jus' in case—don't fergit yer tennis racket."

"Yes, Muther." He shuffled lifelessly out the door and threw the racket in the trunk.

Once on the road, Bruno drove straight to Grumpy's, a dingy saw-dust floored roadside tavern outside of Lufkin off the 59 Freeway that catered to an unsavory assortment of barflies, outcasts, riff-raff, trolls, potheads, lonely men in shirt sleeves, and an occasional down-an-out drag queen. On the old juke box, Peggy Lee was singing "Is That All There Is."

"Bruno Pierce! I ain't seen you in a coon's age! Where you been, boy?" asked Grumpy, a burly mustached and tattooed motorcycle man wearing a black leather cap. He wiped the counter in front of Bruno who had pulled up a barstool and sat slump-shouldered.

"Been dead fer the last two years," he said in a monotone.

"Well the dead has risin! Here, have a bowl of pork rinds. Now, tell me all 'bout it."

"Been trapped in a loony bin outside Lufkin an' near tortured t' death."

"Oh no! Don't tell me—the Madcock Institute."

"How'd you know?"

"Done spent time there m'self as a kid in that dungeon after I doused some Christmas carolers with gas'line an' tried t' set 'em on fire. M' muther thought I was sub-normal an' needed psychic treatments."

"I know all 'bout those treatments. I gotta score t' settle with the butcher inflictin' those treatments—all in the name of Jesus."

"I bet I know who—Dr. Brachman. Is that crazy ol' queen with the tennis rackets an' Bible verses still runnin' that hell-hole?"

"Yep. I ain't never gonna fergive that monster!"

"I swear I seen that gay goose in here wearin' dark sunglasses an' a floppy hat. If you ask me, he's the one that oughta be locked up an' tortured."

"Grumpy, torture's too good fer him. I'm gonna kill that devil."

"Bruno, no trash talk! You don't wanna go killin' nobody. Well now, whut you gonna have? This drink's on me."

"I'll have my reg'lar—a rum an' coke."

"You got it."

Bruno's first sip jump-started his gaydar. He next surveyed the tavern for signs of life only to discover Grumpy's was empty except for a table occupied by a scruffy young redneck with curly red hair, a freckled face, and a T-shirt that read "Born This Way." Bruno locked eyes with the redneck who, smitten, nodded back with a Howdy Doody smile. Bruno stood up—erect.

The redneck swaggered to the counter. "Purty hot weather out there."

"So hot a chicken'll lay a hard-boiled egg."

The redneck smiled. "So hot I could grill a weenie on m' dashboard—if I had one."

"You tellin' me you ain't got a weenie?"

"No! A dashboard."

"So hot the devil farted," added Bruno.

"Hey, ye're smart, funny, an' sexy, too."

The clunky juke box changed records. Liza Minnelli began crooning "Maybe This Time."

After a short pause, Bruno grabbed the redneck by the shoulders and planted a long, deep sloppy kiss on him. The redneck responded lustily as they made loud, wet smacking noises. A near-extinguished ember inside Bruno fanned into a flame.

"Howdy! I'm Bruno," he said musically, grinning from ear to ear.

"'Round here they call me Rattler."

"Rattler, thank you fer the kiss of life!" Bruno grabbed Rattler by the shoulders and looked into his bright blue eyes. "An' somethin' else, I'm fallin' smack-dab in love with you!"

"Well, Bruno, I done fell fer you hook, line, an' sinker the moment I seen you walk through that door."

This sudden connection intensified as their next kiss was longer and louder, much like the slapping of wet, red meat on a butcher board.

"Whew!" exclaimed Rattler. "I gotta come up fer some air! M' brain's in spin cycle."

"Rattler," asked Grumpy, "how long you two lovebirds known each other?"

"'Bout five minutes. Why? You gotta problem with love at first sight?"

"None at all! But at the rate you two are goin', ya'll be holdin' a commitment cer'mony by happy hour."

"How'd ev'rybody like a round of tequila shots!" Bruno pulled a twenty dollar bill from his shirt pocket as Grumpy took the order.

"Wow! Seems like years since I seen a twenty dollar bill. You rich, Bruno?" asked Rattler.

"Dirt poor. An' I gotta git me a bag of dough—fast. Whut little I got ain't gonna last long in this joint."

Rattler sighed half-heartedly. "I'm flat broke an' outa work. Maybe we oughta rob us a convenience store. I ain't never stole nuthin' before—but I'm up fer it."

"Convenience stores are fer am'teurs. Let's hit the jackpot! I'm thinkin' 'bout a bank in Nac'doches t'night."

Grumpy set down the three tequila shots. "Whut's all this buzzin' goin' on? I feel I done walked into a hornet's nest. Come on, Rattler—'fess up."

"Tired of bein' outa work an' broke, Grumpy. Things gonna change real soon—t'night!"

"Ya'll better stay outa trouble. Hate t' see ya'll all end up in the pen at Huntsville. Might be worse than the Madcock Institute."

"I'll take death row over Madcock," countered Bruno.

"That'll be ten bucks."

Bruno handed him the twenty. "An' keep the change."

"Hot dog! Here's t' the future." toasted Rattler. They guzzled their shots.

"Grumpy, another round of tequila. We're cel'bratin'!" He handed him the ten. "Rattler, listen here, I got us a plan. On early Sunday evenin', no one's downtown in Nac'doches. The bank is ours fer the pickins'. But that's jus' the start. We're gonna heist ev'rything that ain't tied down from here t' Houston. We need us a git-away truck fer all our loot. An' we're also gonna stop at the Madcock Institute—I gotta a score t' settle with someone workin' there. Here's whut we're gonna do."

"Yes, sir. Ye're in charge, boss."

"Rattler, with you at m' side, no tellin' how far we're gonna go."

"Sorta like Butch Cassidy an' the Sundance Kid?"

"No, more like Bonnie an' Clyde. Follow me."

The duo drove off in the Chevette, which huffed and puffed onto the 59 Freeway towards Nacogdoches. But about ten minutes into their journey, passing through the sleepy little town of Nazareth, Rattler held his growling stomach. "Bruno, we're gonna have t' stop fer some supper. I'm sufferin' from mal-a-nu-trition. I ain't eaten nuthin' all day 'cept a bowl of stale pork rinds at Grumpy's."

"We ain't got no money fer supper. That last round of shots done wiped me out."

"Then maybe we oughta rob us a convenience store an' then hit the bank. We gotta eat somethin'—can't rob no bank on empty stomachs."

"Whut's that up yonder on the roadside?" Bruno slowed for a closer look.

"Looks like a parked truck in front of an' a ol' silver Airstream trailer. A long one, too! Got something written on the side: 'The Last Supper: In All Its Glory!'."

Bruno strained to see. "It's blindin' me in the sun! Humm… mus' be a roadside food truck. There's a man sittin' on a lawn chair next t' a tent. He's talkin' into a bull horn—prob'ly advertisin'—but ain't no one listenin'."

"There's a girl, too. She's standin' next t' a bar-b-que pit."

"Rattler, dinner's 'bout to be served! Let's eat at The Last Supper—in all its glory. We're gonna take 'em fer whutever they're worth. First their grub an' next their money. An' let's git a good look at that truck an' trailer."

As Bruno pulled to the roadside near a sign reading "This Property Four Sale," they could hear the scrawny middle-aged man with slick black hair wearing a T-shirt that read 'Jesus Is Disgruntled' preaching into the bull horn. "It's the end of times, I tell you! The center can't hold no more! The world's startin' t' darken. Life's c'lapsen' all 'round us. Satan himself is gobblin' up all East Texas!"

Rattler stopped in his tracks. "Bruno, somethin' tells me this ain't no ord'nary food truck."

"Wake up wicked sinners! Fer you there's nuthin' everlastin'. Yer hearts ain't nuthin' but clogged up, stinkin' sewers of sin! God abhors you!"

"That sure don't sound like my God," said Rattler.

"That Bible-thumper would scalp yer naked soul."

"You sinners dangle like insects over a fiery pit! Hell's mouth is wide open an' ready t' swallow whole you an' all yer sins!"

"Rattler, hell's mouth ain't wide enough t' swallow all the sins we're gonna commit."

"God's judgment is upon all who have turned from scripture! Liars, thieves, drunks, tramps, whores, ho-a-mosexuals, sod'mites, human vermin—you stand there like dumb witnesses missin' the very meanin' of yer lives!"

Bruno and Rattler scoped out the crime scene.

"You two rag-a-muffins. You children of the 'pocalypse. Come over here, git on yer knees, an' repent fer yer sins! Yer very existence here t'day disgruntles our Lord! His sufferin' on the cross was wasted on you. He's holdin' back arrows ready t' be made drunk with yer blood!"

"Rattler, I'd like t' be made drunk with some rum an' coke."

"But it ain't too late t' repent! Begin now by steppin' into that trailer an' observin' Jesus an' the twelve disciples sittin' at the last supper. Witness the glory first hand! You there—step forward! Whut's yer name young feller?"

"I'm Bruno, an' this here is…this is…"

Rattler whispered, "M' real name's Nathaniel, but you can call me Nat, like the fruit fly."

"An' this here's m' little brother Nathaniel. We're on a family outin'."

"I'm Rev'rend Joel Jebadiah New Jerusalem Jones. An' that there's my daughter Holy Zion New Jerusalem Jones."

A curious young woman about Bruno's age wearing a modest white cotton frock and unruly black hair tied in a loose bun cautiously stepped forward. "Fer short, ya'll can call me Holly, as in a crown of thorns spotted with blood."

As Holly walked closer to Bruno, he saw she was blind. She had no pupils; only the whites of her eyes glowed like luminous, pearly ceramic orbs in a translucent face. Bruno stood transfixed.

"May I touch yer face, Bruno?"

"All right," he said tentatively, staring into her orbs, as if portals into some far-a-way realm.

She softly cupped his jaw in her palms and lightly fingered his cheeks, nose, forehead, and finally his tense neck. She pulled back. "You poor boy, you done known a lotta pain. I can feel yer pent-up anger. People betrayed you. You jus' need some understandin', that's all. Bruno, there's a lotta good in you! But first ye're gonna have t' fergive those who done hurt you an' let that pain go. You need courage. God helps us all."

Bruno pulled her hands down. "God ain't helpin' nobody. He done played a cruel joke on us all. That includes you too sister. Sometimes you gotta wonder whut all this sufferin's fer. Livin' ain't easy."

"Fergivin' ain't easy. But you got the key in yer hand. All you got t' do is unlock yer heart. That's whut we've all gotta do if we wanna move on in life an' find some meanin'."

"That's jus' whut me an' Nathaniel are doin'—movin' on."

"I understand. Seems like me an' Papa been movin' on ferever."

"She's right," interrupted Reverend Jones. "But me an' Holly are tired of movin' on. Fer twenty years, we've been wand'rin' 'cross the South—t' county fairs, church bazaars, carn'vals, shoppin' malls, even roadsides with that trailer."

"Papa, they've prob'ly stopped t' see whut's *in* that trailer." She pointed to the shiny Airstream glistening in the afternoon sun.

"Inside that trailer, we got Jesus an' his disciples sittin' all life-size in wax. It's awe-inspirin'. I preach, an' Holly gives tours of *The Last Supper.*"

"Papa," she said with growing enthusiasm, "Tell 'em 'bout yer dream."

"Last week the Lord appeared in m' dream an' tol' us t' settle here in East Texas. We started out in Nac'doches an' we're gonna end right here in Nazareth. Gonna buy this land fer sale. Gonna build us a little house an' then a big tent t' hol' spirited revivals. An' of course, I'll have Holly an' *The Last Supper*! I might add a carn'val ride, a clown, an' a pettin' zoo."

"An' tell 'em 'bout the mir'cle—the sign!"

"Yep, done had us a sign yes't'day. I found out these here twenty acres is sellin' fer thirty thousand dollars! You know how much we got saved in a bag after all our years of wand'rin' with The Last Supper? Exactly thirty thousand. Now, that's a mir'cle!"

Bruno looked at Rattler with wonder. "Rev'rend Jones, I'm now a believer in mir'cles! Life ain't such a bad joke after all. Jus' like you said, Holly, God helps us all."

Reverend Jones stood. "Say, why don't you brothers walk up that ramp an' experience The Last Supper. Holly will give you the tour, an' you can each drop fifty cents in her tin cup."

Rattler, hungry and eager for the quick heist, looked skeptical. "Can anything good come from this?"

"Come an' see, Nathaniel," replied Holly. "Here's the door t' the myst'ries! Follow me."

❖

Holly turned on the fans and special lighting effects illuminating the thirty-foot long wax sculpture.

"This life-sized replica of Le'nardo Da Vinci's *The Last Supper* was completed in the 1940s by three nuns at the Mount Rose Convent in Houston. They devoted years of penance fer their past sins t' create this magnif'cent re-creation of the orig'nal 15th century mural in the dinin' hall in the monast'ry of Santa Maria delle Grazie in Milan, It'ly."

"How did ya'll git a hold of it?" asked Rattler.

"When the convent closed, Papa purchased the sculpture, an' since then we've been spreadin' its glory. The work has an inner-life. Note the careful details on the hands an' faces. The nuns used their own hair, which they dyed different colors an' then, usin' a special tool, poked strand by strand directly into the wax. An' observe the fine cloth robes, 'specially the texture an' colors—the intense blues, vivid reds, vibrant greens an' golds. Also note the tablecloth. It's a fine linen woven on a loom by an Italian nun an' then hand stitched."

"Miss Holly, may I touch the tablecloth?"

"Yes, Nathaniel."

He ran his hand across the cloth and felt the delicate stitching. "Makes m' fingers tingle!"

"The moment you experience here is really a moment of moments. All those emotions you see occurs jus' a split second after Jesus announces, 'I tell you the truth, one of you is gonna betray me.' Look at all the disciples' dif'rent hand gestures, body positions, an' faces filled with shock an' anger. They're expressin' the passions of their souls! You can tell Jesus sure done stirred up a hornet's nest! His news ripples 'cross the table, an' they're all wonderin': who could it be?"

"There's an awful mys'try in all this," noted wide-eyed Rattler.

"Yes, there is! The mys'try gains a power over us. An' the best way t' experience it is t' surrender t' it—t' look, listen, an' receive gifts of the spirit—an' let them gifts redden in yer souls!"

The two reluctant pilgrims stood in reverent silence as if a white heat quivered from a forge.

"Why don't we all turn inward fer a moment while I play a canticle I call 'The Music of the Spheres.' As you listen, take some time t' think whut all you've done 'complished in yer lives, where ye're at right now, an' whut good there is fer you t' do t'morrow, fer there is a lotta goodness in us all."

Holly sat on a stool and played a sublime blend of wind chimes, finger cymbals, tinkling bells, and small gongs. Occasionally she would chant in a pure, rich and resonating high-soprano voice that echoed her magical calm.

"There now. I hope ya'll turned inward an' done some spirited an' heartfelt thinkin'."

Bruno stood with his eyes still closed, as if transported far-away in time and space where he, like some ancient astronomer, was urgently attempting to solve a cosmic puzzle.

Rattler put his hands in his pockets and scuffed the floor with the toe of his shoe. Something dark and troubling gnawed within.

"Nathaniel, you got a question 'bout *The Last Supper?*"

"Who's the rude dude with his elbow on the table an' holdin' a purse? He looks sorta sin'ster an' shadowy."

"Ah! That's remorseful Judas, all dressed in green an' blue. I think he's more tragic an' despairin' than sin'ster, for he's clutchin' a small bag—thirty pieces of silver—as payment t' betray Jesus. Note his craggy face. See the stretched veins in his tense neck an' his clenched lips? An' observe he's jus' tipped over the salt shaker! You heard that expression 'Betray the salt'? By the end of the day, he will hang himself."

Bruno wrinkled his forehead. "How is it ye're blind an' yet ye're givin' us this tour an' answerin' questions as if ye're lookin' right at it—colors an' all?"

"I study *The Last Supper* with m' finger tips. I also feel it inside—like a flame. I listen, too! I hear sounds speakin' t' me— like sacred music—'specially at night when I sleep in here with m' pillow at the feet of Jesus."

Rattler spoke: "I'm feelin' goose bumps on m' arms. Bruno, I'm havin' doubts."

"Doubts 'bout whut, Nathaniel?" asked Holly.

Reverend Jones stepped into the trailer. "Now, before you brothers exit, note our table of souvenirs. We got coffee mugs, T-shirts, fly swatters, posters, an even a plastic wall clock all featurin' *The Last Supper*. You can…"

"We got somethin' else in mind fer a souvenir," interrupted Bruno.

"Well then, I hope ya'll enjoyed experiencin' *The Last Supper*." An' speakin' of supper, why don't ya'll join us fer dinner. I'm gonna grill us some hot dogs. We always got plenty t' feed the crowd. Holly, you an' these brothers unfold some extra chairs in the tent an' set the table fer a fine Sunday evenin' meal."

"Yes, Papa! An' I'll git the buns an' grape juice."

❖

Once inside the tent, the four gathered at the table and, after a long-winded prayer, ate heartily as Reverend Jones kept talking, often chewing and speaking at the same time.

"Now, let me tell you, m' daughter here, Holy Zion, she's a good Christian woman. An' when she speaks, she speaks truth—an' truth's rare these days. I think she might be a prophet."

"Papa, don't talk like that. Here, let me pass ya'll more buns."

"She's modest. Now, her mother—she weren't no good Christian woman. She was a sassy tramp who seduced me twenty years ago when I was a young, ig'nrant man workin' outside Nac'doches as the projectionist at the Red Bluff Drive-In movie theater."

"Oh, Papa! Ye're not gonna tell that story again."

"I was showin' *All 'Bout Eve*. Jus' as Bette Davis was sayin', 'Ya'll better fasten yer seat belts—it's gonna be a bumpy ride,' this young strumpet workin' at the concession stand enters the projection room an' starts flirtin' with me. Durin' a moment of weakness, I'm tempted by the harlot an' give in t' m' sinful lust right there on the projection room floor! Well, I force her t' marry me the next day 'cause I thought it was the right thing t' do."

"Bruno, please pass the catsup," said Rattler.

Bruno reached across the table.

"Hey, be careful! You jus' knocked over the salt shaker."

"Bruno, I know why ye're here," said Holly, calmly and resigned.

"Well, as I was sayin', I didn't know it then, but m' new wife jus' had an il'git'mate baby girl by another man. An' whut did m' new wife do the very day after I married her? She betrayed me! She done run off with that baby's father—a smooth-talkin' travellin' shoe salesman from Lufkin who could grin from ear t' ear. An' the two done left me holdin' their helpless baby with no name. I said t' m'self, whut good can come from this?"

As another piece of the cosmic puzzle fell into place, Bruno looked reddened, for there was a world of meaning in the preacher's story.

"Papa, ye're embarrassin' me. Here, ya'll have some grape juice."

"An' that's the moment I saw the light an' started preachin'. Now, one day we was down in Houston when I heard 'bout the wax sculpture of *The Last Supper* fer sale at a convent that done went bankrupt. Well, another light went on! I bought Jesus an' his disciples right on the spot. We've been wand'rin' ever since."

"Papa, you fergot one important part. Tell 'em how you fergave ev'erbody an' moved on with yer life."

"Ye're right! I also done unlocked m' heart an' fergave that sassy tramp an' her smilin' shoe salesman, an' I brung up this dear girl all by m'self. It's a darn shame Holly never had a mama t' help raise her. Guess it wasn't in the cards. You brothers, ya'll take a lesson from me! Don't hang 'round with no sassy tramps."

Bruno—agitated—stands. "Now jus' do as I say, an' no one's gonna git hurt!" The veins stretch in his tense neck.

Holly calmly urges, "Bruno, whutever you mus' do; do quickly."

"Whut!" exclaims Reverend Jones. "Whut's goin' on here?"

"Ya'll better fasten yer seat belts—it's gonna be a bumpy ride." Bruno quickly yanks off his belt, grabs the wiry man's arms, binds his hands behind him, reaches into his front pocket, and pulls out the key to his truck.

"Ye're betrayin' us!" yells Reverend Jones.

"Papa, it's a sacrifice we're gonna make have t' make."

"Preacherman, there's some Judas in us all. Rattler, here's m' car keys. Open the trunk an' find some rope an' a ol' rag."

The brothers in crime sit him in the car and tie his feet. "Rattler, stuff that rag in his mouth—we don't need no more of his Bible-thumpin' t'day. An' when you finish, slide that ramp into the trailer an' close the back door. I'm gonna search fer that bag of dough."

"Bruno," says Holly, "you won't need t' search fer the money. I'm gonna give it t' you. It's locked in the glove compartment—all large bills. You hold the key in yer hand."

"Holly, let's git you in the truck. We got somethin' t' talk 'bout."

"I'll go peacefully. Jus' don't hurt Papa."

"Rattler, you drive m' car. Follow me. Let's go!"

"But, Bruno, where we goin'?"

"M' muther's house."

After a short ride, the pilgrimage pulled in front of Vienna's little house on the outskirts of Lufkin. Wearing a garish 1950s chartreuse cocktail dress embossed with purple amoeba shapes, Vienna paced feverishly across the yard.

"Bruno, I demand t' know where you've been all afte'noon an' who are all these strange-lookin' people? Whose truck an' trailor is that?"

"Calm down, Muther, stop rufflin' yer feathers."

"Where were you at six thirty? The Duckworths arrived, an' you stood us up! I was hopin' Donald would take a int'rest in me. Well, you done ruined that! An' poor Bitsy Mae! You shoulda' seen the look in that poor girl's eyes! Oh! Why does ev'rything always have t' turn out all wrong! One day, when I see Jesus face t' face, I want t' ask him direc'ly…"

"Can it, Muther. Maybe this time ev'rything's gonna turn out jus' fine. Now git in the house an' stop yer babblin'. Rattler, untie the preacher's feet, bring him in, sit him down at the dinin' room table, an' tie him back up. I'll git Holly."

"Whut preacher? Who is Holly? An' who the heavens is Rattler?"

"Muther, I said git in the house an' sit down at the dinin' room table next t' the preacherman! Ye're gonna listen t' me fer once."

As Vienna stormed into the house, Rattler was close behind ushering in Reverend Jones. Bruno helped Holly out of the truck, gently walked her into the house, and sat her at the table. He faced the three of them and was ready to speak when Vienna suddenly noticed Holly's eyes. She pulled her chair close to the prophet and put an arm around her. "Oh, you poor dear girl! You mus' be scared t' death by these demons! A blind girl! Dear Jesus help us all!"

"Muther Pierce, I can see things purty clearly. Bruno knows whut he's doin'. He's a good man. I understand him. We had a talk while drivin' here—a sorta family reunion. An' now it's you who need t' learn how t' understand him."

"Muther, please meet Holy Zion New Jerusalem Jones."

"Fer short, you can call me Holly, as in a crown of thorns spotted with blood."

"An' I'd also like you t' meet her father, Rev'rend Joel Jebadiah New Jersalem Jones—from Nac'doches. Rattler, take the rag outa his mouth."

"Yes, sir!"

"Rev'rend, allow me t' introduce you t' m' muther, Mrs. Vienna Pierce. Watch 'em all, Rattler. I gotta go git somethin' from the truck."

"Mam, you can call me Joel. It's a darn shame t' have t' meet you this way. Yer sinner of a son may be a crim'nal, but I could tell the minute I done seen an' heard you that ye're a good Christian woman. An' ye're mighty purty, too. Anyone ever tell you that ye're the spittin' image of Joan Crawford in *Johnny Guitar*?"

"Why thank you, sir! Ye're a gentleman."

"Mrs. Pierce..."

"Please call me Vienna!" She batted her long lashes.

"Vienna, whutever comes from all this—I want you t' know that me an' Holly are honest, hard-workin', God-fearin', church-goin' people."

"Ma'am," interjected Rattler. "You can believe him. This preacher's a good man. An' his daughter—she's a saint with an inner glow—an' she plays music that makes you see stars an' planets."

"An' who are you? Are you drunk, stupid, or jus' born this way?"

"Muther Pierce," interrupted Holly, "He was born a fine, sweet man. He's gotta' lotta' love in his heart."

"Ma'am, 'round here people know me as Rattler. M' real name's Nathaniel, but you can call me Nat, like the fruit fly."

"A flyin' insect!"

"Vienna, he's a crim'nal." yelled Reverend Jones. "He an' yer son done robbed me an' m' daughter of all our life's savins'."

"Papa, Bruno an' Nathaniel are *not* crim'nals. I gave them the money—as a gift. You an' me, we'll git by. We still got yer preachin' an' *The Last Supper*."

"Whut last supper?" asked Vienna.

"It's the door t' the myst'ries!" exclaimed Nathaniel.

The front door swings open. In walks Bruno carrying a bag of money and the life-size wax figure of Jesus. He sits the figure at the dining room table across from his mother.

"Dear Jesus!" cries out Vienna.

"Muther, as long as I can remember, you've been wantin' t' 'sit down with Jesus' an' have a good, long talk 'bout why yer life's always turnin' out all wrong. Well, here he is. You can have yer talk."

Vienna sat like a dumb witness. "Whut does all this mean?"

"You tol' me t'day you want a good Christian husband. Well here he is—Rev'rend Jones! An' you've been prayin' fer a sweet, pious daughter—well, ye're lookin' at her."

"Sweet Jesus!" cried Vienna.

"Holly, I'm puttin' twenty thousand dollars down in front of you."

"Thank you, Bruno. An' I thank you, too, Nathaniel. I've known you only a short time—but I'm sure there's nuthin' false 'bout you." She held out a hand.

He grasped it. "Thank you, Miss Holly. Ye're makin m' fingers tingle!"

"I don't understand!" exclaimed Vienna. "Who is this Rattler—Nathaniel—Nat—the fruit fly?"

"He's m' boyfriend, Muther. I'm alive—got joy in m' life!" He grinned from ear to ear.

"Oh no!" exclaimed Reverend Jones. "Not ho-a-mosexuals on top of ev'rything else! It's enough t' gag a maggot!"

"Wake up, Papa! You need some new understandin'. Times are changin'. An' you need t' change, too. Rethink whut's everlastin'."

"Nat, come on, let's pack you up an' head t' Houston with the ten thousand Holly done give us. We're gittin' a clean start."

"Yes," replied Vienna. "A clean start—back on the streets, back t' the bars, an' back t' more crime! You'll 'ventually git arrested! But this next go-round, you'll be too old fer me t' commit you t' the Madcock Institute fer more repairin'."

"Muther, I don't need no repairin'! I ain't broken! T'day I took time t' turn inwards an' think things through. When me an' Nat git t' Houston, I'm gonna start college. Gonna become a psychol'gist. An' who knows, one day I might buy the Madcock Institute—an' tear it down stone by stone an' build it up anew. I'm gonna help people become who God 'tended 'em t' be."

"All right; then go! But, Bruno, promise you'll come visit me ev'ry now an' then."

"I will—the good Lord willin' an' the creek don't rise! An', Muther, I'm takin' yer Chevette. Consider it a trade—ye're gittin' a husband, a daughter, a truck, a trailer, an' Jesus with all his disciples. Not bad! You always did like a good bargain—almost as much as an ol' movie with a happy endin'. An' somethin' else, I'm gonna sweeten the deal." Bruno kneels. He kisses his mother's hand. "I fergive you! You did not know whut you had done."

Vienna wept. A curse had been lifted.

"Godspeed!" cried Holly. She grinned from ear to ear.

"Thank you, big sister."

"Sister!" exclaimed Vienna looking with wonder at Holly.

"That's right, I got me a sister. So long, Father Jones. Holly, you help 'em connect the dots. Follow me, Nat, we got one more stop t' make."

"Back t' Grumpy's fer a rum an' coke—one fer the road?"

"Nope. Back t' the Madcock Institute. I gotta score t' settle with someone workin' there."

"Oh, Bruno!" cried Vienna. "Don't drive t' the Madcock Institute—that's nuthin' but trouble. Leave Dr. Brachman alone! If you want a new life in Houston—then leave now. Go! Don't ruin yer chance."

"Little brother," urged Holly, "Don't go plowin' up snakes. Fergive whutever that man done t' you. Move on. Find yer meanin'.'"

"Sister, t'day, some gifts of the spirit done reddened in m' soul. I found the courage t' unlock m' heart, fergive, an' discover m' meanin'. But, don't worry, I ain't gonna kill that beast. I jus' wanna' return his tennis racket."

"Thank goodness!" exclaimed Vienna.

"But I gotta' 'No Pain, No Gain' technique I'm gonna teach t' Dr. Brachman. I'm gonna bend him over, grab that racket, an' stuff it where the sun don't shine. Nat, let's go."

"Bruno, it's me an' you now. We're both cut from the same tablecloth. Hot dog! A whole lotta' good done come from t'day! No tellin' how far we're gonna go!"

THE FAVOR OF A REPLY
JOE LANDRUM

Matt was at the library reading a copy of *Le Chic* magazine when he spotted it. *From Orisons to Opulence* by Muffy McHendricks Morgan. There the book lay, not three inches from his elbow. *From Orisons to Opulence.* That must mean you could pray and get rich!

He'd discovered the word "orisons" last summer when he was doing his best to read *Hamlet.* He hadn't succeeded, of course. *Hamlet* was too much sugar for a dime. He'd scanned the play, though, and some of the language had flashed out at him.

"O heavy burthen!" What could that refer to except his testy Mama and Daddy with their unreasonable demands, temper tantrums, and scolding; they made of his life the most acute affliction 365 days a year. Yes sir, twelve months after twelve months after twelve months. The misery was endless.

"What have I done that thou darest wag thy tongue in noise so rude against me?"

Just what he'd have asked his parents if they hadn't had such ugly dispositions.

"The fair Ophelia! Nymph in thy orisons…"

This bit of quotation had focused Matt on the play's characters rather than his own situation. Hamlet calls Ophelia a nymph in her orisons when he spots her reading a prayer book, right after he's worn himself out fretting whether he should end his misery with a bodkin. A nymph in her orisons had sounded most genteel and, of course, exotic. He'd never heard anybody in Natchitoches, Louisiana, talk like that, so the piquancy doubled.

Matt had used the library since time out of mind. He'd begun there, not with *Charlotte's Web* or *The Wizard of Oz*, but, dictionary in lap, with Frank Yerby's *A Woman Called Fancy*. Every summer he spent afternoons leafing through stacks of *Le Chic* magazine, stopping at pictures of women in designer evening dresses, and glancing at articles entitled "The Seychelles—Ever Truly Sexy?" or "The Duchess—How'd She Do It?"

He threw *Le Chic* onto the table, picked up the book, and took it to the check-out desk.

Arriving home safely on his bike, Matt had endured no hassles, no hurled insults, just the sun beating down on his unprotected skin. He'd arrived just as Ophelia (Matt's, not Hamlet's) was sitting down in her chair to have a cigarette. Any other time he would've rushed to the back of the house to his shadowy, blinded room—his retreat. But he loved talking with Ophelia, and so he sat at the kitchen table.

"Look, Ophelia! Here's this book that's going to make us rich: *From Orisons to Opulence*. Why I don't even need to read it. The title says it all. I'll just pray and the money'll start pouring in."

"Hah," Ophelia scratched her forehead with her cigarette hand then cigarette in mouth, tightened her pigtails.

"We'll move to Palm Beach, at least for the winters, and get a house right next door to Mar-A-Lago. That's where Mrs. Marjorie Merriweather Post lives, you know?" Matt caressed the magic book.

"Naw," said Ophelia, "I don't believe I knew that."

"You'll love Palm Beach. The houses are like palaces and just about everything sits right on the Atlantic Ocean, and it's gorgeous and blue, sapphire even, with creamy white caps dancing on the water."

"Huh, you ain't getting me to no Palm Beach. That ocean can stay right where it's at. Ain't you ever heard of sharks? I don't care a thing about water. Why, I broke into a sweat and nearly lost my breakfast the one time I got in a boat."

"Well, you'll at least have to visit us."

"We'll see."

"As far as I can tell the only bad thing about Palm Beach is Mrs. William S. Paley doesn't keep a house there. You know she's the *dernier cri* when it comes to international socialites." Matt knew it was rude to speak French to Ophelia who likely didn't understand a word, but he couldn't help it. There was no English phrase to describe Mrs. Paley's perfection. "You know one of these days I'm going to be Mrs. Paley's butler. You wait and see."

"Yes indeed, Mr. Butler Man, I'll wait."

"But living next door to Mar-A-Lago will, no doubt, have its advantages. I'm thinking I'll have to take up square dancing. Did you know Mrs. Post gives square dances just about every Tuesday night?"

"I don't reckon you need to move to the Atlantic Ocean to square dance."

"And Mama's got a good figure. We'll hire a professional make-up artist and get her some designer dresses. Before you know it, she'll have invitations to luncheons and teas dances rolling out of her ears."

"Child," Ophelia sounded skeptical, "I don't expect I'll live long enough to see your mama at a tea dance."

"But she's going to have to buckle down and write her thank you notes. You know I've never seen her write even *one*?" Pondering his mother's remissness, Matt looked at Ophelia with sorrow, but pushed on. "And daddy, he's handsome. We'll get him some tailored suits. "Course he's got that terrible temper. Mama too, but at least she doesn't jump and yell like a cave man. She's a pill, but she's definitely going to need less work than daddy." Matt pulled at a tiny tag of his crew cut.

"Lord Jesus, child, if they don't both work on my last nerve. When they come in cussing and carrying own I want to run screaming out of this house." Ophelia closed her eyes, and rubbed her cheek. "Course, you know if your daddy was rich, he wouldn't be nearly as hard to deal with. He's always blasting off because he's always worried about money."

"Ha, you're probably right. But see this book. I'm going to pray us rich, and he won't have to worry anymore."

"Hum. Must be some book."

"But, Ophelia, what about Kathleen, though? She's going to present a special problem. Lord, God, help us—what're we going to do about Kathleen? Wait I know! We'll ship her off to school in Switzerland. I don't think even her obnoxiousness could travel all the way back across the Atlantic." Matt smiled and caressed the book. "Okay, it's all set. We'll move to Palm Beach, become friends with Mrs. Post and her friends. In sixteen years when Betsy needs to make her debut, we'll be ready for it. Why Mrs. Post will probably even throw the ball at Mar-A-Lago." Matt dusted his hands as if he'd solved all the problems.

"Child, tell me again, how did you say y'all was going to make all this money? By praying? I pray every day, and I ain't rich. If I was, I wouldn't be sitting here listening to you."

"No, but look," Matt stuck the book plain in Ophelia's face. "It says it right here: *From Orisons to Opulence*. I'm going to try it. It's got to work. It's in a book."

"Honey, you are a case. Sometimes you act like you ain't got a lick of sense."

Matt clutched the book to his chest, got out of the kitchen chair, and went to his room to compose the prayer. First he opened the blinds, but the sunlight striped and stung his face. So he closed them, sat on his shadowy bed, and began writing. He saw the ink flowing with fluidity and grace. What a good omen—the prayer wrote itself. He read it aloud, "Sweet Jesus, please accept this orison in the spirit in which it's intended and make me and my family rich, rich, rich. In Jesus' name. Amen."

He put the book on the table by his bed. Every night he'd take it up and hold it while he prayed. Days evaporated with no change, as far as he could tell, in his family's financial status. Still he renewed *Orisons* and continued praying.

Two or three days before the book was due back at the library once again, Matt, tiptoed down the hall from his retreat and spotted something on his mother's dresser. He walked into her room, picked up an envelope, and examined it by turning it back to front to back.

It was the most genteel letter Mama and Daddy had ever received. The stationery was heavy ivory. The address was written in fountain-pen. On the back of the envelope at the top it read: *Turquoise Cove, Azure Bay, Florida*

Matt edged into the kitchen, "Mama, why haven't you opened this letter? It looks real nice, and it could be important."

His mama hunched her shoulders, blew at her bangs, and kept peeling potatoes. "I didn't open it because I already know what's in it—an invitation to your cousin's wedding."

"Well can I open it?"

"Why in the world would you care about a wedding invitation? Leave it alone. Put it back on the dresser."

Tottering about, careful as a geisha freshly wound into silver pink brocade, Matt kept his head down and his eyes on the letter. He pretended not to hear his mother's sighs. He could just barely make himself put the envelope down. It felt important. Weighty. Deluxe. Its creamy color and rough texture reminded him of a lace evening dress he'd been studying in *Bridal Bliss* the other day at the library. He flushed, remembering the two public school girls sitting at the next table over—glancing, giggling, whispering.

He pushed the image of those girls back—he didn't care, didn't even know them—and focused on the envelope's handwriting. Perfectly formed in broad, graceful strokes of black ink. He was grateful they hadn't used blue. It was after all a wedding invitation. He recognized this kind of penmanship, having seen samples of it in Emily Post's *Etiquette*—his favorite library book that wasn't a novel. In fact, *Etiquette* was as good as a novel with its butlers and footmen and candelabra and ladies retiring to the drawing room.

"Matt, are you still fooling around with that damn invitation? Leave it alone and call Sarah's mother. Tell her it's time for your sister to come home. Tell her Kathleen needs to be here in fifteen minutes." His mama had finished slicing potatoes and was getting up to rinse them. "Now!"

"Yes, ma'am."

He hated talking on the telephone. People were always mistaking him for a girl. If they were mean people or men—and that amounted to the same thing—they often *pretended* to mistake his voice for a girl's. He guessed it would get lower one day, but he wasn't counting on the confusion to stop. He talked with Sarah's mother, who was the exception—a nice woman who always knew him on the phone—and returned to the kitchen.

"Kathleen's leaving."

"Okay. Get the flour and meal and that bowl I always mix the cornbread up in."

He took everything out and put it on the counter. He inhaled, exhaled, inhaled, exhaled. He knew it'd just make Mama mad, but he couldn't control himself. "Please let me open it. You need to see what it says, where it is, when it is, and all that."

His mama, drying the colander, shook her head but said through gritted teeth "All right, open the damn thing. I know you'll pester the devil out of me out of me until I say yes. Go ahead and open it." She slammed the colander into its place in the cabinet.

He went back to her bedroom and took his daddy's mail opener out of the side-table drawer. Picking up the letter, he closed his eyes and shifted it from hand to hand. How important, how elegant, how *royal* the heaviness felt. His prayers must have been answered. He carefully slit the envelope open and took out the contents.

Good, he thought, *here was the second envelope just as Miz Emily Post dictated.*

On the front was written: *Mr. & Mrs. McPhee*

Good, he thought, they hadn't written out the full name, Mr. & Mrs. Matthew Thomas McPhee, a second time. Miz. Post didn't approve the superfluous.

He unsealed this inner envelope and took the invitation out. *Hup—the tissue paper was in there, right along with the card.* He was almost sure leaving the paper in was what Miz. Post would call a "solecism". At least, though, the tissue meant the card was engraved, not just printed. He decided he would overlook the faux pas and continued to study the card.

Mr. & Mrs. Jason Richard Whittington
Request the Honor of Your Presence
At the Marriage of Their Daughter
Brunhilde Prudence
To
Mr. Jack Ralph McPhee
On
Tuesday, the Fourth of July
One Thousand Nine Hundred and Sixty-One
At Seven 'O Clock in the Evening
King Ethelbald Episcopal Church
And at the Reception to Follow

Turquoise Cove
Azure Bay, Florida
The Favor of a Reply is Requested

The favor of a reply was requested! As a backyard beautician in a small town, his mama got lots of wedding invitations—most of which she ignored. She even got some that said RSVP, but she'd never received one that requested the favor of a reply.

"Mama," he said as he returned to the kitchen, "are y'all going?"

"Are you kidding?"

"Look, you've got to answer it. They want a reply."

"Too bad," she said as she snatched the invitation from him and threw it on the counter, just missing a splotch of cornbread batter.

He went to his room and pulled out the atlas. He wanted to find out just where Azure Bay was located. Sitting on the bed, he opened the book to the Florida map and searched the state. No. Impossible. Maybe he needed to open the blinds, but it looked like Azure Bay was right next door to Palm Beach! His mama and daddy were invited to a wedding that was practically in Palm Beach. He thought of the Charles Wrightsmans, the Duke and Duchess of Windsor, the Kennedys. What a guest list! But he was sure his favorite socialite, Mrs. William S. Paley (also known as the Beauteous Babe), wouldn't attend because the Paley's didn't much go to Palm Beach. Still, Mama and Daddy might meet and make friends with all these society people, and who knew how that could change their lives. Matt thought again about *Orisons* and vowed to continue his nightly prayer. He knew the book *must* be responsible for the invitation.

His belief that one day he would work for Mrs. Paley strengthened. After all, if Mama and Daddy could receive such an invitation as this, anything was possible. He would serve as butler for Mrs. Paley, in fact he'd become her favorite servant. The vision played out in his mind like a movie scene. After a party, up in her dressing room, The Beauteous One would sink like a ballerina into a silk moiré chair (fabulous fabric he'd helped her pick out). He would stand near the door, his head inclined to catch the whispery comments.

"That went rather well, Matthew, don't you think?"

"Yes, Madam."

She would take up a patterned silk scarf—pink, white, lime green—from the onyx table beside her and say, "Next time, no timbales—so heavy. Remind Cook, will you?"

"Yes, Madam."

"And the roses—absolutely garish. What could I have been thinking?"

She would caress the scarf with manicured finger tips. "Tell the gardener we won't use that shade again—muted colors only next time."

"Very well, Madam."

Mrs. Paley's Katherine Hepburn eyes would glitter with naughtiness and her perfect mouth would form the shape of a smile she'd been tactful enough to withhold until then. "The Princess Radziwill adores sweets, doesn't she? She positively haunted the pastry carte," Babe would take up a bulky handbag that had been lying on the floor and would place it in the chair next to her. "The Princess and Mrs. Guest were exquisite, though, weren't they? Yves St. Laurent is a genius, don't you think?"

"Yes, Madam."

"Is everything ready for the move to the apartment on the eighteenth?" She would tie the scarf to the purse strap, study the effect, caress the scarf, and put the bag back on the floor.

"Yes, Madam. The preparations are complete."

"That's lovely, Matthew. You're lovely. I'm not quite sure how we managed before you came."

"Thank you, Madam."

He was pulled from Mrs. Paley's boudoir and zapped back to Natchitoches, Louisiana, by his mother's voice coming from the bathroom, "Shit!" His mama had broken a bottle. Demoralized, he looked around his dark, ugly room. Getting up, he stood at the window, and opened the blinds. Too bright. He shuddered, closed them, but then peaked through. Every way he looked, he saw tacky shingled boxes sitting under giant insect antennae. He looked away, down at the rug-less wooden floor. Clearly, just like a prophetess gazing into crystalline water, he could see the boys playing ball down at the park. Fear, abomination. He shuddered, stuffing back these feelings.

He'd concentrate on this new project instead. He pushed the dreariness down deep, collected himself, and sneaked into the kitchen for the invitation. Back in his room, he sat and studied it. *A wedding practically in Palm Beach. But in July? Wouldn't it be too hot?* He shrugged. *Maybe the Whittingtons' East Hampton house had termites.*

He placed the card and envelopes in his safest drawer. He couldn't argue with his mama, but knew the invitation requested the favor of a reply. Miz Post was uncompromising when it came to responses.

He heard voices yelling, interrupting one another, Daddy's, Kathleen's, Mama's, Betsy's. Supper time.

The next afternoon he sat in his room, alone in the house. He opened the drawer containing the invitation and took it up. Palm Beach, the Duke and Duchess, the Kennedys. He sniffed it. It smelled like what *Le Chic* would call *old* money.

He shut his eyes to see his vision better. Palms surrounding a mauve palace with a red tile roof, the trees bent like dancers with their ruby-orange fronds extending toward the bougainvillea lacing the house. Inside, himself, handsome in black tie. If he'd had time, he could have enjoyed the sea sounds wafting through long windows, the breezes fluttering sun-gilded chiffon, but he had to work. He walked with dignity across a parquet expanse, wielding a gleaming tray of orchid-like canapés. He moved in and out among ladies dressed in pink, violet, and rose taffeta and linen. As he served, he *sort of* tried to ignore the various bits of conversation, but really, he couldn't help overhearing snippets, despite the tinkling glasses of Cristal.

"My dear, she's on her third face lift and fourth husband, no, wait, I think it's the other way round." The platinum-blond lady deftly exchanged an empty wine glass for a full one without detaining the maid carrying the tray.

Another lady raised her diamond and ruby wrist watch causing a pop pop pop in the explosion of lights and colors animating the sunlit mirror. "Darling, I must go. Winthrop insisted I invite the dreadful Texas woman and her solicitor for dinner. I'll need time to compose myself for *that* ordeal. If she'd had the faintest shred of decency, she'd have drowned herself as a toddler, as soon as she realized her name was Ima Hogg."

An arresting brunette shook her head, pill box magenta hat glinting. "Of course, we all *revere* the Duchess, but if one were completely objective, might not one concede her to be the tiniest bit mercenary?"

❖

"Hey, Sissy, Sissy, does Little Snow White want to come out and play?" Today, some boys passing his house yelled and snorted as they headed for the ball field. Matt stuffed his panic.

Their voices and laughter faded. Matt sat and stared at his room's browns and grays. He looked at the imitation knotty-pine chest of drawers from Sears and snorted like the boys had. No matter what his room looked like, it was still his shelter. Outside, everybody despised him. He'd just have to concentrate on his project instead of worrying about things he couldn't change, except his idea meant leaving the cracker box, which was always an ordeal. But he couldn't stay in here forever. He *had* to leave some time. In fact, he had to leave two or three times a week. He'd have to make a run this afternoon. Opening a drawer, he picked up a thin pile of cash. He had to act before his mama could think to stop him.

Matt left the house on his bike and peddled toward town. He rode beneath cathedral-ceiling oak branches shading the intersection of his street and Locock Avenue as a carload of yelling teenagers gunned by him. He crossed the bridge, over the silvery, burbling water, past creamy stucco buildings wearing iron lace, past giant magnolias lining Front Street's river walk. Young drivers honked their horns and pointed. Another cyclist rode right toward him as if to collide, and swerved at the last minute, yelling, "Watch out, Little Girl. Now don't you fall, Nancy."

Matt glimpsed the trees, trying to push down the thought that he was in the sun unprotected. He shivered in the heat but kept repeating his mental list of books and supplies. He stopped first at the library, next at Rexall Drug.

Back at home, he took everything from the bike's side saddles into his room and shut the door. He arranged pen, ink, and stationery. He placed the library's copies of *Etiquette* and *Calligraphy* close by so they'd be handy. Tiptoeing to the window, he opened the blinds. Sunlight striped his bed. He closed them again and switched on the overhead light. It was still pretty dark.

He placed a clean piece of stationery on his desk, took up the pen, dipped its tip in ink, and began to write in shaky calligraphy:

Mr. & Mrs. Matthew Thomas McPhee Regre...

The ink smudged. He'd have to start over. After three or four botches, the reply was about to get on his last nerve. He knew he'd never have a career in calligraphy. Maybe the room was too dark. He rose, went around the bed to the window again, and reopened the blinds. He shook his head as the room illuminated, and closed the blinds again.

In relative darkness he continued working, through sheet after sheet. If he didn't splotch the ink, he wrote the lines crooked. If he wrote the lines straight, he bungled the letters or smeared the ink. But he had to do it. He had to answer, to respond. The favor of a reply was requested, even if it was a refusal. Maybe some of those Social Register types would see the reply and be impressed by the McPhees' elegant manners. He worked on until his back and hands ached, until he could barely see what he was writing.

He was finishing up his twenty-fifth attempt as he became aware of the sounds of Mama cooking supper. Perfect or imperfect, it'd have to do. This had been the last sheet of stationery. He inhaled and exhaled twice then ambled, stationery in hand, to the kitchen. Tentative but regal, he extended the work toward his mother as Her Majesty Queen Elizabeth II would have extended her scepter toward a particularly testy subject. Inhale, exhale.

"Mama, here's the reply to the invitation for Ralph's wedding. If you'll check it, I'll get it ready to mail."

His mother, opening the oven for the cornbread, shook her head and thought, *why couldn't I've had a son like everybody else's? My first child, my only boy, and he is a complete freak, a pantywaist.*

He sashayed around the house like Cinderella going to the ball. She'd told him and told him to pick up his feet when he walked and take bigger steps. It didn't make one damn bit of difference. He swished like Lady Astor. And he couldn't, or wouldn't, do the things that the other kids his age did. Not basketball or around the house, not even yard work. Matt had to keep trying. And now, he'd started going on about how mowing kept him in the sun too long, going on with some stupid idea about the sun being dangerous.

Lately, she was concerned that he spent hours in his room even though it was dark as the devil's own hell in there, even *with* the lights. From what she could tell he never even opened the blinds. She didn't know how he'd survive in this world. It was really embarrassing to have a child like him. He said the craziest things, always talking about the rich women from those library magazines he brought home like he actually knew those people. Always talking about socialites and social status. Social status—she'd never had any, never expected any, never wanted any, never thought about any. She'd started picking cotton at five, and didn't have much time to worry about social status. Now her only son, a sissy boy, couldn't talk about anything but social status, no matter who was around or how crazy it sounded. God, he'd embarrassed her so many times.

Not that she didn't love him. He was a sweet boy, too sweet. But for God's sake, somebody needed to do something with him, talk to him, straighten him out. His daddy sure as hell didn't know what to do. He was too busy carrying on and braying like a jackass with that temper exploding two or three times a week. But she couldn't blame him for Matt's condition—really neither one of them knew what to make of him.

She'd been so thrilled when he'd come, him being the first, not counting the stillborn. When he was a toddler, she'd looked forward to taking him out in his stroller. People would stop her just to admire him. She'd been so proud of his looks, she'd had his picture taken three or four times a year for the first few years. Well, the handsome child was now going on thirteen and, in many ways, he was still as babyish as he'd been at three or four. Certainly he was as helpless—not at all like the mature young man she'd expected him to become.

Mature. Well, in some ways he *was* ahead of his time. She'd caught him from the earliest age doing things that made her, a grown-up woman, blush. Why, she hadn't even been able to tell his daddy the first time she'd caught Matt. From time to time after that, she'd catch him again, and he'd always get so upset, you'd have thought she'd slapped him or beaten him. She'd felt like doing just that too. He might have gotten upset, but the behavior went on and on, and somehow she could never bring herself to mention it to his daddy.

How Matt would ever make it, she didn't know. Lord, she hated raising children. Thank God for the women in the beauty shop. She could always find something to laugh about with them, even if she was working herself to death in the process. Thank God for Miz Perry and her card parties. Thank God for duplicate bridge. Thanks to Jesus for any distractions from her kids.

Having kids—marriage, for that matter—wasn't all it was cracked up to be. She bet she could've made it on her own in the world. Of course, now she'd never know. But she'd been a star player on the girls' basketball team. Matt couldn't even dribble a damn ball, wouldn't try. She'd been a good student, especially in math. Matt wasn't good at anything but sissified subjects like English and French. French for God's sake. They hadn't even taught French at her school in Pinewood. *What possible use could a boy ever have for French?* But he made straight A's in it. It probably had something to do with all those magazines from the library.

In her opinion, he read too much and he read the wrong stuff. You couldn't get him to sneeze at *Huckleberry Finn*, but he'd damn sure eat up all those old book-of-the-month club books she had laying around. He had a vocabulary as large as any adult she knew, whether they'd been to college or not. That'd do him a lot of good when he was trying to—she hated to think about it—get a job, or, God help them all, when he was drafted.

Now this fancy wedding invitation had come. When she'd heard about his cousin Ralph's engagement to that rich girl in Florida, she'd known that just the invitation would put Matt in a snit, and she'd been right. She'd wanted to put it away so he wouldn't see it, but the telephone had rung. She'd gone to answer it, and had forgotten all about the unopened invitation. And now Matt was sticking something in her face while she was trying to get the cornbread out of the damn oven. *Why couldn't I've had a son like everybody else's?*

She put the hot pan on the counter and took the sheet he'd extended and read it.

Mr. & Mrs. Matthew Thomas McPhee regrets that they must decline Mr. and Mrs. Whittington's kind invitation for Tuesday, the Fourth of July One Thousand Nine Hundred and Sixty-One.

She snorted when she was finished and said, "If I was to answer the invitation, it wouldn't be with this. The penmanship's terrible, and the grammar's not even correct." She read from the sheet aloud to him, "'Mr. and Mrs. Matthew Thomas McPhee Regrets'. If I sent this, we'd look like yahoos."

She let the paper drop to the floor. She stomped and ground her foot into it. She turned back to putting the cornbread on a plate.

Matt picked up the paper and, scanned it as he retreated to his room. She was right. He'd written *Regrets*. He'd concentrated so hard on his fancy letters; he'd forgotten to check subject-verb. He stacked the library books, including *Orisons* on the table. He'd return them tomorrow, and wouldn't be praying tonight. Matt put pen and ink away in a drawer. He threw the used stationery—including the battered reply—into the waste basket.

Light and movement in the dresser mirror—glimmering pearls, a varnished nail touching a glossy lower lip. Mrs. Paley, the Beauteous Babe, shook her seraphic head. "Matthew, could one really abide so slipshod an effort? One would have thought better of your grammar." The brilliant face dimmed as the angel head continued shaking.

Tiptoeing to the window, Matt opened a Venetian blind. The sun striped his face. He shut it.

Thou Shalt Not Lie
N. S. Beranek

From a block away the jalousie windows of the vestibule resembled a faceted gemstone glittering against the navy blue night sky, but now that he is standing inside of it, Reed's impression of the space is far less favorable. It seems to him to border on seedy, something he never would have expected from a high rise on a residential street so near downtown, prime real estate in the city of Chicago.

The harshness of his assessment triggers a wave of guilt that causes him to backpedal. *No, not seedy,* he silently amends, *but definitely tired.*

The layered panes of glass are cranked open to catch the cool breeze coming in off the lake, in spite of the fact that the air is ripe with the stink of rotting fish and algae and the borrowed scent of car exhaust. Underneath those smells, seemingly coming from the tiles beneath his feet, Reed detects the faint odor of urine.

Like the ones covering the solid portions of the walls, the floor tiles are aquamarine in color, reminiscent of the shower room at the Y.M.C.A. in the small central Illinois town where he attended Bible College. Reed smiles, recalling with fondness the countless Friday and Saturday nights he spent splashing around in the pool with Cam and some of their fellow students. Then he remembers: *Cam is dead.* His stomach does a flip. He pushes the thought from his mind.

Unlike the tiles in his memory, the ones currently beneath his feet are worn to a matte finish and marred with black streaks from decades of abuse by hard soled shoes and boots caked with snow and road salt, rather than the barefoot traffic of naked boys.

He steps to the intercom panel. The names of the building's residents are written in faded ink and protected by yellowed plastic rectangles. Reed reaches up to press the correct black Bakelite button but is stopped by a sharp pang of doubt. *He won't answer the door.* It astounds him that he hadn't thought of it earlier, either before he set out for Tobin Jones' apartment building or while he was circling the blocks surrounding it, searching for a parking space. He's all the more amazed because he understands exactly why the young man won't come to the door, knows how it feels to have a stranger hell bent on being granted an interview leaning on the bell. Reed has spent the better part of the week and a half since the accident that took the life of his boss and dearest friend, trapped inside his home with his cell phone turned off and the receiver of his real phone out of its cradle.

It would have been even more of a madhouse, he knows, were it not for the fact that on the day of the accident Hurricane Isaac was battering the Gulf Coast and threatening the start of the Republican National Convention. The storm stole the focus of the twenty-four hour cable news channels and relegated the events in Chicago to a line or two on the scroll beneath the talking heads. Because of Isaac, it has been mainly reporters from local news outlets who have been hounding and isolating Reed, magnifying his grief. His torment by them began the morning after the accident, when the Tribune ran the front page headline: Chicago Pastor Who Prophesied End of Days Dies Good Samaritan, along with a color photograph showing the large cross left by an unknown person on the curb nearest the spot where Cam was struck and killed and Tobin Jones injured. The cross was of the "Taken" variety, with an arrow point cut into the top of its vertical arm to indicate that the person killed had been lifted to heaven by the Lord. The special crosses came into being because of a dream Cam had in which, he said, God revealed to him that the first phase of the Rapture was about to begin. He explained that each of The Chosen would be given an opportunity to sacrifice their life to save another person's; those who did would be taken directly up to heaven. A Good Samaritan craze would ensue, and it would be the last opportunity for the unsaved to repent their sins and accept Jesus as their Lord and Savior.

Though the photo in the paper was snapped only hours after the accident the Taken cross placed for Cam was already piled high with flowers, teddy bears, and hand-written notes. The thing that caught Reed's eye, however, was the bloodstain on the asphalt in the photo's background. Thinking of it now makes him frantic; without deciding to he presses the button three times in quick succession, then gives it three longer presses, holding it for a full count each time, and finishes with three bursts as short as the first set.

A car horn bleats in the distance. Almost immediately it is answered by angry honks from sedans and the beeps of economy cars, even a deeper blast he imagines comes from a big rig. He's fairly sure the ruckus emanates from North Halsted. He imagines the scene: a herd of young men has just spilled from the popular avenue's many bars. They've staggered drunkenly into the street, directly into the path of the cars. In his imagination they are all European fashion models sporting tight jeans and even tighter t-shirts, thumb rings and long, asymmetrical bangs. He listens for shouting, curses, and laughter, but hears only the rushing water-like white noise of faster traffic coming from beyond Halsted, way out on Lake Shore Drive.

A rumbling catches his attention. As he listens it grows sharper, developing into the clack-clack clattering of an elevated train which passes unseen somewhere very near before fading back into the din of the city.

He decides that the younger man has done the smarter thing and gone to stay at a friend's. Just as he turns to go, the room is blasted by an electronic racket so loud it makes him jump. It is several jarring seconds more before it dawns on him what the noise signifies—Tobin Jones granting him entry.

The lobby last underwent a makeover in the late eighties, Reed surmises as he glances around. A Nagle print overlooks a pit grouping of black leather sofas, which in turn sit atop a rug that reminds him of a sweater Bill Cosby once wore on the cover of Parade magazine. Knit using a multitude of vivid yarns, the sweater was a natural entry point into a sermon about Joseph's coat of many colors. Bringing that photo to Cam's attention had been something of a coup for Reed, then the education minister for the church Cam's father Lebbeus Burke founded in the forties, because his best friend loved pop culture references that lent themselves to biblical discussions.

He steps up to the brass and black marble elevator surround. *What was he doing in that intersection?* Thursday afternoon was Cam's designated time for writing his weekly sermon; everyone was under strict orders not to disturb him after lunch on that day of the week—for any reason short of the return of Jesus Christ himself. As his assistant pastor, Reed never booked appointments for Thursdays, so as to be free to deal with any crisis that arose. Sometime in the evening Cam would bring the finished sermon to Reed's house to give it a test run, usually arriving between eight and nine, a few times not until after midnight. He'd never failed to turn up, freshly-penned sermon in hand. The habit served them well for three decades.

So what, Reed asks again, *was he doing crossing an intersection a half dozen blocks from the church at nine-thirty on a Thursday evening?*

❖

"Excuse me. Are you alright?"

He turns and finds an elderly woman standing just to his right. In the crook of her left arm she cradles a small white bundle of fur he believes must be a dog.

"Yes, ma'am, jus' fine," Reed replies, forever a small town Nebraska boy raised to respect his elders. "Thank you."

She gives him a dubious look. "You haven't pushed the button."

Sure enough, the button marked with an upward-pointing arrow is unlit. He had not called the elevator, yet has been patiently waiting for it to arrive. "Oh, thank you," he says, feeling his cheeks redden. He jabs the button, which lights instantly and causes a bell to chime. The door begins to slide open, revealing that the car was there all along.

"Well, we need to go do our business," the lady says, lifting the dog higher to indicate it.

The idea of her standing alone in the dark at this late hour, even just a few feet from the door, alarms Reed. "Should I wait?" he asks.

Already at the doorway to the vestibule, she turns back and squints at him. "What for? We're fine. Don't worry about us." She turns her back and gives him a dismissive wave over her shoulder.

Just before the vestibule door closes behind her he hears her call, "You're the one staring off into space."

The elevator walls are covered with grey industrial carpeting and the space has a noxious yet strangely familiar odor. Reed pushes the button for the fifth floor just before the realization hits him of why he knows the scent. When they were first married, his wife Kim, inspired by a Sunset do-it-yourself home improvement book, spent days turning one wall of their fourth bedroom into a hive of pressboard cubbyholes, each hidden behind a door laminated with orange, mustard or avocado-hued glossy plastic. The plastic was affixed with adhesive that emitted the same offensive odor he smells now; he guesses the carpeting on the elevator walls was adhered using the same product.

The project was intended to transform the guest bedroom into a multi-purpose space, a den/library/playroom for their daughter Sarah, but in Reed's opinion it only ever adequately achieved the last. The outlandish color scheme gave it the atmosphere of one of the "daycare centers" that were springing up all across the nation. Cam had said, and Reed agreed, that the facilities were the inevitable result of the nation's skyrocketing divorce rate. Reed remembers worrying that Kim was trying to subtly suggest they should enroll Sarah in such a place, that his wife wanted to join the workforce and "find herself", as so many women were then doing. But she hadn't been proposing any such thing; she was merely trying to be fashionable and frugal at once.

He follows the ascending apartment numbers around a corner to the butt end of a hall containing only two doors. One is marked "Maintenance"; the other has no markings at all, but Reed spies nail holes where numbers must once have been affixed. Though he thinks it is the door he wants, because the number he seeks is next in the sequence and because there was no other hall to turn down that he saw, the fact that it is unnumbered unnerves him; he is about to double-back and look again when the unmarked door begins to swing away from him. It halts after only a few inches due to the security chain, which has been pulled taut.

Nothing is visible through the sliver of an opening except a thin slice of bare ecru wall. "Hello?" Reed says. "Are you Tobin Jones?"

Instead of answering directly, a husky voice replies, "Why are you here? I did the interview with the Trib so that people wouldn't have to...wouldn't...have..." The end of the speaker's sentence is lost to a spate of coughs. "Ow!" he says as soon as the fit is over. "Dammit, that hurts." His words are clearer, crisper than before. "Sorry."

It is important to Reed that he sees the young man's face when he asks him the question that brought him across town so late at night. "There's something that I...Would you please move to where I can see you?"

To his great surprise Tobin Jones obliges, sliding sideways along the wall until his right shoulder rests against the doorframe. "Ta da," the young man says, without a trace of humor.

He looks very little like the high school graduation photo the newspaper published and very much the way one might expect of someone who was recently hit by a car: his left arm is in a cast and sling, his corresponding cheekbone appears to have been scrubbed raw with sandpaper, and his hair, tawny in color, stands out at odd angles.

Grainy black and white images flood Reed's mind, images of Cam and Tobin Jones entering the crosswalk in that order; of the younger man spying the car Cam never saw and running forward into its path; of his grabbing Cam and trying to pull him back but failing because of the difference in their sizes. Terrible images of the car barreling down on them as they tumbled separately to the asphalt. Cam had somehow ended up at just the right angle in relation to the vehicle so that when it struck him he'd rolled, and would have been pushed clear had it not been for a pothole. His body had wedged in it, and the car...

Reed shuts his eyes tight, as if the scene is playing out in real time in front of him, not in moving pictures planted in his mind's eye three hours ago by a poor-quality video from an outdated surveillance system. The images defy his actions and keep playing out. Over and over the car rolls over Cam, crushes his ribcage.

According to his eldest, Caleb, the coroner had said it popped his heart "like a water balloon".

Don't tell your mother that, Reed remembers saying. He opens his eyes again, finds Tobin's gaze. "Cam wasn't the Good Samaritan; that was you."

The boy's jaw tightens. "No."

"It's on tape."

The young man's eyes widen with fear, and then quickly narrow again, "Bullshit."

The owner of the videotape was also the owner of the dry cleaners located at the intersection where the tragedy occurred. He said he'd heard, simultaneously, the roar of an engine at full throttle and the squeal of tires sliding across asphalt. Seconds later people had come rushing into the store shouting that he should call 911, a ludicrous request given that he could see, even through his steamy shop windows, at least fifty people with their cell phones already out. Then a woman said she'd recognized one of the men who'd been struck, that he was famous, or sort of famous, anyway. The dry cleaner gloated that he'd duped the police, explaining how he'd removed the videotape on which the event was recorded, switched off the VCR, and inserted a different tape into it, one which he'd first partially unspooled. When detectives arrived and asked about his surveillance system, he told them the machine had been broken for months and ejected the dummy tape as proof.

"There is a tape. I've seen it." Reed wishes with all his being that he hadn't; wonders if he will ever be able to stop seeing flashes from it.

"No way. If there was the cops would have it, and they…" Tobin lets his words trail off. His expression is one of unease.

"What? They would have come here and asked you why you lied?"

"No," the younger man says, again defiant. "They would have shown it to me before you."

There's a protocol, Pastor Samuelson. I'm sure you understand, the officer said. *We're only allowed to talk to his wife. If she isn't available—and I'm talking incapacitated, not just off shopping or whatever—then we can speak to one of his children. After that, to the spouse of one of his children. Or, if there isn't one of those, to a sibling. Can't imagine it'll come to that, but while I've got you on the line, did—, I mean, does Pastor Burke have any siblings?*

It was how Reed had known Cam was either dead or so badly hurt they didn't expect him to survive whatever had befallen him. Shock and grief fueled his indignation and sent words he'd never before used flying out of his mouth. *Screw you!* he'd hollered, before slamming down the phone.

"I was his assistant for longer than you've been alive," he says.

Tobin Jones seems unfazed. "So? I'm the one who was involved with him."

The resident assistant who checked him in on move-in day at the dorm told Reed that his roommate had already arrived, but from the doorway of his assigned room the scene inside was inscrutable: twin beds that looked equally unclaimed, a pair of empty desks, and a single bureau at the midpoint of the narrow space. At a loss to determine where he might put down his burden, Reed found it impossible even to enter the room. *If yer looking for 213, you've found it,* a voice said. Reed felt the handle of the hard-shelled case being pulled from his grip. Seconds later an outstretched hand was thrust into his view. *I'm Camon Burke, but everyone calls me Cam,* the would-be hand shaker said. *What's your name?*

Reed had made a vow to himself that at college things were going to be different; he was going to be a different person. He was going to make eye contact with his classmates and firmly shake their hands and project an aura of confidence, because all the advice he'd gotten was the same: if you can just pretend to be confident in yourself, son, everyone else will believe it, and pretty soon you'll believe it, too. And so Reed answered the proffered hand with a firm squeeze and a few quick pumps of the arm. To his amazement he found that it was true, he immediately felt better. He felt that yes, he could turn things around simply by deciding that they would change. It was so clear. Why hadn't he been able to see it before? One by one, he would win over all of his new classmates and things would be good.

Determined to make his desire reality, to look his new roommate in the eye, assert himself, and finally gain respect, Reed had looked up and been immediately undone by Camon Burke's faded denim eyes, golden hair, and winning smile.

He'd never gotten any indication that Cam felt the kinds of things he did or saw the world in the same unusual way, so he never let on about the odd desires that moved his heart and nothing ever came of them. And yet, everything had. Instead of returning to Nebraska after graduation he followed Cam to Chicago to take a job as the education minister at Cam's father's church. It was a fire-and-brimstone affair, totally unlike the lukewarm congregation he grew up in, and Lebbeus and Marian were nothing like his own parents, who'd sent their son to Bible College not because they wanted a minister in the family, but to keep him safe from the influence of the secular world for just a little while longer.

He'd stayed by Cam's side for thirty-five years, first as his roommate and friend, then as his co-worker, and finally, after Lebbeus had a fatal heart attack, as his Assistant Pastor at The Light of God Assembly of Greater Chicago.

Never in all those years was there the slightest hint that Cam harbored thoughts similar to his; still the question always haunted Reed: what if? What might have happened all those years ago if he'd told him how he felt? What if Cam secretly felt the same way and was simply every bit as scared to say so?

The strange phone call he'd received an hour before meeting the blackmailer in the back room of the dry cleaning business struck right at the heart of his fear. *I have a tape I think you'll be very interested in,* the caller said. *If you don't want people to know the truth about Cam Burke and that boy that got hurt in the accident with him, bring your checkbook and meet me at this address in one hour.*

A light bulb goes on in Reed's mind. *This young man means he was involved in the accident with him, not 'involved' the other way!* Jubilation and relief wash over him. His knees threaten to buckle.

"Are you okay?" Tobin Jones asks.

"No," Reed admits. "I just watched my...my...oldest friend...," he cringes at the grossly inadequate but technically apt description. "...get killed. I also saw you trying to save his life. I know you're lying about what happened, and I'm not leaving here until I know why."

"That was pretty smart, what you did down there," Tobin says after Reed is inside the apartment and the door is bolted and re-chained. He leads the way down a narrow, dimly-lit entry hall into a room that isn't any shape Reed remembers from geometry class. An odd conglomeration of walls, windows and doors, it feels more like accidentally-created negative space than anything anyone planned.

"What I did?"

"S.O.S." The young man points to a small, picture tube-type television sitting on a wheeled butcher block cart. The scene it shows is a nearly overhead look at the empty vestibule, captured by a camera Reed hadn't noticed. "If you hadn't done that I never would have switched the channel to see who it was."

The revelation that the young man let him in because he saw his face and recognized him takes Reed by surprise. He was so happy to be granted entry that he hadn't stopped to contemplate why the other chose to buzz him in.

"You know who I am?"

Tobin snorts and rolls his eyes but doesn't answer. He lifts a powder blue polar fleece throw from the back of one of two black metal folding chairs which are pushed up to a bistro-sized blond wood dining table. Down the center of the table are seven votive holders: red, orange, yellow, green, blue, indigo, and violet. The sight makes Reed's stomach lurch.

To make up for not being able to use his left arm, Tobin grips one corner of the fleece throw between his teeth while he winds it around his shoulders, then pads barefoot across the hardwood to a nubbly brown plaid sofa. As he carefully lowers himself onto it Reed notes that the right leg of Tobin's worn jeans is ripped open—not, he guesses, from the accident, but as more of an anti-fashion statement. It makes it possible to see the graceful way his leg narrows below the knee and swells again at the top of the calf, and that fine golden hairs cover his shin.

That pastor of yours was no Good Samaritan, the dry cleaner said by way of greeting the minute Reed was safely inside the stock room of the store. *The only thing really getting 'Taken' is your flock, am I right?*

The dry cleaner had had the idea that they were on the order of televangelists, when nothing was further from the truth. Cam's fanciest physical possession was his Mercury Grand Marquis, but what he valued most was his wife, Joanne, their boys, Caleb and Joshua, and their grandkids. There were no mansions with gold faucets or heated dog houses. Joanne drove a Chevy Suburban because it was a good vehicle for getting donated items from the church to the many members of the congregation who barely got by on disability or social security checks. Chicago was a hard place to be poor, and the church held drives throughout the year, collecting coats and space heaters in winter; fans in summer; school clothes in fall; and bags of food continually.

The tape wasn't what Reed thought it would be, but it was just as bad, and he'd paid dearly to keep it out of the media's clutches. His hand shook as he wrote out a check for "ten thousand dollars and no cents" but he didn't have a choice; the tape threatened everything Cam had worked his whole life to build, and was gruesome besides. After spewing the contents of his dinner on the stock room floor, he'd vowed never to let Joanne or the boys see the awful images the tape contained. His plan is to rip the offending celluloid or whatever it is that videotape was made from out of the case and burn it. First, though, he wants to know why Tobin told the world that it was Cam who saw the car and threw himself into its path to save a stranger.

"Tell me why you lied."

"You should be happy I did. Isn't that what he would want?"

There was a time when Reed would have felt confidant saying what he thought Cam would or wouldn't want—saying no, absolutely not, he would never condone dishonesty; but four months ago Cam had revealed that he'd received a transmission from God via a dream. It was behavior worthy of Lebbeus, and that frightened Reed. Cam had never been his father. He ran an entirely different sort of ministry, seeking to inspire people to come to Jesus instead of scaring them into doing so. Reed never expected him to have a revelatory dream or start preaching the commencement of the Rapture. Since those things happened, he hadn't been certain of much.

"No, he wouldn't want you to lie," he says, hoping he sounds convincing.

"Why? Because it breaks a Commandment?" Tobin's tone is condescending, but Reed is used to encountering that.

He takes a deep, calming breath and nods. "Yes."

❖

A new understanding of Matthew 16:24 has been laid on my heart, Cam announced during the sermon in which he revealed his dream to the congregation. *It will now have a new, literal meaning, for He is about to begin calling His Chosen home! Each of us will be confronted by a situation that will determine whether we sit by His side for eternity or suffer eternal damnation. Ladies and gentlemen, He asks you—what will you give in exchange for your soul? Will you take the opportunity presented? Will you follow His example by giving your life to save that of another?*

Because the Mayan calendar was believed by many to predict the world's end on December 21st, prophesies such as Cam's were particularly good for selling newspapers and attracting people to websites and blogs. News of it spread quickly from the congregation to the rest of the city and then out to the nation and the world. The church began fielding a steady stream of calls from various media outlets, and Cam had been more than happy to grant an interview to anyone who asked.

Just as the hubbub was beginning to quiet down, a jogger in Grant Park threw himself between a lunging rottweiler and a toddler he did not know and was killed. Cam, seeing a place where a Good Samaritan "fell before being raised up", placed a cross tipped with an arrow point at the site of the attack.

The media had a field day. The reporting of incidents of selfless behavior became a daily occurrence almost overnight. Some people questioned whether the frequency of the acts had actually increased or just the rate at which they were being reported. Others took issue with the acts themselves. When two women rushed to help the driver of a car that struck a hydrant and then a telephone pole and were electrocuted along with the man they were hoping to save, people asked: Did it count even though the driver died? What about the fact that the women likely never imagined they would die? Did that mean their sacrifice didn't qualify? When a couple drowned while trying to save their dog, the debate raged: Did saving an animal's life count? Would it still count if it'd been their child, or was it a parent's duty to try to save their offspring? And speaking of duty: Were police, firefighters, and members of the military true Good Samaritans, or were they something else? Some of the 'Good Samaritans' were even revealed to have been up to no good when they died. A man who saved a little girl who'd fallen from a zoo tram car turned out to have lured her away from her parents and into the tram because, it was speculated, that was the fastest route back to the main entrance and escape. Witnesses said that just before she tumbled into the path of an opposing train, the little girl had been struggling to get away from the man and frantically calling for her mother.

It got worse. Journalists and talk show hosts began to accuse people of setting out to get killed to secure entry into heaven, or at least fifteen minutes of posthumous fame. For Reed, that line of questioning culminated three days ago, when a television personality postulated that Cam had orchestrated the accident that took his life so that he would be revered after death, and perhaps also because he'd been secretly diagnosed with a dread disease. It was all Reed could do to not to throw something through the front of the set. Instead, he'd switched it off and vowed not to watch another minute or read another word of such drivel.

❖

"I'm sorry," Tobin says. "That was rude. It's just…everything hurts."

One of Reed's jobs as assistant pastor is to sit with the sick and dying and their families in hospital rooms. Even before his wife Kim was diagnosed with the ovarian cancer that took her life six months later, he'd heard more than his share of pain-induced outbursts and paranoid rants brought on by powerful drugs. "It's alright. I understand," he says. He pulls out one of the folding chairs, turns it around, and takes a seat. "Tell me, how did you know it was what Cam would have wanted?"

Tobin looks aghast. "Seriously? Those f—" He catches himself. "…freaking reporters were at the hospital when we pulled up in the ambulance. How could I not know he was the prophesy guy?"

Reed shakes his head. "No, you lied right after it happened. I saw you on the tape. Before the reporters. Even before the ambulance. You gestured to the first people who rushed up to you, and it was obvious you were telling them he tried to save you. Why?"

Tobin's bottom lip begins to quiver. "Because he would have, if he'd seen the car first. I know he would. And because I, I owe him."

He drops his gaze. "He never would have been in that intersection if it wasn't for…if I had just…" When he looks up, there are tears welling in his eyes. "I'm so sorry," he says. "It's my fault he's dead."

After the coughing fit that followed Tobin's declaration has dissipated, Reed asks, "What do you *mean* 'your fault'? Was he meeting with you? Did you know him? How? From where?"

"Ouch, now that really hurts," Tobin says, flashing a crooked smile. "No, I get it. You were looking at him the whole time. I can't blame you. Those blue eyes, and the way the crinkles appeared beside them every time he smiled? I wouldn't have seen me either."

Reed has heard it said that men who are attracted to other men can sense it in one another. If it's sometimes true, it's a skill he doesn't have. Being exposed unnerves him. He's worked hard to keep others from seeing the truth because in his youth even boys he thought of as normal somehow knew that he was not like them.

"You're mistaken," he says. "I'm not—"

"Lying is a sin, remember?"

"There are even worse ones."

Tobin startles him by laughing. "Not being gay." He scowls. "Wait, you don't believe it is one, do you? But…Cam said Jesus' problem is with hate, never love."

Reed finds it hard to breathe. "He said that?"

"Duh. He didn't preach that Leviticus crap. I know. I checked out your website." He pulls the throw tighter around his shoulders. "Didn't you two talk about this?"

There were subjects they'd deftly avoided. Thinking about that fact makes Reed queasy. He steers the conversation back on course. "Tell me where you met him."

Tobin chuffs. "Same place I met you. I was your waiter at Menu@1957."

Menu, as it is referred to by the editors of the Tribune's "Eat This!" section, is a hot new retro diner located on Montrose just a few blocks from the church. The paper has done no less than three features on the establishment, each accompanied by splashy color photos of its glitter-red booths and gleaming chrome lunch counter. Not surprisingly, at its grand opening in April hordes of the city's foodie and hipster sets had shown up, as had Guy Fieri from the *Food Network*, camera crew in tow. Cam and Reed had stopped by on successive Thursdays, hoping to get in, but each time found a line snaking out the door and halfway to the Starbucks on the corner.

It was shortly after their second attempt when Cam thought God spoke to him and everything went mad, and another two months before things died down enough for them to try again. Reed remained skeptical about their chances to get in, owing to simple math. Chicago was a big place; it took quite a while for all the people who wanted to avail themselves of a new opportunity to do so. His fear, though, was unfounded. That third time the wait had been only fifteen minutes long.

They'd spent the time awkwardly, crushed into a small pocket of dead space just beside the door with a handful of other hopefuls voyeuristically eyeing the already-served. But while the rest of the would-be patrons commented on the food, Reed and Cam whispered to one another about the people crowding the space, an expensively and outlandishly dressed group of souls sporting tattoos and the glint of polished metal coming from rings at the crests of their eyebrows and studs at the centers of their tongues. The two men of God agreed that they'd never seen a single diner or member of the staff at a Sunday service.

"But he didn't talk to you other than to place his order," Reed says.

"He did that evening at Starbucks," Tobin explains. "I was on my break. He asked to share a table, because the place was packed." He drops his gaze again; a gesture Reed now understands signifies feelings of guilt. "I thought he was hitting on me. I shouldn't have said okay."

"He wanted to know if you'd been saved," Reed says confidently. Cam had once explained to him that whenever someone caught his eye he took it that the Lord was tapping him on the shoulder, pointing out a soul still lost. Because of it, he was relentless in his pursuit of those persons. It was conceivable he'd followed Tobin into the coffee shop; that he'd engineered the "accidental" meeting.

Reed had witnessed Cam's fervor many times but had never been the focus of it, because his roommate quite reasonably assumed that a person enrolled in Bible College was as impassioned as he. Not wanting to lose him as a friend, Reed had simply let him believe what he wanted, the same way he'd let him believe that friends was all he wished they could be.

"My parents would be so disappointed," Tobin says. "We're freethinkers. I was raised to know better, to steer clear of religious weirdoes." He catches Reed's gaze. "Sorry."

"Go on."

"Normally I would have told off someone who came over and started trying to run that kind of head trip on me, but I couldn't help it; I just liked him so much, right off the bat. I wasted my entire thirty-minute break listening to him, and when he asked if we could meet again the following week, I agreed. We just sort of kept on meeting."

"Every Thursday evening," Reed says. "The night of the week when he was supposed to be with me, test driving that week's sermon." Suddenly, he understands. If Cam had harbored thoughts like his, the weekly sneaking off with this boy would have had a different flavor. "It couldn't have gone anywhere," he says. "He wasn't that way."

"Even if he was, I swear I wasn't really going to do anything!"

"Because he was married?"

"Yeah, and because," Tobin reaches up, takes hold of a chain around his neck which Reed hadn't even noticed, and from beneath his shirt pulls out what appears to be a gold question mark affixed to it with a twist tie. "I am." Reed realizes the object is a mangled wedding band. "My hand swelled. They had to cut it to get it off," Tobin says. He begins to tremble. "Oscar's gonna freak. I couldn't tell him over the phone. I had enough trouble keeping him from coming back here as it was." He swallows hard. "He's…he's an insurance adjuster. He's down in Orlando dealing with the mess Isaac left. They need him because he speaks Spanish, and we need the money. We're saving up to buy a house."

❖

When Reed steps from the apartment back into the hall, he sees the lady from the lobby, sans dog, coming toward him, carrying a plate of food—a pork chop, two eggs, and toast under cling film; it reminds him of the plates Kim would set aside for him whenever he was out keeping one or the other of the flock company in their time of need.

The woman narrows her eyes. "I didn't know that's where you were headed. You aren't a reporter, are you?"

"No, ma'am, I'm a…I was a good friend of the man who died."

"A minister? Oh, lord. You leave that boy alone. There's nothing wrong with him."

"Yes, ma'am," Reed says. "I know that."

Now.

As the elevator door opens onto the lobby, Reed hears the echo of his daughter at age five. "Ah-bee-air-toe means 'open' in Span-itch, Daddy! Did you know that?"

It was one of the many clues he'd had that Kim sometimes let Sarah watch "Sesame Street". He'd asked his baby girl where she'd learned the word, but she was too clever, even then. She'd clammed up and stayed that way, remaining to this day close-lipped about a variety of topics. Reed suspects she is far more liberal than she lets on. For one thing, she married a man who wasn't raised with a strong faith. For another, they'd moved just far enough away to make it plausible that they do not attend Sunday services. Reed pictures weekend mornings at their house, imagines his grandchildren watching programs that make Big Bird and his friends look like "Leave It to Beaver".

Thinking of Sarah, all grown up, makes the time left to him quantifiable; a number he can wrap his head around. *Twenty good years if I'm lucky*, he thinks. *I might get to see Beckett and Willow enter college.*

What do I want for myself in that time?

❖

Through the vestibule's jalousie windows he spies the paler blue sky over North Halsted. Pushing open the street door, he realizes he already has a plan. First, he will go home and erase the portion of the security tape that shows the impact. Then, he will give the thing to Tobin, to burn or show to the world as he pleases, since he was the one 'involved'. Reed hopes he will choose the latter. After all, why shouldn't people know that a married homosexual atheist risked his life trying to save Cam Burke from a speeding car? It's the truth.

Next, as soon as the banks open he will stop payment on his check to the blackmailing dry cleaner. After that, he will stop at the office long enough to write his letter of resignation and pack his things, because he has no business running a church. He can scarcely believe that in eulogizing Cam he'd quoted Job 5:26, "Thou comest in full age unto the grave, as the going up of a stalk in its season," because it has been something of a hallmark for him to minister without ever quoting verse, and the source of the majority of the compliments he has received. *You didn't preach at me, but listened when I needed someone to hear. You made me feel less alone*, people have often told him. It occurs to him that he hasn't read the Bible of his own accord since he was maybe six years old; that listening to Cam's weekly sermons has been all the religious teaching he has been able to stand, because he and Tobin have a lack of faith in common, too. He realizes he has been using the church as a place to hide. *I used my friendship with Cam the same way,* he thinks. *Because it could go nowhere, I didn't have to be honest and face being rejected.*

Lastly, he will make the drive across town and tell Sarah in person that he's decided to step down from the church. He'll call it "retirement" though he's too young for that by a decade. He imagines she'll bring up the subject of his starting to date again, because for most of the eight years since her mother died she's been pushing him in that direction. He was never interested before, but now he wants what Tobin has.

I don't have to tell her everything right away, he reasons. *I'll open the dialogue today, and eventually we'll get there.* He breathes deep, stands taller.

But there will be no more living a lie.

Contest Winner

IN A CHAMBER OF MY HEART
SANDRA GAIL LAMBERT

L awdy, the noise in here is almost worse than anything. Someone dropped another tray on the floor, and the staff never stops yelling to each other down the hall. Well, now I'm lying to myself. Nothing's worse than the pain or even how it itches inside the cut on my stomach. Abdominal incision the doctors call it when they come poke. Opened me up, closed me up. Seems they could have known there was nothing for it without all this. But their drugs work okay, and morphine's my favorite word these days. I could use some now.

"Here's your lunch tray, Ma'am."

He's rattling his cart on down the hall before I can tell him not to leave it. The drugs make me slow. Cheap deli meat, too much mustard, a hard slice of cantaloupe on a lettuce leaf—I can tell from the smells what's under the plate cover. I wouldn't eat that on a day I wasn't sick in my stomach. I reach around for the spit-up basin and hold it close. Slow breathing and recalling the river is what keeps me from gagging.

I use my mind to walk past a bay tree all in white bloom and the sweet of it follows me. The earth softens, and I step through a rattle of palmettos and then around the humped roots of cypress trees until the cold of spring water rises along my legs. I hold my breath and imagine diving down through darker and darker blues to the spring's mouth and, for a moment, I'm past the teeth of rocks, past where light can reach, and into the caves. The current beats against me, rushing out of the earth. I stop swimming and rise. Around me, braids of water spin to the surface in long strands. Flashing like a mullet, I flop to my back. I put the basin to one side. I think I'm safe, for now. The door opens.

"Excuse me, Ma'am."

So much ma'aming. I don't seem to have a name anymore. But she's waiting for me to answer and hasn't walked in my room like it's a broom closet and I'm the broom. Whoever she is, I'm disposed in her favor.

"Come on in. And who are you?"

"Ma'am, I'm a volunteer for the County Historical Society. We want to put together a book of oral histories from long-term residents of the area. Your chart says you were born here. Is that correct?"

Everyone seems allowed to read my chart except me. But she seems nice enough.

"Yep, right across the Silver River."

She's not paying attention. She's rummaging in her big purse. The color matches the linen suit. Periwinkle, they call it, but to me it's more like pickerel weed blooms. That suit, with the pressed white shell, means she's one of our society ladies—must we have them? Pain ripples around my spine. I brace before it attacks. This time it's just a quick bite and lets go. I look over at the women again.

She's sitting on the edge of the fold-out chair that my gal sleeps in sometimes. A spiral bound notebook covers her chest like a shield. She twists a finger through her necklace, and a cross flips over her neckline and dents into the blouse. The cross is a tiny thing, so she's Methodist most likely, and I'm a good work. I feel sick in my stomach again. That tray must have warm mayonnaise on it.

"I'll make you a deal. You take this food out of here, and I'll talk to you. At least until my gal comes."

She looks at the tray like it might give her something, but she summons up a sense of duty. While she's gone, my favorite nurse comes and squirts the nice stuff into my IV.

"Here you go, dear. I'm going to load you up the most allowed before you leave tomorrow. It'll make the trip home easier." She holds my hand.

She's got one of those crushes people get on old ladies. I'm only ninety-two, but I guess with my hair mostly gone and weighing as little as I do and smelling like I'm rotting from the inside, my time of women wanting me for real is over. But I'm not going to let her think I know that. I tickle inside her palm.

"Hey, watch it, Lady. I'll tell on you to that jealous girlfriend of mine down in the lab."

She's still wagging her finger at me as the historical society lady comes back in the room. We stop laughing like kids getting found out.

"If you need anything else, just buzz." Her voice goes professional, but she winks over the woman's head as she leaves. I like her so much. I like this society lady. I like everyone when the drug first goes in.

"Ma'am, are you awake?"

My chin rubs on my chest. There might be drool. I give it a wipe on the sheets before looking at her.

"Where do we start? Do you ask questions?"

"However you'd like, Ma'am. I do have a basic information form to fill out, but otherwise I'm just here to record whatever you have to say. We're not to judge or censor. But I will say that most people start with their parents."

"I'm a bastard."

"Excuse me?"

"Write it down. I'm a bastard."

"Now, that's not a word we use these days."

"Aren't you supposed to let me tell it my way? And in 1920, when I was born, people used that word. I heard it a lot."

She studies her notebook even though she hasn't written a word.

"Write it down."

And she does, best that I can tell.

"My mother ran a jive joint during the Prohibition. A whisper sister, that's what they'd call women like her. Our family had always had a bit of land along the river, out of the way of city law, and people could drink right in their boats and listen to the bands. Coloreds and whites both played. So many people had died—in the war, from the Spanish Flu. Ma said something wild and desperate got in their hearts."

It feels so good, the drug. I stop talking to enjoy the moment like all the cancer society pamphlets say to do. I think they meant loved ones and sunny days and kittens and such, but they should have included the drug rush. I hear the sound of linen against vinyl and know she's thinking of leaving. I find I don't want her to go.

"My mother had grown up out there on the river and didn't care much about the proper way of things. You add that with how soft she felt towards hurt people and strays and mix in all those broken-down boys coming back from Europe and that's how I figure I got born. And with my skin darker than hers and hair that never would lay flat, not that you can tell that now, I've always thought there might be some mixing in me. Ma said no, but she'd say that no matter what, wouldn't she?"

The woman's pen stops. She's staring at me. I give her my old lady eye, and the pen moves again.

"But she always took care of me. Especially those first years when the money just poured in. Hah. That's a play on words, get it?"

I'm laughing too loud. The drugs do that. But I'm not strong enough for it to go on very long. I finish with a squeak and pant for a while before I speak again.

"So, she sent me to school with books and nice clothes. The other kids called me names, but I looked good. Better than some of them. Ma made sure of it. Then came the Depression, in the middle of that Prohibition ended, and the money disappeared, all of it. My mother said that she made good money but had spent gooder. We'd have been hungrier if Ma's grandmother hadn't taught her about roots and such. We'd dig up the arrowhead plants in the water and roast their tubers. And, of course, we fished. But one day, after another meal of roots that left our guts sort of messed up, Ma washed in the river, put on the best clothes she had left, and told me to stay put until she got back from town. When she did, we had money. And we kept having money so I could keep going to school, at least for the months they kept it open. Did you know the government closed the public schools to save money?"

"Really?" The woman writes as fast as she can. She flips over to a new page and fills half of that before she catches up.

"Still, I managed to do pretty good, and when a teacher decided I was smart enough for bookkeeping training, the money showed up for that. I was sixteen and, I'll just say it my own self, good looking, so Ma kept me close. But she didn't need to worry. I studied hard, and I was never one for men, anyway."

I raise an eyebrow at the historical society lady. She smiles.

"We need more nice girls like you these days. Our young women, well, you know how they are."

"A nice girl. Oh my, if my gal heard you say that. Anyway, Ma kept doing whatever it was she was doing until the Depression lifted. And she'd gotten to be a good saver so we managed fine. Then the next War started just in time to help me get a good job."

I'm staring at the ceiling. The past moves over the squares of pitted tiles like a movie and I'm just the narrator. But that last bit sounded bad. I look over, and the woman has stopped writing again.

"Don't stare at me like that. Of course, it was terrible, especially what happened to those Jews over in Europe, but we didn't know anything about that then."

"Yes, Ma'am. Of course."

The pen moves again, and I rest my voice while she catches up. The pain drugs have leveled out, and I'm not saying everything that comes to mind anymore. I can pick and choose. The War started my life and in another way, stopped it. But I don't know if I'll tell her about that. I stare at the ceiling. My pilot's face looks down at me, and she's mad that I'd leave her out of my story. She was the one always so careful, so hidden. If she wants this, who am I to get shy at this late date?

"Okay. I've decided. I'm going to tell you something I've only ever told my gal. Have you got enough ink in that pen, because I'm not saying this again?"

"Yes, Ma'am. And I have another one right here in my purse."

She flips to a fresh page. I've got her interested, I can tell. Let's see if she keeps writing.

"Over on past the highway, that's where the airport used to be in the forties. And that's where they brought in military boys and taught them to fly. I got a job out there handling payroll. They don't tell you this, but a woman pilot helped with the training. And let me tell you, they paid her so much less than the men, not that she was questioning that when she came to see me about a problem with her check. Her zoot suit fit too big so she'd rolled the arms and cinched the waist, and the way the cloth billowed, she looked like the Sultan of Arabia, but with hips. Those pilot goggles sat on top of her head, and hair stuck out the sides of them. I stared at her so hard my ears went deaf. She leaned in and put a palm on my desk to point at her pay stub, and I had to wring my hands into each other to keep them from cradling hers, it was that sudden. She said later it felt the same for her, but she had that military training. You could never tell anything just by looking at her. I started dropping by the women's barracks after work, and the best memories are how we'd jitterbug to Benny Goodman in those narrow aisles between the bunks. My pilot kept care that she and I didn't dance together more than with anyone else."

Up on the ceiling, my pilot smiles at me like she would on those weekend furloughs when we'd pretend to fish along the river. We're remembering together the place where the current curled around on itself. Behind an old lightning-scarred cypress, we found a bank hidden from view. Pain kicks at the backside of the drugs and mixes with an old grief I thought I'd left behind.

"Ma'am? Are you tired? Should we stop? Ma'am? Ma'am?"

Her words come from far away. I can't see anything. Will this sadness be what I take with me? I wish my gal was here, but this will do. I relax into what is to come. I wait. But I keep hearing the noise from the hallway, and all I feel is cold metal hurting against my ribs. I've slumped into the bed railing. My arms are just strong enough to push back to center.

"Ma'am, should I call someone?"

"No. I want to get to the end of the story."

I manage a deep breath. It might be my last. I'm going to run as many words out on it as I can.

"The first time I took her to the river was in winter, but I knew that spring water would feel warm, and we had to push through bushes of purple asters all in bloom, and they scratched against us, but we didn't notice. We stripped bare and jumped in, and when she came and laid her body against the whole length of mine in water so clear that we could see ourselves all the way down to our twenty toes, it hurt like a scald and then it didn't."

I breathe again. It seems I'm going to live awhile longer.

"Ma'am. Perhaps you need some assistance."

The woman has her face tilted up and pinched, as if she smells something bad.

"No. You need to listen. No one remembers her anymore but me and, secondhand, my gal, and soon it will just be her. This is important. Write this down."

I hear a pen scratch paper.

"On the river, we could take our time. She told me about her parents dying of the Spanish Flu and how an old aunt had raised her and how on the exact day of her tenth birthday a flying circus buzzed over the town, the planes doing loop-de-loops, dives, and barrel roles. A Curtiss JN-4 biplane—I still remember the name because of how her face looked when she said it. We'd talk about the future and how when the war ended we'd live near an airport somewhere close. She understood that I couldn't stay far from my mother. She'd work flying, even crop dusting if she had to. It didn't matter, we'd be together. The War got bigger, and orders came for her to join the other women pilots in Texas to ferry bombers out to the west coast. We'd always known she'd have to leave for a while. That last morning she took off her flight scarf and wrapped the white silk around my neck. We only kissed that day, but it was over and over with me pushed up against a pile of broken wing struts lying in the back corner of the hanger. I never heard from her again."

Did I say all that out loud? I don't care. This is my life or it was. When do you start using the word was for your life? I've heard other old people do it, but I never have. I don't think I'll start now. This is my life. I fumble through the sheet until I find the call button. I have all sorts of hurt coming through the drugs. I close my eyes against it until my nurse comes. I hear her talking to the historical lady.

"Perhaps you should go. I think she's talked enough."

"Oh, certainly. We're not supposed to intrude."

"No, let her stay. Just give me another dose." I've grabbed my nurse's wrist, but let go so she can do her work. I hear the flap of the tubes against the IV pole and feel heat race through my body.

"There you go, Lady." She cups my fingers with hers and whispers. "I'll send in the aide to help you with that little accident"

From far away, I feel the wet under me. You'd think I'd be ashamed, but that's all done with now. I open my eyes, and the society woman's nose is still wrinkled. She should get used to it. Sick people smell.

"I waited for a long time. You couldn't just call or send messages over the computer like now. And showing too much interest wasn't safe. They watched for that sort of thing in the women. I wondered if she had left me, if everything had been a lie or a dream. When the paperwork came through our office about a plane accident and asking for her records and my pilot's name had comma deceased after it, for a second, just a second, I felt a strange relief. I had been loved. What came next wasn't pain. Instead my hands were on hers, gripped on the rudder. They felt the stutter and drop that sent clouds rushing over the cockpit. Together, we saw the curved horizon of a blue sky drop into a swirl of browns, then greens, then a sweep of branches, a stream, a field of purple and yellow flowers. I heard the great noise of everything ripping apart."

The historical society lady wipes her eyes. But I feel good. And not just from the morphine. Talking about it makes me know that sadness got left behind years ago. My pilot salutes me from the ceiling tiles and fades into the speckled paint.

"I fell down right there on the floor behind my desk. They found me and took me to the flight surgeon who decided I was pregnant so they fired me. I didn't argue with them. I didn't care. I ran all the miles to the river, but I couldn't even put a hand in that water. I couldn't for years after that."

The aide comes in with linens under her arm. She shakes the curtain, and the hooks rattle along the ceiling tract. The society lady becomes a shadow in the material. I yell out to her.

"Sorry about this. The cancer, you know." That usually gets them to excuse me anything. Except for my gal, she doesn't let me get away with it. The latex glove squeaks along my skin as the ties on my gown are loosened. The lady's voice comes from the other side of the curtain.

"Perhaps this is a good time for me to ask some of our questions. Ma'am, do you go to church or have any other religious affiliations?"

I raise my voice the best I can so it'll reach beyond the curtain.

"No, my mother either. I guess not going to church was our tradition. I mean we had a Christmas tree and presents, and Ma told me her grandmother had words she said over the corn when it came in, and my mother gathered river water every new moon and made me drink it. Is that what you mean?" Now I'm just messing with the poor woman.

The washcloth slaps cold on my behind and drips, but the aide is good at what she does and finishes quick. She gathers the dirty linens and swishes back the curtain on her way out. The historical lady's pen dithers over her form.

"Well, we don't really have a box to check for that. I'll just put Christian."

I ignore her. I want to finish my story.

"I had a low time after that, in my mind. I'm ashamed to say I ended up living off my mother. I couldn't get myself out of bed. When I was able to do for myself again, there weren't bookkeeping jobs for women what with the veterans coming home. My mother used some connections and got me hired on to help the potter they had out here at the Silver Springs Park. He let me work the clay some, and it surprised us both that I could see something in my mind and then it would form between my hands. The clay gave me some peace. And that's all I did for a while. I put my pottery first and let the loose ends drag on everything else in my life. Except for taking care of my mother. She'd started having trouble with her heart."

"Tray pick up." The cafeteria man yells into the room and makes the historical society lady drop her pen. I wave him away and wait for the pen to be ready before I talk again.

"Every day I worked in a studio close enough to hear the glass bottom boat captains tell their tales. They'd turn the odd shapes of underwater rocks into tragic stories of bridal chambers and lover's lanes. Me, I didn't go to the river, didn't even look out over it until the winter after Ma died. I'd gotten in a bad way again. It's odd the way my mother passing brought on a flood of grief for my pilot. I hadn't let myself think about her in years. But one day, after work, I walked to the river. The asters bloomed in great sprays everywhere. I walked through them, and they cut over my face and hands. Blood stung into my eyes and tasted sweet in my mouth."

The lady rattles her form. She wants to leave. I don't want to be alone. My gal will be here soon. I force another breath and keep talking.

"I fell down at the edge of the river, and my face splashed into plants, mud, and water. When I rubbed my cheeks, I felt clay. My hands searched into the underside of the bank and found more clay. I scooped out an armfuls and carried it dripping back to the studio. I didn't know what the heck to do with it. It was nothing like the clay we had delivered. First I cleaned it, but I knew it needed tempering. The park had made a fake beach with brought-in sand. My clothes were still stained and wet but I didn't care. I ran through all those pale-skinned tourists and got a bucketful of that sand.

"Silver Springs had a beach?" The lady's voice surprises me. I'd forgotten she was here.

"It sure did. But it got closed with integration same as the swimming pools."

She writes that down. I don't know if she's been writing the other stuff.

"Then I sat at the wheel and remembered my pilot while I worked the clay into a pitcher. I can't tell you how long it took, but I didn't sleep, even during the firing. I brushed it first with sky colors and then poured coils of coneflower yellow. I sponged on prairie iris purples and sprayed streaks of tangerine earth around and around in a rush of color. I fired it again and slept, maybe for days. I bathed and washed my hair and got dressed nice before I opened that kiln. The pot seemed perfect. I went and pretty much stole a boat and got on the river for the first time in all those years. I found our place, me and my pilot's, and dipped the pot into the river. It filled for the first time. It didn't crack and the colors glittered in the water. I kissed the rim, took a long drink, and let it rest in my arms. Around me marsh hens bobbed and strutted over mats of plants, and frogs called for one another. Manatee noses broke the surface and huffed."

I pull my mother's star quilt over my belly. I'm always cold. The pain is close again, but talking keeps it still. It quivers like an animal ready to leap. I don't look at the lady. It would give her a chance to interrupt with some made-up excuse to leave.

"I was all right after that. Every day my hands made something real. When the potter retired, I took over. He'd studied the Indian way of making pots some place up north and added to that. I added some more. The way yellows hold their color thick on the pot, that was my doing."

"Ma'am, did you ever marry?"

I just ignore her. My gal will be here soon.

"Do you remember the show "Sea Hunt"? They filmed it here. The first time I saw my photographer was in springtime when the limpkins screamed and flapped across the river in their lustful ways. I'd been making mold pottery all week. Stamping 'Silver Springs, Fla.' on piece after piece made me antsy. But I might have had more patience for the work if I'd known about the plans to hire it all out to China. Anyway, I took a break to watch them make an episode of the show. The underwater photographer pirouetted like a dancer. When she rose up out of the spring, water streamed down the slick of her wetsuit and when she shook off her cap, red hair spread out into the sunshine. She traveled a lot, but when she was in town, we were together. She didn't seem to mind how much older I was than her. Still doesn't."

I'm glad I've talked past most of the hard times. The pain chews at me right through the middle, but I'll win against it in the end. I'll die, and the pain will have to die with me. My gal will arrive soon. I lick my lips so I can keep talking until she gets here.

"May I pour you some water?"

"No, I'll wait. My gal has promised me mint tea from our garden. She mixes lemon balm and spearmint and drips in a little honey. And she'll have her camera. She keeps taking pictures of me. I complain, but she says I'm more beautiful than ever. She better arrive soon. The evening shift nurse makes her leave at the end of visiting hours like she wasn't family."

"So you had a child."

"Bless your heart, Ma'am, but you're missing a few things. Of course, we could have adopted like the girls do these days, but that never happened."

I stop talking to the woman because my gal is at the door, her silver hair lit up by the light from the hall. It still has sparkles of red in it. She has stems of spider lilies in one arm and a pitcher of tea in the other. She sets the pitcher down and leans over to let the flowers fall around my body. She kisses me and kisses me and rests her forehead against mine, and we breathe each other's breath. How she can stand the smell, I don't know.

I look to see how the society lady takes all this. She's out the door, in the hallway, and the pages in her notebook are half-ripped off their black plastic coils. Another woman dressed like her, but in an early spring shade of green, puts a hand out.

"Oh, we can't use any of this material. Read this part." The society lady has one of those whispers that carries. Her friend reads, it couldn't be more than a few sentences, and shakes her head. I hear the lid of a metal trash can raise and drop. I hear her ask if the man in 213 is well enough for an interview.

I don't regret talking to her. And here's my photographer pouring me tea out of my pitcher. The purples have faded and there's a chip along the rim, but this is still the best work I've ever done. My gal tilts the plastic hospital cup to my face, and I sip. I wish I could enjoy it. But I pretend that I do and am remembering the taste of fresh-cut mint when my throat snaps shut.

My arm flings out and smashes the cup into the air. My legs shake against the sheets. Something tries to rip through my spine. Telling stories distracted me for too long, and now I'm helpless inside the pain. I grit my teeth not to scream. My gal runs out of the room, and she does the screaming for us. People talk over my body about whether they should do anything, and my gal hisses at them to just give me something for the pain. Someone must have listened because the drug overflows into my muscles like the river after a summer storm. The evening shift nurse says anyone who isn't family has to go. My photographer tells her to fuck off, she's always had the worst language, and climbs into bed with me.

❖

She's still here beside me. Best you can tell in a hospital, another morning has come around. I feel better than I have in weeks. Today I'm going home. My nurse comes in and puts coffee beside the bed and wakes my gal and tells her to drink it quick, that the doctors will make rounds soon. She's a slow waker, always has been. Her arms spread in a long stretch that ends up as a hug around my shoulders. She kisses my mostly bald head and goes into the bathroom. While she's in there, all the white coats gather around me. My gal stays in the bathroom and listens. They know she's there, but the compromise covers them legally. I nod and smile at everything they say just to be pleasant. I'm going home no matter what.

The doctors leave, and I work myself to sitting while my gal packs up around me.

"Here you go, my old lady." She hoists me the rest of the way. She's seventy-five this year but still the athlete. "Let's get some real clothes on you."

"Wait. I've finagled one more dose of the good stuff for her. Then I'll take out the IV. It'll make things easier." Our nurse comes to my side. She's brought a wheelchair.

My skin tugs as she pulls out the needle, and part of me is scared to be without it. The two of them stand on either side of the bed and slide pants up my legs. She turns away to get one of the menstrual pad things they use for 'leaking' as she delicately calls it. My gal takes the moment to give me a squeeze back there, and we smile at the memory of our desire. They lift my arms and pull a sweater over my head. The nurse flips the one wisp of hair I have left out over my collar, and she winks at me. A few days ago she took care of my gray roots as a going home present. "We girls have to look good," she said as she ripped open the Clairol package and shook the bottle. Our nurse hands my gal a bottle of pills.

"These aren't as strong, but they'll hold her until Hospice gets to your house and sets up the IV. And here's our favorite lab tech with all the supplies we could put together."

I can hardly see the tech behind a wheelchair piled with those diaper things and pads for the bed and all sorts of basins and who knows what else. She gives my gal a hug and comes over and kisses me on the cheek. I guess now that I'm going home they don't have to act as professional. I want to tease about just how well her girlfriend took care of me, but I'm still too high to say anything.

"Let's get you out of here." My photographer lifts me out of the bed as if I were her bride.

I don't weigh enough to hold down paper in a wind, but I know that later she'll complain about how I ruined her back. I'll pretend to hide my pain drugs from her, and we'll joke about my drug addiction. I put my head under her chin and rest in her arms. This is how it must have been with my mother before I can remember. But my body remembers, and I hear my mother singing and feel how it used to make a breeze through the hair on top of my head.

Our nurse pushes the wheelchair closer, but we stand like that together for a little longer. She's so gentle that I hardly know I've been put down. The nurse fits pillows around me, and my gal wedges the pitcher into the crook of my arm.

"Can you hold on to it?"

I can. I'm coming out of the drug haze, but the pain only licks at my back. This is my best time. My gal pulls something long and beige out of her pocket and wraps it around my neck twice and lets the ends fall into my lap.

"I thought she'd want to keep you warm on this trip."

The silk has gone yellow and thin, but I smell my pilot on the scarf.

We head out into the hall with my gal holding my hand and our nurse pushing the wheelchair. The lab woman whistles and pretends she doesn't know us as she rolls the supply-loaded wheelchair a few feet behind. We must be quite the caravan.

At the car she lifts me again, but we're all business this time. She doesn't have a back seat or much of a trunk in her Alfa Romeo, so supplies get tucked in all around. She bought a stupid car for around here, but there's no getting the Hollywood out of my love. She got it from some actor whose movie sales went south and says it wasn't that expensive. I never pressed her on the exact price, because I like being driven around town in a yellow convertible with a black leather interior. It looks good on me.

"Now, we'll come by tomorrow. We'll bring dinner, and I'll check on things. You've got my number, right?" The nurse hugs my gal and now she's hugging me. And now she's crying. My gal reaches in and fastens the seat belt around me and the pitcher. She smooths the scarf over my neck.

"A seatbelt?" I cock my head and give her the look I do when she pretends that I'm not dying.

"Well, for the pitcher."

She drives slower than she can usually manage and turns to check on me over and over. I want to snap at her to watch the road like I usually do, but that good feeling I woke up with rushes out of me. I don't hurt yet. This is something else. My skin doesn't hold me anymore. The heart of me moves out through it, and all the world comes inside. I've never felt this way before.

"It's time."

"What, do you need a pill? I can pull over right here, and I brought water."

"Darling, it's time."

"No, no, no. We're almost home. I had a hospital bed delivered and put downstairs right where it will look out over the garden. We'll take that quilt there and put it on top. I have the new portfolio to show you. It tells your story, our story, even your pilot's story. I have plans. We have plans."

"Don't take me home."

"Okay, we'll go right back to the hospital. They probably haven't even stripped your bed yet. Do you need one of these pills first?"

She's like a soon-to-be father losing all sense.

"Darling, take me to the river."

"Oh, no. That's too much to ask. And you'll ruin my back if I have to lift you again. And the park has river access locked up tight. We'd have to pay, and I can't see them letting me carry you in past all those tourists."

"I'll show you. There's a back road. We're going to scratch up your car, maybe even knock it out of alignment. It'll be something for you to remember me by."

"Shit. You are so damn stubborn. And mean to the last. Where do I turn?"

I show her, and soon we're driving through an opening that almost remembers it used to be a road. The loose sand pulls at the tires, and red bays slap against the sides. She rolls down the windows, and my scarf flickers around my neck. The smell of new leaves washes the rot off my body. The car nosedives into a pit of sugar sand and stops just before where the river makes a sun-bright gap in the trees.

She carries me to the shore and there—as there needs to be—an old canoe, its aluminum beat up and stained, waits for us in the marsh grasses. We're in one of the old stories where the hero is provided what he needs as he needs it. She lays me on the bank in a meadow of blue-eyed grass that spreads between the cypress knees until the blossoms drip down into their own reflections. My love gets the pillows from the car and stacks them into the bow of the canoe. She nestles me among them. She spreads the quilt and puts a cap on my head. She tucks and folds and rearranges things until she's satisfied I'm comfortable. But those sorts of feelings—warm, cold, the press of a rivet against my side, pain cracking my bones—don't matter anymore. She puts the pitcher into my arms, and it settles between my breasts.

We stare into each other's eyes as she leans forward to wrap her arms around the stern and launch the canoe. It slides into the water, and at the last moment she hops in and kneels in front of me with her bottom perched on the center strut. There's no mistaking that moment when you leave land, when the boat floats. Through all the cushioning and drugs and death that is so close, I feel it. My love paddles and looks over my head. She sees what comes. I see what passes—patches of star rush in the shadows, the green, blue, white of hemlock puffs. Yellow butterflies unfurl their tongues over the red triangles on the quilt. I see a wood duck with her Cleopatra eyes.

We hear voices, splashing, and women in blue, red, green, purple, and yellow kayaks come up on us. They are polite, each one, as they pass us by. I know who they are the way I knew in the barracks. I nod my head that certain way and grin. As each one passes, their reflection lingers behind them. The last one, in the blue kayak, begins her polite nod but changes it into a real smile. She recognizes me. Now the last reflection pulls forward, out of my sight.

"Oh, my God. You are still looking."

"Yes, my love. Always."

"You know, you probably gave them nightmares the way there's not much left of you but your teeth."

"My mother had good teeth right to the end." That's all the words I have left.

I watch the water. The cobalt blue in the shadows I figured out, but these mirror glints of teal I never got on a pot right. The canoe slows and turns in an eddy, and now I see what is to come. I recognize where we are even before the lightning-scarred cypress slides into view. Her spring leaves make a green mist along the branches. She's lost some over the years. The canoe finds the path behind the tree, the place where a bit of the river hides behind itself. My gal puts down her paddle and lays her face into my lap. I don't know what I believe, but she believes in a heaven where loved ones wait. She has brought me home. She's giving me over to my pilot. I guess this is what I believe—that gestures of love are never lost.

I feel so many things. The annoyance of the great blue we've flushed is in my throat, the beat of her wings in my lungs. Arrowhead stalks stretch up my spine and bloom their white flowers into my breasts. I list towards the edge. A turtle swims away from us, the flip of her turtle feet a tickle along my ribs, and an alligator splashes off the sunny bank. My love's hand pulls me back, and I slip flatter into the boat until only the sky is above me. I see the alligator's old relative, the crocodile, thirty feet long and hungry, blinking its transparent eyelids and swimming in the ancient ocean that existed here before us all. The manatees are gone from this river, I know this, but I feel one resting between my hips. I feel it all. I feel the scarf unwrapped from around my neck. The heart of me goes with it, and we're slipped into the pitcher and now we fill with water and tumble down into the grasses and rich muck. Dragonfly nymphs with translucent bodies swim into us and snap their jaws.

In a chamber of my heart, plum purple grief pours out of my gal. It adds hue to the last circle of blood that swirls through my cells. It adds love, love, and love into the mix of the world.

Mountainview
James Russell

Nick has a morning ritual: he imagines bus crashes. In one scenario, he pictures a deer running into the road. The bus, having swerved to avoid it, careens into Mrs. Paulson's giant Oak. In Nick's favorite scenario, a tire pops, making the bus skid on its side, smearing the road yellow, sliding to a stop in front of his house. The bus still arrives for him, but the door can't swallow him because it's ground into the road.

Nick hears the grinding engine before he sees the white roof and yellow face of the bus. There is no deer. The tires remain whole. Nick abandons fantasy and shoulders his burden of books. The breaks sound their steam release. The door scrapes the bottom step, folding itself to the side. Ms. Anderson has a big white smile across her thick black face.

"Mornin', Nickie!" she blares.

"Morning," Nick confirms. He slouches up the stairs and gazes down the awful aisle.

On the left, two girls argue with an opened math book on their laps. They debate who's right about some Greek thing, and this is only the fifth day of school. On the right, there's a big sixth grader who looks and smells like a meatball.

Nick steps down the aisle.

On the left are two seventh-grade girls who just discovered makeup. They sneer at Nick like his very presence emanates fart. On the right, a tiny boy with a large head stares forward at nothing, wearing a purple sweat shirt, looking like a lost grape.

Nick steps down the aisle.

On the left, a skinny girl digs through her bag. She emerges with an asthma inhaler as she spews a repellent sound. The effort to board the bus used all her allotted energy for the day. The right seat is empty.

Nick sits. He cradles his head in his hands. He jerks back as the bus growls forward.

He hears Kyle McGillis and Paul Johnson in the back, or at least he hears the lowness of their voices. It reminds Nick to take inventory of what he hates about himself. He starts with his voice, the highness of it, the rodent squeak quality it has, especially compared to the manly baritone of boys like Kyle and Paul.

Nick leans forward and stares down at his feet, remembering to hate them, remembering to hate his body for starting its puberty renovations here, of all places. It's like the puberty gnomes cut off his old, proportionate feet in the middle of the night. Then they took a coffee break and played his Play Station. Then they realized they'd wasted their work shift and, with the first morning birds singing through his window, they tacked these giant flippers on his body and climbed out his window, laughing.

Before Nick can move on to hate his scrawny chicken legs, a ball of paper lands in his lap. Kyle grunts laughter from the back of the bus. "Three-pointer!" he yells.

"Mistah McGillis, it's much too early in the school year for this!" Ms. Anderson says, turning the wheel. "An' I know someone's mom and pop from church, don' forget!"

Nick smiles. Kyle is silent.

The ball of paper shifts as the bus makes the sharp turn onto Franklin Street. It has one word scrawled across the flattest end of its crumpled side—Open.

Nick thinks about what his mother always says when he's honest, when he tells her what school is really like. She says other people only have power over you if you let them. She says, "When they put you down, it only has power if you chose to believe they're right." She tells Nick to make a safe place in his mind, where he can go whenever he's in danger of letting them win.

Nick tries to think of other things, to find his safe place. Nick thinks of his mother and home, of safety and shelter. He thinks of his room and his shelf. He loves his shelf. It has his Play Station games and pro-wrestling DVDs. It has notebooks full of awesome hypothetical video game sequels and pro-wrestling events. It has books by King and Rice, Poe and Tolkien. It has *Metal Gear Solid*, *Summerslam*, and *The Silmarillion*.

The shelf means escape to elsewhere.

But he isn't there—that is what his mother never understands. No matter how bad he wants, he isn't safe; he isn't at home in his room. He is nowhere near his shelf. He is on the bus, five minutes from school. And the paper ball is telling him what to do—Open.

Nick opens it. He hears Kyle's guttural laugh from the back of the bus, in response to the crackling of paper. Nick recognizes his tiny girl ears in Kyle's drawing. He sees the blue dots of his eyes. Kyle gave Cartoon Nick a full-blossom chin zit—a blazing red circle, the putrid head represented by an absence of color. Nick rubs his chin, remembering how much it hurt to burst it three nights ago, how much Windex it took to clean the bathroom mirror afterward.

Kyle took the time to find a red marker, just for that one detail. Nick thinks it is almost flattering, how much effort Kyle put into this. On the paper, Nick's hair is pencil flecks, so it hangs down limply over his forehead, cut like it always is, since Nick doesn't know what else to do with it. The nose is small and sharp, girly as his ears. There's no trace of facial hair. It's everything Nick hates about himself, and the worst thing isn't even his head.

Cartoon Nick's mouth is open. A leg-like penis complete with a pair of basketballs nut sack aims at his face. It's veiny, another use for the red marker, or maybe the zit was the afterthought. There's no body attached to the floating dick and balls, but Cartoon Nick's face is coated with a torrent of jism, just the same. Underneath the drawing is a sentence: *Nick M. sucks cok.*

Reading that, Nick thinks of the dreams and the wrecked pajamas and boxer shorts. He remembers of how good it feels, physically, but the things he dreams about when it happens, the showers at swim camp and what happens there with the other boys—things like what's on the paper in his lap—they leave him with questions he isn't ready to answer.

How does Kyle know? How does everyone know what Nick doesn't want to feel?

The school building speeds toward the bus. The sign out front reads: *Welcome back!* Underneath that, *First School Board Meeting Thursday, 9/13.*

Nick realizes this is only his fifth day as an eighth grader. He thinks about how much fun Kyle is going to have this year, again, treating him like toilet paper.

Unless he finds a way to fight back.

Nick digs through his backpack for a pen. He folds Kyle's drawing flat on his English textbook. He draws an insertion mark between the O and K in Kyle's *cok.* Nick realizes this will mean an ass-kicking, but he doesn't care. He'll lose, as sure as his body is that of stretched taffy boy and Kyle's is that of a meaty bull man. But it's fine. Nick has been here before—with Kyle and with other bullies. He'll survive the beating and Kyle will be suspended. Then Nick can have a month or two of life under a log. He gave up on popularity years ago. All he wants now is peace. If peace isn't worth a beating, Nick reasons nothing is.

He writes a sentence above Kyle's: *Cock has a C in it you stupid sped douche bag.* It feels wonderful, all the heat in his face. He re-balls the paper. The bus grinds to a halt in front of the school. Some kids stand while others stuff books into their backpacks.

Among all the frenzied movement, Nick turns and throws the ball back toward Kyle.

He doesn't wait to watch Kyle's reaction. He squeezes through the aisle, using his skinniness to lank past the new make-up girls. One of them grunts at him while the other sings, "Hi-ii, Nick." He hears paper crackling behind him, even among all the other noises. Nick hears Paul laughing at Kyle. He hears Paul say, "You didn't know how to spell *that?*" Nick regrets his tiny rebellion as he squirms his way out of the bus.

❖

The ceiling is too high in the first-floor boy's room. The aquatic sounds of Nick's morning pee thunder up the walls like a monsoon. He can't imagine what it would sound like in Mr. Stevenson's Math room next door if someone had a tug-of-war with a determined turd.

He giggles—sometimes he makes himself laugh. The bathroom acoustics carry his titter farther than he intends. He zips up, flushes, walks over to the sink, and washes his hands. He looks in the mirror.

Nick's grandma has this thing lately—she pinches his cheeks and goes, "Look how handsome! Ya' must hafta beat the girlies off ya' with a stick!"

It makes Nick think there should be a word between awkward and annoying—awknoying. His grandma talking about dating? Nick isn't ready—for all that.

But as he looks in the mirror Nick wonders what it might feel like, if someone who isn't his grandma would tell him he was handsome—someone who didn't have to. It feels too impossible to imagine. He feels greedy even hoping for something like that.

But what if someone he liked said that to him? How wonderful might that feel?

Nick sighs and checks his watch. Seven twenty-four. No way he's going to homeroom yet. No way he's sitting there for six minutes while Ms. Hoss checks her e-mail, giving Kyle time to retaliate. Nick walks away from the mirror and goes into the stall. He closes the door, lowers both seats and sits with his head in his hands.

"You're wrong, guys," he says to no one. "I must be cool. My grandma thinks I'm handsome."

The bathroom door slams open.

"...corrects my spelling. I mean, what a fag! Who does that?" Nick knows it's Kyle. He pulls his legs up and sits Indian-style on the lowered toilet lid.

"Maybe he wanted to mess with your head," Nick hears Paul say. Paul runs the water. Nick guesses Paul is fixing his hair—something he usually obsesses over.

"I know how cock is spelt! I mean, not as good as fucking Nick probably does but c'mon! Who takes the time to correct spelling on a dis-note for fuck's sake? What a loser! And he called *me* a fucking sped? He didn't even know how to spell *douche*!"

"I didn't notice that. How did he spell it?"

"There was a CH in it, like 'couch.' It was all fucked up."

"No," Paul laughs, "Dude, he had it right."

"Fuck off, smartass."

This moment is what Nick was afraid of. Teachers never come in the bathrooms. But he had nowhere else to hide until seven thirty.

It was stupid, his little bus rebellion. It will end with his head in a toilet. Nick pulls himself in more, feeling the tension as he presses his arms and legs and the whole structure of his body. Nick tries to compact himself, to compress his spider legs and stick arms.

"Just leave him alone. I still don't get what he ever did to you," Paul said. Nick is surprised. He always thought Paul enjoyed watching Kyle torture him.

"He never *did* anything. It's just like, I look at him and I *have* to fuck with him, you know?" Paul walks over to the hand dryer and turns it on before responding.

"No. I look at him and I don't *have* to do anything. I mean, you're probably right and he's a fag and all, but like, why do you care so much?"

Kyle pauses before answering, like a contestant unsure of a prize answer. "We change with him in gym!" he says suddenly.

"Not really. He always runs in ahead of everyone. Can you remember one gym class last year where you were in your underwear and he wasn't already out at his warm up spot?"

Another pause. "No." The hand dryer turns off.

"So why do you care?"

"He's a *fag!*"

Nick hears Paul walk over to the mirrors. "Why does it matter?"

Kyle laughs nervously. "Maybe you're one too, since all of a sudden you like him so much."

"Maybe you're one, since you draw dicks for him on the bus."

"Why are you being such an asshole?" Nick almost feels bad for Kyle. He actually sounds hurt.

"You're the only one on the team who can shoot three-pointers! Three detentions and you're off the team. You already got one on Friday, the first *week* of school, for throwing that orange at lunch. You could've got another one for throwing your stupid dick art project at Nick on the bus."

"So?"

"So I want to win this year! Our first game isn't even 'til October. So stop being a jackass for two minutes so our team won't suck." Paul walks over toward Nick's stall. Nick tries to compress himself into even more of a ball, but his damn flipper feet...

"Alright, shit, relax coach," Kyle finally says.

Paul tries Nick's locked stall. Nick wants to move over, to be undetectable if Paul looks through the sliver of space on the door's side, but there's no way to do it without noise. "Anybody in there?" Paul pulls the handle again. Nick thinks he sees Paul's eye in the sliver, despite Nick's best amateur contortions.

"Well?" Kyle asks. Paul hesitates.

"Nothing, janitors probably locked it by accident."

"How? There's no key for those, I bet I could..."

"Forget it. I'll crap during Spanish. Let's not be late for homeroom." They leave. Nick exhales, waits. He unfolds himself, stretching. He unlocks the stall and moves out into the bathroom, and then, the cacophony, the frenzied movement of the halls.

Nick stumbles through the door to Science just as the bell rings.

"Take a seat," Mr. Jordan says. From behind his tall desk, Mr. Jordan motions across his sterile, hospital-like room. The last open desk is in front of Kyle.

"Mr. Jordan, can I talk to you in the hallway?" Nick winces as he says it.

"Can I afford to waste instructional time talking to you in the hallway?" Mr. Jordan asks. "No."

"Please, it'll only take..." Mr. Jordan interrupts with an exasperated sigh.

"Mr. Morella, please tell me the seating arrangements for my eighth grade Science class."

"First come, first serve," Nick replies, half-groaning. They spent half the first day of school listening to Mr. Jordan talk about it.

"Why?" Nick realizes Mr. Jordan is doing that thing where he plays dumb just so he can quiz.

"Incentive," Nick says, "to show up early."

"Did you show up early?" A couple of girls giggle.

"No, but..."

"In fact, you were almost late." Nick feels his rage as facial heat. Mr. Jordan couldn't talk in the hall for a minute, but he can waste all this time interrogating him.

"I dropped my books," Nick says, presenting the awkward pile of books and folders he's barely holding. Kyle snickers. Nick hadn't dropped his books. Kyle pushed him into a gargantuan seventh grader, a kid whose puberty gnomes were dedicated professionals. That kid slapped Nick's books out of his hand, and once they were down—book soccer.

"But you have them now." Nick wants to kill Mr. Jordan with his eyes. He hates the way Mr. Jordan's lower gut flap hangs over his belt. He hates that waddle of skin under Mr. Jordan's chin and how it shakes when Mr. Jordan talks. He wants to slice all the fat off this man, cut him down to size.

"Yes, I have my books now," he mumbles.

"So take a seat in front of Mr. McGillis."

Nick sits.

"Now, yesterday we were discussing adaptation, migration, and extinction. These are the three options any species faces when their habitat is threatened."

The phone on his desk rings. Mr. Jordan walks over and picks it up. He's quiet for a minute.

"I understand," he finally says.

He walks over to the far side of his desk, where his computer is. Nick watches Mr. Jordan's eyes scan the screen.

Kyle leans forward and flicks Nick's ear. The rage heats Nick's face again. Kyle sits back just as Mr. Jordan looks up. For just a second, he looks a little panicked; he seems a little human.

"Is everything okay?" a girl asks.

"Some announcements," Mr. Jordan says, his expression returning to its default setting. "The east wing will be closed today for emergency maintenance." Nick is sad. Mrs. Hanson's class is in the east wing. She's nice. That makes it a safe place. Plus, you can see New York from her windows. Nick loves looking at New York. It reminds him there are so many other places out there, where nicer people might live.

"How do we get to gym?" Paul asks.

"You'll go around the west wing. Coach Palumbo will understand if you are reasonably late. Also, those of you with cell phones are to hand them in." There's a pause. None of them are supposed to have cell phones, but everyone knows the cool kids have them—it shows your importance; it shows people might maybe want to talk to you whenever. Mr. Jordan sighs, realizing their reluctance. "Look, you'll get them back at the end of the day."

No one moves.

As if on cue, Tiffany Winters' phone rings with a tinny instrumental. Everyone laughs but Mr. Jordan. "Do not answer that. This is exactly the type of disruption we were trying to avoid." He stalks over to Tiffany's desk and snatches her little, purple phone in his fat mitt. She huffs but doesn't object outright. The ring is muffled by Mr. Jordan's palm-blubber.

"Who else has one? I'm not playing around here!"

Nick doesn't have a cell phone. Who would call? His best friend Ronny moved away at the end of sixth grade. Nobody else talks to him. He watches as Mr. Jordan stalks the aisles, pausing in front of the students he suspects of some combination of wealth and popularity. Tiffany's best friend Becky hands in a shining pink clamshell. Paul hands him a sleek black sliding phone. They drop them reluctantly—they're handing over the entirety of their social existence, handing over limbs.

Nick feels good watching that. Now their friends are out of reach. Now they know how Nick feels all the time.

Mr. Jordan moves up the aisle toward Cassie Van Hall. Nick knows her dad owns a movie theater and some candy stores. That makes her a cell phone kid. But Nick can't feel the same joy at Cassie being stripped of her phone. Cassie has money and friends, and Nick has seen a few boys stare at her all dopey-eyed—she has every reason to act like a snot if she wants, but she never does. In fact, Nick remembers one time, at his locker last spring, when she told Kyle to shut up and leave him alone.

"Miss Van Hall, your phone please," Mr. Jordan says. Cassie looks up at him, unsure of how to proceed.

"Mr. Jordan, my father gave me my phone in case of an emergency. It isn't even turned on. I can show you." Nick sees how calm she is. He knows that will only frustrate Mr. Jordan.

"If ever there was an emergency, you could simply use the office phone or the phone on my desk." Mr. Jordan levels an expectant palm at Cassie.

"Mr. Jordan, I'm not sure the school has the right to take our phones, or any of our personal property."

"Yeah," Tiffany Winters adds. Cassie has turned Tiffany's earlier scoff into an organized thought. Mr. Jordan doesn't look at Tiffany. He keeps his eyes on Cassie.

"That's where you're wrong, Miss Van Hall. We are allowed to ask you to change if we deem your clothing, your 'personal property', to be a distraction. You are allowed to refuse, but that means you are sent home. You can hold on to your phone if you want, but you'll be taking it with you to the Main Office." He moves his palm closer to Cassie's face. She looks at it, and then looks away. Mr. Jordan sighs. "Is this really your decision? Do you really think you're better than everyone else? That the same rules all your classmates have to follow somehow don't apply to you?" Some of the students giggle. Nick knows this is a master stroke—some kids are jealous of Cassie's family and their money.

Nick feels like saying or doing something to stand up to Mr. Jordan, to stand up for the only popular kid who's ever been decent to him. He could run out in the hall and pull the fire alarm—something crazy, something totally out of character, something that will force his school and the people in it out of their cruel normalcy. But before he can muster his courage, Cassie places a light blue phone in Mr. Jordan's hand.

"She was right," Kyle says. "You can't just take our stuff." The room is already quiet, but now it's eager and attentive as well. Mr. Jordan walks over to Kyle's desk. He leans in close, but speaks loud enough for everyone to hear.

"You don't have a cell phone, do you Mr. McGillis?" Nick is surprised that he pities Kyle. Kyle enjoys certain perks of popularity. He has friends through the basketball team, popularity-by-association through Paul, but when he isn't wearing jersey number 66, he's a torn-jean-and-band-shirt kid. His father works construction and his mom is a glorified secretary in the city. Kyle lives on Lower Mountain Avenue—Mountainview's poorest stretch of road and everyone knows it.

"No." Kyle says it loud, but he's facing down. A girl at the back of the room laughs. Nick turns back toward the front of the room, afraid to make eye contact with Kyle.

"Anyone else?" Mr. Jordan asks. Nick knows how smart Mr. Jordan is. He knows Mr. Jordan understood the viciousness of publicly asking Kyle that. Nick feels like saying something, getting that hot feeling in his face again, like when he fought back on the bus. He feels like standing up to another bully, the worst kind—an adult trusted with power. He feels like fighting for Cassie, for all abused students.

Even Kyle.

But when he looks up and sees the impossible height and pure girth of Mr. Jordan, the little revolution dies in his throat.

"Then let's move on. We were discussing adaptation, migration, and extinction." Mr. Jordan passes Nick's desk, walking towards his own.

Kyle flicks Nick's ear lobe again. Nick jumps a little in his desk. It stings worse than the first one. It takes him completely by surprise.

"Adaptation has been called the cornerstone of Evolution," Mr. Jordan says to the board.

How could Nick have been so stupid? How could he allow himself to think that Kyle was worthy of sympathy?

"Who can give me an example of adaptation?" Mr. Jordan asks. Cassie Van Hall's hand shoots up.

Nick turns to his notebook. He isn't going to allow Kyle to make him furious. He's going to try what his mother always said. He's going to find a safe place. At the top of the page he writes "Adaptation, Migration, or Extinction." Underneath that, he starts a hypothetical pro wrestling card, the lineup for the World Wrestling Federation's September pay-per-view, "Unforgiven".

"Adaptation is when a species changes its behavior somehow, in response to the changes in its environment," Cassie says.

Nick changes the Edge vs. Christian match for the Intercontinental Title into a Ladder Match by writing the word "ladder" above their names. It makes sense. They're both famous for ladder matches already.

Mr. Jordan turns toward the board, making shorthand notes of Cassie's response.

Kyle flicks Nick's ear again. This time, his whole ear is hot as if it is infected.

You stupid fucking cave boy! I felt bad for you! We had something in common! We had the same enemy! We could've been friends, but you're too chicken shit! You can't take it out on Mr. Jordan 'cause you're just as scared of him as I am. So you take it out on me? Fuck you. I hope your stupid shack house collapses on you and your whole fucking family!

"That's a good definition of adaptation," Mr. Jordan starts, "but what I had asked for was an example."

Nick takes a deep breath. He chooses to ignore. He can escape into the cartoon world of wrestling, even stuck here, in an old bully's class, sitting in front of a young bully. Yes, that's right. There is no class, no cruel giant of a world outside of it—the whole world is right here. It's a white world of possibility with one red vertical line and twenty-four blue horizontal ones.

W.W.F. Unforgiven 2001—that's the world. Stone Cold Steve Austin is going to defend the W.W.F. Title against Kurt Angle, that's a given, especially with how their *Summerslam* match ended. But what type of bout? The Intercontinental Title bout was already a Ladder Match. What about a steel cage?

Kyle flicks Nick's ear a fourth time. Nick punches his desk reflexively. The structural supports of his safe space buckle from the heat in his earlobe.

Nick stands up and turns around.

"Can you please stop flicking my ear? I'm trying to learn about adaptation!" He says it with as much bass in his voice as he can muster. He stands there, ear on fire, rebellion heat in his face, staring at the mountainous boy in the desk. Kyle's arms and shoulders are thick, his back and chest broad, but under his shaggy hair his face is completely surprised. Nick expects Kyle to get up and punch him, but he just sits there with his mouth open, like a walrus waiting to be thrown a fish. Some girls laugh. Some boys join them.

"Mr. Morella, why are you disrupting my class?"

Mrs. Springfield comes through the door. She is the Special Education teacher, responsible for students like Kyle. Nick sees sad confusion on her face and sits down. He feels bad, again, suddenly. He called Kyle a sped in his note. Kyle looked dumbfounded like a sped, just now. Nick's bus rebellion suddenly feels like a cheap shot. And he yelled at Kyle—belittled him just like Mr. Jordan. Nick doesn't want to imitate Mr. Jordan, ever, even if Kyle provoked him.

"Good morning, Mrs. Springfield," Mr. Jordan says. Nick is happy to see her too. She's young and pretty. Mean guy teachers like Mr. Jordan are nicer when she's around.

"Morning," Mrs. Springfield says. Nick notices how red the white parts of her eyes are, how purple and puffy the skin beneath. She looks like Nick's mother, when she's been crying behind her bedroom door. Mrs. Springfield walks slowly to the back of the room and drops her binders next to the student computers.

Nick wonders what's going on. Between Mrs. Springfield's face, the west wing detour, and the cell phone collection, something is just not right. Nick has never seen a teacher cry, or evidence that any teacher ever cried. Nick's mind lingers on it a moment, but then a larger and more concrete anxiety casts a shadow over the thought.

Science is almost half over and gym is next. Nick has to be ready to run, so he can change before everyone else. He doesn't want to be exposed while he sees the other boys exposed. He doesn't want to feel anything he isn't ready to feel.

The run around the school's west wing delays him, but it's okay, Nick reasons, it will delay everyone else too. He loves to run. He loves the burning in his lungs and the tension in his legs. He runs past lockers and trophy cases. He loves to see how fast he can make everything and everyone blur by him. He loves to believe he can run right to high school and graduation and goodbye hometown; he wants to run past it all.

"Easy!" Coach Palumbo says from his office as Nick rounded the corner. Once he's in the locker room, Nick hurls his backpack off on a bench and flips the plastic bag with his gym clothes inside-out. The contents land haphazardly on the cold tile floor. Nick kicks off his sneakers and thumbs his mall shorts down, stepping out of them and into his gym shorts. The most dangerous part—

the underwear part—is over. Still, he doesn't want Kyle to have a chance to say anything about being able to count his ribs, or how Nick's chest looks like a little girl's. When Kyle did that back in sixth grade, all the guys looked at Nick and laughed like goats. Nick hated their laughing more than anything. Nick hates how Kyle can make himself large at Nick's expense.

Nick flings his collared shirt over his head like it has caught fire. He wriggles into his gym shirt, stomps back into his shoes, and hops out to his warm up spot, sitting and pulling the back of his sneaker out from under his heel, just as the first boys round the corner by Coach Palumbo's office.

He sits and stretches and catches his breath. He savors being alone. High above, the lights buzz like electric nests. The giant gym smells like sweat and sawdust. Sometimes, on days like this, he imagines the roof collapsing, burying him alone.

Like every other day, the ceiling remains far above.

The boys trickle out of the locker room in pairs and trios, pushing and punching and laughing. The girls pour from the far end, from their locker room, in chattering clumps of five or more. They mix effortlessly, the boy and girl lumps; they're all gab and movement, and soon Nick is surrounded by a buzzing cloud of others. Paul walks to his usual warm up spot, in front of Nick, and grabs his ankles to stretch. Kyle is a row over and three people up. Far enough, Nick reasons.

His eyes catch it by accident. When Paul bends over to grab his ankles, the entirety of his ass is visible, underneath the layer of cloth that is his shorts. Nick can see the shape of each cheek, like muscled melon. He can see exactly where Paul's crack begins and ends its southern journey.

With that, Nick has an erection.

As if he heard Nick's thoughts, Kyle turns to Paul and says, "Hey, better hang a 'do not enter' sign on your ass," nodding his head toward Nick, the perceived anal threat.

Paul laughs so hard a lime snot wad fires from his nostril, landing on the polished gym floor like a confused slug. Next to Paul, Tiffany Winters screams, "Ewww!"

Coach Palumbo emerges from his office. "Johnson, get a paper towel and handle that. Everybody else stand up!" he says.

As Nick rolls forward to stand, he reaches into his pocket. While he's hunched over, he pushes the unwelcome boner to the side, where it'll be less of a visible lump, less of a target for Kyle.

"Jumping jacks!" The students all jump and slap at odd intervals. Nick wants to savor the thrill of pushing his body's limits—the only part of gym he usually likes—but each jump threatens to loosen the erection from his briefs. His usually crisp jumping jacks are impossible to execute while he leans halfway forward, hoping to hide his arousal.

"C'mon Morella, push it!" Coach Palumbo says.

"He wants to," Kyle says. Still cleaning the floor, Paul cracks up again.

"Quiet, McGillis! Two detentions in the first five days of school is a record you don't want!" Palumbo says. Kyle is quiet. "Everybody down for leg stretches!"

Nick is relieved. Sitting down and leaning forward is the best way to get rid of a hard-on. Maybe Palumbo knows what Nick is trying to hide. That's gross, but at least Palumbo's trying to be nice. Nick remembers how Coach Palumbo tried to get him to join the Track team last spring. He remembers Palumbo saying how it would make Nick a part of something greater than himself.

But Nick couldn't imagine being at school any longer than he had to. He couldn't imagine school as anything but a source of pain.

The little phone by the gym entrance rings. Nick can't remember a time it ever rang, in sixth or seventh grade.

"Johnson," Coach Palumbo says to Paul, "ten laps! You lead it!" Then he runs to answer the phone.

The cluster of students slowly becomes something like a line behind Paul. He runs, with Kyle and some of the prettier girls. Kids fall behind them in descending order of social importance. Nick allows himself to be last. He watches as Coach Palumbo nods with the phone on his ear, like they can hear him nodding. Then he hangs it up and fumbles through the pockets of his tracksuit pants. Nick watches as Palumbo runs back into his office.

Nick runs, rounding the gym perimeter with the others. He runs fast enough to keep Paul and Kyle from lapping him. He runs slow enough to keep from passing Amanda, the overweight girl in front of him. Nick doesn't want the attention passing anyone will bring.

His first lap around, Nick sees Coach Palumbo going outside, having emerged from his office with a big jangly set of keys in hand. He locks the first set of fire doors. Nick's place in the running hierarchy puts him right by his Coach, as Palumbo re-enters the school and closes the locked door behind him. Curious, Nick slows his pace. The Coach's eyes meet his.

"Don't worry, son," Coach Palumbo says, "the doors are still open on our side." Nick runs past him. He tries to think of another time a teacher offered him an explanation when he hasn't even asked a question.

On his second lap, Nick sees Palumbo moving toward the second set of fire doors. He decides he's curious. He passes Amanda, who's too busy huffing at her shoes to take any notice. Then he passes some girls who make phlegmy noises as he speeds by. Then he passes some slower boys. One tries to trip him but Nick jumps to his left as he darts by. Nick is back around the gym, gaining on Kyle and Paul and the pretty girls. He has that wonderful strained feeling in all of his lower body. He sees Palumbo stop, as he reaches the second set of fire doors.

One of the doors opens from the outside. A man steps into the gym. Everyone in front of Nick stops running. Nick stops running.

"Cassie!" the man calls, scanning the students. He wears a suit and he's balding with glasses, but he doesn't seem like a teacher. Then Nick recognizes him. Besides being a successful local business owner, Mr. Van Hall speaks at events like the Memorial Day Parade because he was in the army once. That's how Nick knows his face.

"Cassandra!" he spots his daughter, toward the front of the stopped running line.

"Dad?" Cassie says.

"You can't be here!" Coach Palumbo says, stepping between Mr. Van Hall and his daughter. "Sir, please, we're trying to avoid a panic."

"You were all just going to pretend nothing was happening? A lot of these kids' parents work in the city! Don't you think you have a responsibility to tell them?"

"What's wrong with the city?" Cassie asks her father. Nick wonders the same thing.

"We're just trying to avoid a panic here, sir. I'm going to have to ask you to calm down."

"Calm down? Are you crazy?" Mr. Van Hall tries to maneuver around the larger man, but Palumbo keeps in front of him, like a defender blocking a net.

"Sir, please," Coach Palumbo says. Mr. Van Hall stops moving and wags his finger in the Coach's face.

"I'm taking my daughter home! You're not stopping me!" He moves to the left and then quickly to the right, Coach Palumbo trying to mirror his movements. Then there's shoving. The line of students becomes a crescent, so everyone can see. This is far too entertaining. Even Nick wants to see how it will end.

Cassie decides to listen to her father. She tries to walk around Coach Palumbo and he turns and grabs her arm. To Nick, it doesn't look like he hurt her, but apparently Mr. Van Hall doesn't care. He's smaller, but when he connects with that first punch, a bloody piece of Coach Palumbo's tooth rattles across the gym floor.

The kids don't rush in right away, like they would for a normal fight. This is a parent fighting a teacher. There is no precedent here, no point of reference. They stand back and stare.

"Kick his ass, Coach!" Paul yells. And with that, they circle around like they would for any other fight.

"Do it!" Kyle yells. "Fuck him up!" Coach Palumbo wrestles the smaller man to the ground. His first punch bounces Mr. Van Hall's head against the gym floor like a basketball.

"Stop! Stop!" Cassie screams.

Nick is the only one looking at the other students, instead of the fight. Their faces are contorted with rage. They shout and shake their fists. They become a single buzzing cloud, a swarm of hate.

Nick walks briskly, behind the students. His legs take him out the first set of fire doors.

Outside, it still feels like summer. But something is wrong. When Palumbo took them outside to run the mile last year, there was always this one old guy trimming his hedges, and someone, somewhere, was usually mowing. Today there is no sound from any yard. Nick's legs decide to trot, they decide to run. He wants no part of the ugliness in the gym, and because of what Mr. Van Hall said, he wants to see the city.

He quickly rounds the corner of the school building. He runs along the third base line of the ball field and, over the crest of the hill, the city reveals itself.

Manhattan is on fire.

Smoke covers the southern third of the island, and only one of the two Twin Towers is there. There's a hole towards the top of it, like a mangled mouth. Smoke billows forth from it.

This is what the school was trying to hide—the world was ending, and they thought it would be better if Nick and all the other kids just learned about adaptation and did jumping jacks.

Nick hears something behind him. He turns. Kyle lumbers towards him. Nick braces himself for the punch, but Kyle walks past him, his jaw hanging as he views the hell-scape. Nick remembers.

"Your mom," he says to Kyle, "she's a secretary there." He feels sorry again, about calling Kyle a sped. "I remember from Social Studies, those stupid reports we gave on what our parents do."

Kyle doesn't turn to look at Nick, but he responds.

"She says I give her headaches," he says, looking at the city. Nick is horrified, knowing Kyle's mom is somewhere in that dust cauldron. Kyle turns and looks at Nick.

"Your dad," he says to Nick. "He's a city cop, right?" This is a tone Nick never heard from Kyle before. He doesn't know the word yet; he doesn't know "empathy", though he appreciates the sentiment and the authenticity behind it.

"He works there," Nick confirms. "He takes a ferry in, from Atlantic Highlands," Nick explains, "We haven't seen him for two Christmases, though. He lives down the shore with some girl."

Kyle nods. He and Nick stand face to face.

"You're not worried about him being stuck in that?" Kyle thumbs toward the city.

"Honestly, I'm more worried for your mom." Nick feels hollow saying it. But it's true. He refuses to waste feelings on his father. After what his school has done all day, Nick doesn't want to lie about anything. Kyle just stares at him with a blank face.

Nick figures the moment is over, and everything will go back to normal now. He waits for the punch. He doesn't care anymore. He can endure this beating and many more like it. He realizes, after seeing the city, how small the violence in his life actually is.

Kyle doesn't throw a punch. His massive frame buckles and he collapses forward, toward Nick.

Kyle's face crashes into Nick's. His giant hand cradles the back of Nick's head. Kyle closes his eyes but Nick's are wide-open with shock. Lips are on lips. "W" words swirl behind Nick's open eyes.

Warm.

Wet.

Weird.

Nick pulls his mouth away. He has a question; he has no way of knowing a form of this question will appear on the cover of Time Magazine the following week, in response to the attacks. Like his country, Nick is desperate for an answer.

"Why did you hate me?"

Kyle turns back toward the city as grief becomes moisture on all parts of his face.

"I dunno."

Kyle chokes and sniffles. Nick attains height by lifting his heels, so he can put a hand on Kyle's shoulder. He still half-expects a punch, or at least for Kyle to brush his hand away. Instead, Kyle's giant hand envelops Nick's, as his broad back quakes with sobs. Nick stands there off-balance, in excited terror, feeling swept up by the storm of sudden, uninvited, and irreversible change.

LOOKING FOR PHILIP
GEORGE E. JORDAN

New York City, September, 1981.

I have walked down these cross streets on the Upper East Side a hundred times in the past year, Steven thought. Between First and Third avenues, they all look alike—apartment houses, doctor's offices, an occasional restaurant—but he never knew there were gay bars in the area. He thought they were all downtown in the Village. He continued walking towards First Avenue.

A few feet from the sidewalk stood a brick building. It wasn't one of those old 19th century brownstone row houses New York is so famous for, but an ordinary early to mid-20th century building. The few windows on the street level were tinted so dark that it was easy to walk past the building and not really notice it. Steven took a piece of paper from his pocket and doubled checked the street number. There was no name or sign on the door. A black bouncer, dressed in an expensive dark suit, looked carefully at Steven's silk shirt and pants before opening the door to the bar.

It's a good thing I dressed for the part, Steven thought. He stepped into a hall and immediately turned left, down three steps into a longer hall. On the right was a large checkroom. *It must get pretty crowded in here in the winter*, he thought. The fall chill had not yet arrived, so it was empty. The walls were covered with rich, dark green velvet. The place was crowded and it wasn't yet 11:00 p.m. Steven continued to the end of the hall which opened into a large room with a long bar on one side. At the end of the bar, in a small mirrored lounge, was an ebony grand piano. Mirrors behind the bar reflected every part of the room making it easy to see everyone there once your eyes adjusted to the dim lights. *Convenient*, he thought. Looking into the mirrors, he saw several men his age—early forties—and older, watching each new arrival. There were no women.

Steven ordered a bourbon and soda and carefully examined each face reflected in the mirrors. Philip was not there. Steven looked at his own disappointed image in the hall of mirrors and leaned against the bar. He stared toward the hall. *At least I can see everyone who enters and leaves*, he thought. He sipped his drink and carefully observed the crowd. Although he had lived in New York for several years, he wasn't a bar person. The numerous years he was married, he and his wife usually entertained their guests in restaurants. Cocktails and after dinner drinks were offered at home. The local bar scene had never become part of his life. *God*, he thought, *what am I doing here, drinking alone, in one of the most expensive bars in the city—and a gay bar at that—no, worse yet, a gay hustler bar!*

He noticed that many of the older men appeared to know the younger ones quite well. They talked to some and bought drinks for others. The drinks were expensive.

At least it's a nice place—no, Steven thought, *it's an elegant place. The music is good, very good. The piano player must know every Broadway musical*, he thought, *and he doesn't miss a note*. He looked at a large vase filled with real pink and white lilies on the piano. Next to it rested a crystal bowl, filled with money—tips for the entertainer.

Several young men smiled at Steven. If he glanced at them, only for a second, they started to approach him. If he turned away, they stopped. *They aren't pushy*, he thought, *I'm glad for that*. He was nervous and he knew it probably showed. He motioned for the bartender.

"Have you worked here long?"

"A couple of years," the bartender answered hurriedly.

"I'm looking for Philip Knight—dark green eyes, dark hair, exceptional looks and body."

"Look around, man, do you see anybody here who isn't exceptional looking?" The bartender walked away.

"Good old New York," Steven sighed

"Maybe I can help you." Steven turned. The quiet voice belonged to an older man. He was elegantly dressed with a carefully folded paisley pocket square perfectly placed in the left pocket of his blazer. His dark hair had already turned to salt and pepper and he sported a goatee and mustache. *He looks like a librarian*, Steven thought, *or a professor.*

"Thank you," Steven replied. "I'm looking for a young man in his early twenty's—looks younger—with dark, medium-length, sort of shaggy hair, shorter than me, but with a beautiful and well developed body. His features are chiseled; he looks almost like a male version of the 1950's screen beauty, Ava Gardner. But his most memorable feature is the color of his eyes—they are a piercing emerald green."

"I do remember him," the man answered. "An exceptionally beautiful face and his eyes were so green, I wondered if he wore contact lenses—those new tinted ones."

"Have you seen him lately—the past two days?"

"No. I come here every other night. I know most of the working boys here—by sight at least—and I haven't seen your Philip in several months."

Steven's face fell. He sat next to the older man.

"Did he steal from you?" the man asked. "You have to be careful with some of them, not all, but some, especially the ones who are on drugs."

Steven looked at the man and nodded no. He couldn't speak. He tried to imagine Philip in this place—a *working boy*. He hated the term. He was well aware that Philip had worked as a hustler. He and Philip had discussed it numerous times. But sitting in a place like this and discussing it with a total stranger, this was another kind of revealing light.

"No. I can see it in your face," the man continued. "I would say that you are in love with him. Am I correct in my observation?"

Steven nodded yes. *How can this be*, he thought, I'*m not gay, yet, I'm in love with a boy I've only just met, who is half my age.*

"That is bad. Most of these young men don't know how to love. They often want to be loved, but they don't know how to accept it or how to return it. I'm afraid that most of the ones I have known, and I have known a lot of them, come from pretty awful backgrounds.

They will try and make you think differently, but I know them better than they think." The man drank and continued, "It's all right to buy them for sexual pleasures, they don't mind that, that's what they are here for. Some of them go with each other just for the fun of it. But don't make the mistake and fall in love with one of them. How long have you known the boy?"

Steven blushed. He couldn't bring himself to answer, only a few weeks. *This doesn't really happen to adult people*, he thought and remained silent. *Perhaps I'll wake-up soon and it will all go away.*

The man studied Steven's face. It was handsome, not pretty, kind but not sweet, determined, yet filled with pain. He was like a figure out of a Pre-Raphaelite painting still searching for the Holy Grail, unaware of the dangers ahead. "I'm afraid my advice is too late for you."

Steven looked at the older man's smile. *He is kind*, he thought, *a nice man. He doesn't look like the type who would pay young men to…* The sexual pleasures he had learned from Philip flashed before him. "Did you go with Philip?" Steven heard his own voice ask.

"Oh no," the man chuckled. "Your Philip is too dear for my budget. He brings a very high price as well as I remember. I have never played in your league." He looked at Steven's expensive shirt, tailored pants and handmade Italian shoes. "You're lucky that you can afford someone like Philip, especially while you are still young. It's harder when you become as old as me. I know that they want only money from me." He studied Steven and drank. "You are very handsome and still young, you might find a lover, but I don't think I'd look for one in a hustler bar, unless that's what turns you on. Are you one of those?"

"What?" He didn't know what 'one of those' was.

"Some men only like whores—men or women. He needs to feel always in control. Emotions have no role in the game, only complete control. It's another insecurity."

Steven was impressed with the way the man spoke—slowly, genteel and seemingly with great knowledge.

"I think older men who pay for sex," the man continued, "are like the beautiful young men in here who are selling sex. The same insecurity. Neither one knows how to love or how to receive love, for that matter. Are you one of those?" he asked again.

"No," Steven shook his head. "I don't think so, not now, now that I have—had—Philip." His last word drifted into a whisper. There was silence for a moment.

"Is he your first love?"

Steven nodded yes. *I don't want to go on with this,* he thought. "Where else can I look?" He asked and abruptly stood up.

"If he is working in New York, he will most definitely come in here, at least once during the night. This is still the most expensive and most popular meat-market in town."

"If he were dancing in one of the strip clubs, where would he be?" Steven looked anxious.

"Hummmm. I haven't been to one of those in a while. Let me get the local bar guide for you." He leaned over the bar and took a small magazine from a stack. Glancing at the black and white photograph on the front, he looked startled. "Isn't that you?" The older man looked carefully and handed the magazine to Steven. On the cover of the publication was a photograph of Steven and Philip. They were kissing, but it was easy to recognize each one.

"Oh, my God," Steven whispered. "What is this publication?"

"It's a weekly guide to what's going on in the gay community. It is in every gay bar and club in the greater New York area—probably in Connecticut and New Jersey as well." The man looked at the picture and smiled. "It's a nice photo, but I must say, you certainly look silly in that costume. Whatever are you wearing? It looks like a worn-out tutu—but no, there are fairy wings and wands! You're holding fairy wands as well! He looks stoned and you look very drunk!"

Steven moaned, "He was, I was, we were."

"It's probably in all the gay newspapers as well. Let me see," he leaned over the bar again. "Yes, here they are. Most of them arrived this evening, or they would be stacked by the door. It's okay to take one—they are free to the customers

Steven looked at the newspapers. Photographs of him and Philip were on the front pages of all of them. Some were full length, some were close-up, some showed Philip kissing him. These photos of their hairy bodies stuffed into the worn-out fairy tutus were more ridiculous than anything he had ever seen. *How could I possibly have gotten myself involved in such an insane moment,* he thought.

Then the pleasure and feeling of joy of being with Philip flooded his mind. He wanted to cry out, 'Philip.'

"You're quite a celebrity. You and your Philip are leading one of the oldest Gay Liberation Parades in America. Wait until the crowd in here recognizes you.

He opened one of the newspapers and looked from page to page. "Here it is," he handed it to Steven. "Here is a list of all the gay bars and clubs in New York City."

Steven took the paper and looked at it. He couldn't believe it. "This many?" There were several columns on the page. "There must be hundreds of them!"

"There are categories," the man pointed to the columns, "and notice that they are arranged by sections of the city." He glanced at Steven. "You really are new at this, aren't you?"

Steven nodded, looking at the long list. *New at this*, he thought, *I know nothing about the gay world or these bizarre places.*

"Here, note how each one has this symbol by its name. Now look at this chart," the man's finger slid to the top of the page, "that tells you what kind of gay patrons usually go there. Let me see the list of clubs with dancers. There are quite a few."

Steven drank his bourbon, while the older man studied the list.

"This one, I think. Your Philip is too beautiful and expensive to be associated with any of the others. Has he danced in the clubs before?"

"Yeah, when he needed money in a hurry, he used to work in a couple of those places."

"Humm, I'd like to see that."

Steven got up to leave.

"Wait," the man touched his arm, "it's too early. You don't want to have to sit there all evening, go after midnight. If he really knows what he is doing, he'll be in the last show and it will have the best crowd of serious lookers. The boys who don't get purchased there, will come here, or to some of the other bars. It's best to go later."

Steven reluctantly sat down again, "Thanks. Can I buy you a drink?"

"Why, yes, I would greatly enjoy that. Certainly something new for me—to have a younger man pay for the drink." He motioned to the bartender for another round.

He obviously is well known here, Steven thought, *by the way the bartender jumped to attention.*

"Do you always go for the young beautiful ones?" the man asked.

Steven looked at the newspapers and magazine on the bar. He stared at the photographs of himself and Philip. *There's no way this guy or anyone will believe me, if I say I'm not gay, especially after seeing these photographs.*

"No, this is my first exceptional beauty—and my last." Steven heard himself reply. Then, without hesitating, he blurted out to the man, "We met only a few weeks ago by accident at a gay resort where those photographs were taken. I never gave him money. As a matter of fact, he seduced me. I know this sounds stupid, in the light of those photographs, but I'm—I'm not really gay."

"You mean you have never come out to anyone, not even to yourself," the man calmly replied. "Don't worry; these photos will do it for you. You won't have to say a word. Although your names are not printed, your friends, family and enemies—certainly your enemies—will recognize you. And these photos will be all across America by the end of the week. That parade you and your young, beauty are leading has become an important gay liberation event. I'm sorry, but even your best friend and mother won't believe you aren't gay after seeing this." He held up one of the papers, showing a full length photo of the two of them hugging each other.

Steven groaned, "Then it's even more important that I find him."

They drank quietly for a while. Steven watched the reflections in the mirrors—flirting, probably bargaining, buying. "Are all of these young men for sale?"

"Most all of them. Some probably live in the neighborhood and come in just to socialize. If you talk to one, you must immediately ask him if he is working or just playing. That way you will know for sure."

"I've never seen any place like this. It reminds me of what a real whorehouse must have been like in the 19th century."

"Same mentality. Some of them are charming, and you often get more than you bargained for, but some aren't worth the money. They promise everything but when they go home with you, all they can think about is how to get out as fast as possible with the money."

"What happens to them, later in life?" Steven sipped his drink.

"I'm not sure. By their mid- to late-twenties—certainly by the age of thirty—they have too much competition. A new generation takes over. One thing about the flesh trade, for men anyway, they have to be young and in great shape—usually well-endowed or exceptionally beautiful. Some aren't really gay."

Steven looked surprised.

"You didn't know that? No, some do it only for the money. Some, perhaps, for the thrill. If he tells you that he only gets sucked—nothing else—you can be assured that he is probably straight. I often think that's why some men come into these places; they want to think that they are seducing a straight man—not a gay one. There are bars filled with gay men, young ones especially, but no, these men—the ones who are buying—want a straight young man." He looked carefully at Steven. "You could do very well in the bars. You're handsome and very natural looking, the all-American dream guy. You don't act or look like the usual gay man. That's always a plus. You're too much of a gentleman to have been a hustler when you were younger, but you certainly could have been a boy-toy."

"A what?" Steven was startled, but fascinated and a little flattered by the older man's admiration.

"A boy-toy. He isn't the same thing as a hustler. There's a natural, dangerous animal, sensual sexuality in the mind of the kind of male who hustles on the streets and in the clubs. It's much more than a survival instinct. He's usually well-endowed and extremely macho acting. He certainly isn't the type you would invite to your mother's home for dinner. There are no emotions involved. He knows you want him only for sex and you know he wants you only for money. As Oscar Wilde described it, 'It's like feasting with panthers; the danger is half the excitement.' But a boy-toy, that's another animal. He may be cute, sexy and sensual, but he possesses none of the wild threats hiding beneath the surface of the hustler. If we were back in college, the boy-toy was the one in the khaki pants, penny loafers and pale pink cashmere sweater. Neat and sweet. All of our mothers' friends smiled and commented what a nice young man he was. We introduced the polite young thing to fine wines, elegant restaurants, theatre, opera...of course our mothers and their friends had no idea we were buggering him ragged every night, or vice versa. He became our young protégé and we were such a good influence on the young man. Either way, the older man pays. But some pay for yearnings other than sex."

Looking over Steven's shoulder, he said, "Good evening, John."

He lowered his voice and spoke again to Steven, "That's a strange one, John there. I know several of the young men who have been with him. He wants one thing and one thing only, and he doesn't mind what it costs."

Steven looked at the man named John. He was about his own age, pleasant features, good body, clean-cut and certainly straight looking.

"Watch the type he likes," the older man whispered.

Steven followed John's glance in the mirrors. Each time his glance paused, it fell on young men with open shirts exposing hairy chests.

"Did you notice?"

"Yeah, I'd say he likes them hairy."

"You are very observant," the older man smiled. "I asked one of my young friends what John likes in bed. At first he wouldn't tell me. They are very protective of their clients and of each other. Competitive—but protective. I insisted, and since I was a regular for the young man, he explained John's passion."

"What?" Steven asked glancing at John.

"John always explains in great detail to the working boy, young or old, before he leaves with him. The young man must have a hairy chest, the more hair the better. When they go to John's apartment, the young man strips and gets into bed. He has to lie on his side and pretend to be asleep. Then John goes into the room, naked, and quietly slips into bed with his back to the hairy young man. After a few moments, the young man must turn over and put his arms around John, gently pulling his back to his hairy chest."

Steven waited. "That's all?"

The man nodded yes. "Nothing more. I asked my friend, why? He said that John once explained it. When John was a little boy, he used to get out of bed very early in the morning and run to his parents' bedroom. He climbed into bed on his father's side, and snuggled close to his father. His father always placed his arms around him and let him sleep for the remainder of the morning."

Steven drank his bourbon. "Do you think the father...?"

"No. It's the feeling of the hairy chest against his back. That feeling recalls a sense of security, long since lost. He doesn't try to have sex. That is the feeling he wants—that sense of security, if only for a little while. It is more important to him than sex."

Steven stared at John. *How sad*, he thought, *that a joy from one's youth can become such a demanding demon in adulthood.*

"The young men are very nice to him, watch when they see him," the older man continued. "The pay is good, I'm told, and they don't have to spend the night. An hour or so is sufficient, and they don't have to reach a climax."

"Is everyone into games?" he asked the older man.

"Everyone is looking for some kind of fantasy to soften the blows of reality," he looked at Steven. "Aren't you?"

"I'm not sure. Maybe I haven't had so many blows of reality, yet. So why are you here? What type are you looking for?"

"My type? He no longer exists. I'm under very heavy medication for advanced, inoperable cancer. The same medication that keeps me alive has destroyed all of my sexual desires."

"Then why do you come into a place like this?"

"For company and conversation with people like you. A drink with a stranger is cheaper than a visit to a psychiatrist and a whole lot easier than confession to a priest. I was a priest, so I know."

Steven looked startled.

"No," the man continued, "I was not defrocked for enticing under-aged choir boys. I left the priesthood once I realized that I really could not turn down an available young man, and they are so available, everywhere. If I have sinned, I'm being punished for it. My greatest pleasure was fine sex. It has been taken completely from me. My erotic dreams turn into nightmares."

Steven just looked at the man and continued to listen. *How odd*, he thought, *for this total stranger to be telling me something so personal. Is this what happens to lonely people in old age?* Suddenly he was aware of a quote he had heard: 'What growing old does not do to you, living alone will.'

"See? How easy it is to tell you this? And I don't even know your name. I'm cursed to spend my old age alone. I have absolutely nothing to offer a lover. No security, no sex. I couldn't be any good to even John, there. I have no hair on my chest. So I come here and watch other people act out their lives." He paused and studied Steven's face. "What if you don't find your young beauty or what if he doesn't want to come back?"

"I'll find him, I've got to," Steven partially whispered. "He'll come back, once I explain all of it to him."

"But what if he doesn't want to come back?" the man insisted.

"At this moment, my answer is I don't want to survive without him. I don't think I can even try."

The man studied Steven's reflection in one of the mirrors. He looked confused. "Just remember this, in case you don't find him, regardless of how rare or unique something or someone is—there is always a comparable—not a replacement, but a comparable. Always.

Steven rose to go. "I don't want a comparable or a replacement. I'll find Philip."

The older man took his arm. "And remember, when you meet someone—anyone—in a place like this, be very careful. You have no idea if anything I have said to you is even remotely true.

He stood up and looked at the man. His eyes had a sparkle in them. "This is my truth, my reality," Steven pointed to Philip's picture, "I think before him, I lived in fantasy. Thanks for the information," he said taking the papers and magazine from the bar, "and the advice. I have to find him soon—before he becomes fantasy."

Steven walked past the doorman into the street. It was getting crowded and several limousines were double-parked. Some of the chauffeurs were dressed in full livery waiting for their bosses to select their evening's pleasure.

"Taxi!" Steven called and entered the darkness of a cab.

BUCKY AND THE WOODS COP
JIM STEWART

When Conservation Officer Woodward Scott had come in for supper he'd loosened the forest green uniform tie and unbuttoned his collar. Reddish-blond hair had sprung aggressively from the open neck of his shirt. He'd rolled up his sleeves, exposing his thick forearms, and dug into his usual—the meatloaf plate special.

He pushed his chair away from the table, ran his big hand over his neatly trimmed mustache and beard to remove any last particles of the meal, stood up, and brushed the crumbs off his gray Conservation Officer uniform shirt. It fit snug over his well-defined chest. The Department of Natural Resources patch on his sleeves over his biceps caused many to notice his muscular arms.

Scott rolled down his sleeves, buttoned them around his thick wrists, tightened his tie, and donned his regulation Pershing uniform hat. It matched the color of the tie and his twill trousers and fit snuggly over his close-cropped red hair. In his uniform CO Scott was the idol of most women and the envy of many men.

The North Pines Cafe was closed. CO Scott looked out the front windows onto Main Street. It had stopped snowing. He laid a ten on the table for his supper. His beefy hands folded a twenty dollar bill in half and slipped it under the edge of his ketchup stained plate. He glanced at the waitress, gave her a slight smile, and looked down at the folded twenty. The waitress knew what it meant. She returned a faint smile that barely hid her bad teeth.

Halfway down the narrow hallway to the back door CO Scott glanced over his shoulder and saw Weesie pick up the twenty and pocket it. She headed toward the hall. Besides the dishwasher and cook cleaning up in the kitchen, he and Weesie were the only ones left in the restaurant. Just before the back exit Scott entered the men's room on the right. He left the door unlocked.

Joe Campeau finished the pots and pans and used his dirty white apron as a towel. He had a dilemma. The night before in the Sun Dog Saloon he'd been propositioned. Not the usual down-state dude who wanted to swing on his tool. He always managed to pick up a few extra bucks that way. No, some dude offered him cash for a trophy buck. At least a ten-pointer, the guy had said. A twelve-pointer would be worth even more. The dude wanted bragging rights back in the city. He didn't care about the meat. Campeau thought of the old Kelvinator freezer in his grandpa's lean-to. It could hold a whole deer carcass once it was cut up and packaged in freezer paper. The meat would help them both through the winter. Campeau knew of a trophy buck in the cedar swamp over by Prison Camp Road. He also knew what the dude wanted was illegal.

"Bucky!" the cook yelled, "Get your fucking ass back to work! You want to be here all night?" The cook, like everyone else, called Joe Campeau Bucky.

Bucky bagged up the trash. He was stripped to his white stained wife-beater under his apron. Even in November it got hot as hell in the kitchen, especially when he opened the big dishwasher and the steam rolled out. He opened it now to take out the last tray of pots and pans. Sweat ran down the underside of his bare arms. It dripped off his forehead and was caught in his patchy young-man beard. He flexed his pecs under the wife-beater. More sweat trickled down his chest through the few dark hairs that had sprouted there. The smell of the sweat aroused him. He smiled to himself, revealing two prominent front teeth—the grin that had earned him his nickname.

"Aren't you about done in there?" the cook yelled through the service window.

"Done!" Bucky yelled back and took off his apron.

He pulled a grungy long sleeved waffle-weave shirt over his uncut hair and down across his body. The waffle-weave didn't get tucked in. Bucky flexed his pecs again. It felt good. He pulled on his old gray hoodie.

"I gotta' take a piss and then you can lock up," Bucky yelled back at the cook.

"Weesie left?" the cook said.

"Last I saw she was headed for the back door."

Damn, he really did have to take a piss. Bucky headed down the hallway and pulled open the door to the head as he unzipped his fly.

Weesie was down on her knees in front of the woods cop.

"Shit! What the hell?"

Bucky stared at what was protruding from CO Scott's unzipped uniform trousers. Weesie turned her head to see who had come in. The conservation officer splattered her green waitress uniform obliterating half the word *Louise* on her nametag.

"God damn, kid," CO Scott muttered under his breath as he adjusted his Smoky-the-Bear hat trying to regain his dignity.

Bucky backed out of the toilet, his eyes still on the conservation officer. He hustled out the back door, grabbed his black watch cap from the pouch of his hoodie, pulled it over his long dark hair, and headed for his pick-up parked in the corner of the lot.

Bucky lived with his grandpa, Hank Campeau. The old man was crippled up pretty bad from the action he'd seen during the dying days of Vietnam. He lived on a small veteran's disability pension, food-stamps, and whatever squirrels he could get with his twenty-gauge from the back porch. Hank Campeau was Métis— part French, part Indian. His ma had told him so. Since none of his papers confirmed the fact, he received no shares in the new casino that went in just outside of town.

Since the old man couldn't drive anymore, he had given Bucky his pickup and snow plow blade. Everybody said it was going to be a bad-ass winter this year. Bucky knew he could make money snowplowing in town. With money from that, the dishwasher job he'd had since high school, and the occasional "tip" from down-staters that he let swing on his north-woods pole, he got by.

If things didn't work out he could always go into town and enlist at the Army recruiting office on Main Street, but that would leave grandpa on his own. The old man had taken care of Bucky since his dad had ended up at the Big House down-state. Bucky's ma had followed her man to Jackson, enrolled in beauty school, and wrote to the kid for a while. When his old man's parole fell through, his ma took off with her new boyfriend. Bucky hadn't heard from her since the eighth grade.

Bucky climbed into his truck, started it, and let it warm up a bit. He thought about the trophy buck offer again. The more he thought about it, the more he convinced himself it was the right thing to do. Just as his windows were starting to fog up he saw the woods cop come out the back door of the North Pines Café.

Bucky's fly was still unzipped from when he'd walked in on Weesie and the woods cop. He stuck his fingers inside past his zipper. Damn that felt good. With his other hand he cleared a circle the size of a saucer in the fog on the windshield.

A light skiff of snow had settled on the dark green DNR vehicle. Bucky watched the woods cop head for it. Parking-lot lights lit a lone pine in a circle above "Department of Natural Resources" stenciled on the truck's door.

He saw CO Scott hop up into his truck and heard it start up. Bucky put his whole hand through his fly and squeezed his tool as he panted softly.

❖

"Time for this woods cop to leave," the game warden said under his breath.

It was seven-thirty and already dark. The snow had stopped falling, but the wind had picked up. Tomorrow, the first day of firearms season, would be a long one. CO Scott didn't know who gave him more grief—the drunken downstate hunters looking for trophy racks and pussy or the local poachers trying to feed their families through the winter.

As he left the parking lot CO Scott noticed a ten-year-old black Chevy pickup with a red passenger door and a gray-primer hood. Junkyard replacements. Firewood was randomly tossed in the back, exhaust came out the tailpipe, and the windows were fogged.

I'd like to know what's goin' on in there, the game warden thought to himself. *Maybe Weesie's earning another twenty.* He rolled down his window to get a better look.

As the dark green truck passed him, Bucky was sure its driver was staring out the open side window at him. Bucky stopped what he was doing and waited a few minutes after the DNR truck left before he put his pickup in gear and pulled out of the parking lot. He could see the taillights on the DNR truck as it turned right a couple of blocks down the street. Bucky kept his pickup far enough behind so as not to be an obvious tail.

A few minutes later he saw the woods cop pull into the driveway of an old frame house on Oak Street. Bucky pulled over and parked about half a block back on the one-way street. It was cold and the snow had started falling again, so he left the motor running.

Conservation Officer Woodward Scott got out of his pickup and went inside. He lived alone. It fit his job. He liked it that way.

When Operation Desert Storm ended the first Iraq War, Woodward Scott was shipped home and mustered out of the Marines. The wild life was his for a while as he adjusted to being a civilian again. But then one day he saw where it was taking him. Nowhere. He knew his military training would give him an advantage in a law enforcement career. Scott passed the entry level law enforcement exam and enrolled in the twenty-two week class at the Commission on Law Enforcement Standards Academy in the state capitol. He graduated near the top of his class and spent another eighteen weeks working for the Department of Natural Resources in different field assignments throughout the state. He then applied for and got his current job as a woods cop.

Bucky saw a light go on in the back of the house. In a minute an upstairs light went on in the room over the front porch. Old pull-down shades covered the double windows in the room's dormer. Bucky could just make out movement behind the shades. It looked like the big bear of a man was stripping.

Scott stripped off his uniform. He got the DNR-issued black snowmobile suit from the closet. It had lots of pockets for things he might need in the field. He patted down the suit checking the contents of the pockets. His compass, power bars, folded heat sheet, buck knife, Maglite, and two pair of Flexi Cuffs were all in their proper places.

He carefully folded his dress uniform and laid it on top of his old Marine footlocker. Stripped down to his olive drab boxers, he glanced at himself in the mirror. The light reflected off the curly copper-gold hair that covered most of his body. *Not bad for an old college linebacker*, he thought. He hadn't worked out in years. His job kept him fit. The size of his arms caused him to carry them slightly out from his torso. His massive chest dominated his still hard belly. CO Scott stepped into his double-XL snowmobile suit and pulled up the long zipper that ran all the way up the right leg, across his crotch, and up the middle of his chest. The suit was built to wick away sweat. He liked the way it rode across his bare nipples and brought them to attention. He fingered the DNR patch sewn over his left chest pocket.

Bucky inched his truck closer until he was directly across the street from Scott's house. The silhouette of the woods cop filled the worn shade. Bucky glimpsed a flash of bare flesh covered with reddish-blond hair along the edge of the shades where they hung away from the windows. Bucky's hand went back through his unzipped fly.

The upstairs light went out.

Bucky kept the lights off, put the old truck in reverse, and backed up the street to where he had originally parked.

The downstairs light went out.

CO Scott left the house, walked past the DNR truck in the driveway, and got into his Jeep Cherokee parked on the street. He was going undercover tonight. The old black pickup with the red door and gray hood with the motor running that was parked across the street caught his eye.

The Jeep pulled away from the curb and headed down the street. Bucky let it get ahead of him before he followed.

It started to snow as CO Scott headed out of town. Just before he turned off the old State Highway onto County Road 42 he glanced in his rearview mirror. A pair of headlights rode half a mile behind him.

The Jeep started to leave tracks in the fresh snow. *Good tracking snow for opening day tomorrow*, the woods cop thought. *Hunters will like that. So will I.* He smiled to himself.

Fifteen miles later the woods cop slowed down when he spotted the two-track everybody called Prison Camp Road. There was no road sign. There was no prison camp. The State Prison Board had closed the camp decades ago. The woods had reclaimed the land and most of the road.

Bucky hung back about a mile so as not to be seen. He could now easily follow the tire tracks of the Jeep in the snow. He saw every turn where they went down first a gravel road, then onto the old Prison Camp Road.

Bucky almost blew his cover when he suddenly saw brake lights flash ahead. He had been driving without lights. He quickly stopped and rolled down the window. Bucky could hear the Jeep advancing down the two-track.

A couple miles further Conservation Officer Scott turned left through a stand of poplars. Their bare branches brushed against the Jeep as it crept along, bouncing over the rutted trail. The officer stopped at a weathered wooden gate. It wasn't locked. He got out and pulled it open. Back in the Jeep he shut off the headlights and proceeded along the trail. CO Scott knew his way in the dark.

Bucky eased his pickup forward until he saw an open wooden gate. He pulled his truck off the path into a little turnaround and parked. Bucky reached behind the seat in the old Chevy and pulled out his 32 Winchester Special. He'd had it since he was fourteen. His grandpa had given it to him when he graduated from the eighth grade. It was a light rifle, but good for deer. He checked the safety, quietly hopped down from the truck, slung the rifle strap over his shoulder, and started down the two-track. The moon could barely be seen under the cedars. After a quarter mile Bucky felt the path start to rise. In a moment he was out from under the cedars and slowly walking up an incline. At the top was an old hunting camp surrounded by second-growth white pine with a light in the window. The jeep was parked next to the cabin.

Bucky crept toward the cabin keeping the rifle close to his side on its sling. He stood back from the window in order to see through it without being seen. Large shadows loomed across the inside walls as he saw the game warden adding more wood to the fire. Bucky crouched down when the woods cop came to the window and glanced out. CO Scott appeared naked. Firelight shone off his chest and arms. The sight of the big man aroused Bucky. He readjusted the rifle slung over his shoulder. The conservation officer moved away from the window. As he bent over to get more firewood Bucky could see he wore his olive drab boxers.

CO Scott turned down the Coleman lantern and lay back on the lower bunk. Its old mattress had no sheet and was scratchy on his naked back. It felt good. He wondered how many other men had used the old cotton wadding and horsehair mat with its stained striped ticking. Inside it was warm even though the fire was burning low. Years ago somebody had built a stone beehive bake oven inside to hold heat and keep the small cabin warm once the fire burned out.

The image of Bucky staring at him and the waitress on her knees flashed through his mind. He had seen the bulge that had been in the dishwasher's Levis. Somehow the kid looked familiar. Once on his way out of the North Pines Cafe CO Scott had glanced into the kitchen and saw the dishwasher standing in a cloud of steam wearing a wife-beater. The white tank top had accented his dark shoulder muscles and beefy pecs. He had looked like a wrestler in a singlet. The kid had always caused uneasy stirrings in the woods cop. Tonight those feelings were strong. The game warden panted softly.

Outside Bucky could no longer see the Conservation Officer through the window. He looked around. The November moon came out from behind a cloud. He saw a pine stump a couple of feet high a few yards from the cabin. He climbed onto it. He could now see inside the cabin. The light from the dying fire lit up the nearly naked man on the lower bunk. Bucky almost lost his balance. CO Scott was running his big hands over his hairy chest. The conservation officer's tool had freed itself from the confines of his boxers. It looked even more formidable in the dying light from the fire than Bucky remembered when he'd burst in on Weesie and the woods cop in the restroom a couple of hours earlier.

Bucky's equipment strained against his Levis. He leaned forward on the pine stump, trying to get a better view of the woods cop inside. This time Bucky did lose his balance, falling sideways off the stump into the dried brush. He wasn't hurt but had grunted slightly when he fell. Bucky made more noise as he scrambled with his rifle into the cluster of pines near the cabin. He watched the cabin window.

The game warden came to the window, cupped his big hands around his eyes, and looked out. CO Scott had heard something outside.

Bucky walked down the path toward the cedar swamp about a hundred yards and stopped. He pulled a flashlight from his hoodie pouch and waited.

The Conservation Officer moved away from the window, picked up his snowmobile-suit from the chair, stepped into it, and zipped it up. The residue of his sweat inside the suit felt cool on his naked flesh. He pulled on his watchman's cap and out of habit patted his pockets for the Maglite, buck knife, and Flexi Cuffs.

CO Scott stood to the side of the doorway and slowly opened the door. All was quiet outside. Then he heard a branch break about a hundred yards away on the path that lead to the cedar swamp. The woods cop stepped outside and closed the door. He waited. Another branch broke near the edge of the swamp.

Bucky heard the door of the cabin open. He picked up a small dead branch from the side of the path and broke it in two. In a few minutes, he heard the woods cop walking towards him. After a couple of minutes, Bucky left the path and deliberately broke several braches as he made his way toward the swale where he knew deer bedded down.

Just as the first deer started out of the swale Bucky turned on his flashlight. The beam fell directly on a small startled doe. She froze. The next instant a powerful beam of light lit Bucky's face. For a moment both men stood still anticipating the other's action.

"Conservation Officer Woodward Scott. Turn off your light and put your hands on your head," he said.

Bucky turned off his flashlight, put it in his pouch, then slowly put his hands on his head. A bank of clouds shifted to the northeast and allowed the moon to dominate the night sky as CO Scott approached. When the game warden was about five feet from Bucky he stopped, his Maglite still on the younger man's face.

"Damn," he said under his breath. CO Scott tried to place the young man in the beam of his Maglite. He knew it was the dishwasher from the North Pines Café, but the kid looked familiar for some other reason. Then it came to him. The dishwasher had been a star high-school wrestler. It was Joe Campeau. Years ago Scott had seen him wrestle in the heavyweight class when the kid was in high school. Whenever the young Campeau and his opponent had assumed the neutral starting position his team-mates had all shouted "Pin him to the mat, Bucky, pin him to the mat" *Yes, it's the wrestler*, the woods cop thought to himself. Scott had last seen Bucky wrestle a couple of years ago when he was a senior. The kid's body looked beefier now, even under his hoodie, than it had when he'd won the state Class-C regional heavyweight championship.

"I'm going to have to see a picture ID," CO Scott said, "and a hunting license."

"They're back in my truck," Bucky lied.

"I'm going to have to take you in Mr. Campeau," the conservation officer said. He fingered the Flexi Cuffs in his pocket.

"Not a problem, Officer Scott." Bucky grinned. Everybody knew who Conservation Officer Scott was but nobody had ever called Bucky Mr. Campeau before.

"I want you to keep your hands on your head while I get your rifle," CO Scott said. He left the Flexi Cuffs in his pocket.

Again Bucky did as he was told. His body ached for release when the woods cop nearly hugged him as he un-slung the 32-Winchester rifle from Bucky's shoulder.

"We're going back to the hunting camp," CO Scott said. "You're not going to give me any trouble are you?"

Bucky grinned, showing the officer his namesake front teeth, and shook his head. "I promise not to run away, Officer."

"Let's go then." Yet again Bucky did as he was told.

The game warden locked the 32-Winchester Special in the Jeep. The two men went inside the cabin. The fire was nothing but a pile of coals. Heat still radiated from it and the warm stones of the bee hive oven.

"Take care of that fire," CO Scott ordered Bucky, nodding toward the wood stacked along the edge a wall.

Bucky carefully placed some pine and split oak on top of the dying embers. It soon brought the fire back to life. He pulled off his watch-cap, hoodie, and waffle-weave undershirt all at once and stood in the glow of the fire in his white wife-beater. A sheen of sweat covered his dark shoulders and arms. Scott's gaze traveled down to Bucky's hands, to broad thick fingers with flat nails chewed to the quick, to knuckles scabbed from a slipped socket wrench.

"You used to wrestle didn't you?" CO Scott said as his voice cracked.

"I was regional champion at a hundred eighty-two pounds my senior year," Bucky said, pride creeping into his voice.

"I used to wrestle too," CO Scott said. "When I was a grunt in the Marines."

Bucky and Scott looked at each other the way men sometimes do. A message was telegraphed with that look. They both grinned. It was a challenge, a friendly man-to-man challenge. They were no longer the woods cop and the poacher, instead they were just two men. Without another word they lifted the mattress from the bunk and laid it on the floor in front of the fire. Bucky stripped to his camo shorts. His body trembled slightly despite the heat in the cabin. The game warden pulled down the full-length zipper of his snowmobile suit and shed it. He now wore only his DNR-issue OD green boxers.

"Take the defensive starting position," CO Woodward Scott said to the younger man. His voice cracked slightly again.

Bucky got down on both knees. He leaned forward, bent his arms at the elbows and placed his palms on the old mattress in the defensive position. His bent arms lowered his upper body. The game warden got down on both knees behind the younger man, leaning over him with his hand around his waist in the offensive starting position.

Bucky could feel the sweaty fleece of the game warden's chest and belly along his naked back. The conservation officer moved in closer. The smell of the young man's sweat excited the woods cop. He inhaled deeply.

"On three," Scott said.

On three Scott grabbed Bucky's thick right wrist and jerked it out to the side. On three Bucky used his powerful bent arms as springs to push back against the heavier man, lift him, turn his sweaty torso around, and set it back down on the mattress. In doing so he allowed his head to be scissored between the woods cop's powerful thighs. Scott put his hands behind Bucky's bull neck in a finger interlock. He pulled Bucky's head toward him. Bucky inhaled the older man's musk.

"Takedown, Sir," Bucky said. He grinned up at the conservation officer.

The pitch in a pine knot burst at the bottom of the fire and erupted in a volley of hot embers. The split oak settled down into the warmth of the coals. As it flamed, long shadows of the two men were cast against the walls of the cabin.

Again the younger man took the defensive position. This time he put his weight on both knees and braced the palms of his hands on the old mattress. This time his elbows were not bent to spring and throw the older man, but instead they were braced to take his weight. Again the heavier man got down on both knees behind the younger, leaning over him. Both were ready.

Male grunts as if from boar bears staking out territory reverberated across the tiny room. A circle of man flesh turned on the old mattress as power muscles entwined and the two men explored the other's masculinity. They wrestled until both had reached the edge of ecstasy. The burnt remains of the oak logs shifted down further into the bed of coals and shot out a shower of sparks.

Both achieved rapture in the glow of the dying fire. They lay panting softly, collapsed on the old mattress. The smell of woodsmoke, man-sweat, and testosterone hung heavy in the air as the two men dozed in the hour that belongs to neither yesterday nor tomorrow. The last dying embers cast low shadows against the cabin walls.

CO Scott woke. It was not yet first light. The fire had died to half a dozen red coals. He watched as Bucky opened his eyes and gave him his namesake grin.

"Want to be my shadow, Bucky?" Scott said.

"I'm ready when you are, Boss," Bucky said.

The two men exchanged a long bear hug, dressed quickly, and quietly left the cabin. Within a matter of minutes they were near the stream that led to a beaver dam on Blind Biscuit Creek. Two does came down to drink. A few yards behind a twelve-point buck followed them. A bright beam of light suddenly stopped the buck in his tracks. A rifle shot cracked the morning stillness. The game warden instantly shone his high-powered Maglite in the direction of the shots.

"Conservation Officer Woodward Scott. Stay where you are. Do not move."

It was silent for a moment. Then the sound of branches breaking as someone ran blindly through the woods. The game warden ran down the trail searching the woods ahead with his light. Bucky ran behind him.

They both spotted it there on the trail—the twelve-point buck. Its hind quarters twitched slightly as it died. The sound of an all-terrain vehicle racing away shattered the morning air. CO Scott made as if to take chase, then stopped. The groomed snowmobile trail along the edge of the cedar swamp provided the perfect escape route. The noise of the ATV faded into the distance.

"Now what, Boss?" Bucky said.

"As a Conservation Officer I confiscate the carcass."

"Then what?"

"The practice is to donate the meat to the needy."

"Do you mean somebody like a crippled old man on a disability pension?"

CO Scott thought for a moment. "Yes, somebody like that," he said.

"I know somebody like that, Boss." Bucky grinned at the game warden.

"We better get it gutted out so it can cool," CO Scott said.

Together they dressed the buck carcass.

Scott handed a rope to Bucky who tied it around the base of the buck's rack to hold it high while he dragged the gutted carcass back to camp. CO Scott went inside to secure the cabin while Bucky headed down the two-track through the cedar swamp to his pickup. He hoisted the twelve-point buck into its bed, covered it with a blue tarp, and headed home to the single-wide trailer, Grandpa Hank, and the second-hand freezer in the tar-paper lean-to.

CO Scott made sure the fire was out. He adjusted the padlock so the door looked locked but wasn't. It was fully light now and most of the snow had melted. The woods cop was about to leave when he spotted two fresh cigarette butts on the ground under the window. He didn't smoke. Neither did Bucky. On the wall under the window the game warden saw a big honker that had been spit out at the wall. It had run down over the weathered boards of the cabin and had almost dried in the morning sun. As the game warden stared at it longer he realized it wasn't a honker. The escaped poacher had evidently enjoyed their wrestling match last night.

Bucky spent the morning in the lean-to cutting up venison while Grandpa Hank wrapped it, tied it, and packed it in the old freezer. Around noon Bucky headed to the Sun Dog Saloon. Inside he spotted the man he was looking for. He motioned him outside to the back parking lot. Bucky took a big bulky feed-sack from his pick-up. He handed it to the man who looked inside. Bucky saw him counting until he ran out of fingers. The man pulled out his wallet and handed a wad of twenties to Bucky, who counted them and slipped them neatly into his own wallet. The man put the feed-sack in the trunk of his Buick and drove off to the south. Bucky went back into the Sun Dog Saloon and made a phone call.

Half an hour later Conservation Officer Woodward Scott, now in full DNR dress uniform, complete with Pershing hat, was driving his dark green half-ton pickup with the pine tree emblem on the door when he spotted a car speeding south. He pulled it over.

"Good afternoon, sir," he said. "Conservation Officer Woodward Scott of the Department of Natural Resources." The driver looked up at CO Scott's mirrored aviation sunglasses. "We're conducting a survey," CO Scott said. "I'm going to have to ask you to open your trunk."

Silver Pumps and a Loose Nut
J.R. Greenwell

Daphne sat alone in the booth, stirring the half-empty glass of vodka and tonic in front of her with her fingertip, the fourth in the past hour. Her eyelids drooped from the weight of the oversized, false eyelashes glued to her aqua blue shadowed lids. She drifted in and out, thinking about being at the beach at sunrise to pay homage to Ursula Andress. As she listened to the honky-tonk country music in the background coming from the dusty jukebox, she gently shook her head and rolled her eyes in disgust with the selection of music. *Whoever heard of a honky-tonk angel,* she thought to herself. She hated country music, as it brought back memories of the time she lived with her evil stepmother in a trailer court south of Birmingham. Daphne knew well the perils of being a modern day redneck Cinderella.

The soft amber lights cast a glow on Daphne's bright blond hair, teased high and hanging down past her shoulders. Her lips lacked color as her dark red lipstick had worn off. Too tired to reapply more gloss, and with the bar ready to close and no one there to even notice, she thought it would be a waste of time to even look halfway seductive at this hour of the night. Apparent that she missed the bar's prime time, she took off her four-inch silver heels and placed them next to her purse as if she were protecting them from some unknown foot-fetish thief. The pumps, two sizes too small for her size eleven feet and making her already six-foot tall willowy body even more towering, were her prized possessions. More than anything else, walking in those glorious shoes gave her the swagger of self-confidence and womanhood that no pair of flats could. She stretched her legs under the table until her feet relaxed on the seat across from her. Her black dress barely covered the top of her thighs, and each time she flexed her legs and pointed her toes, her body shifted forward and the hem of her skirt would rise, exposing her bright red lacy panties.

Sitting alone wasn't the way Daphne pictured she'd be celebrating this night in Daytona. It was almost closing time and the only people in the place were the bartender, Daphne, and her ride for the night, Sam. Sam was a forty-something drag-gofer from Birmingham who offered to take Daphne and her mentor, Stella, to Daytona for a contest at Club Diva. The trip was really his excuse to visit with his old boyfriend, the bartender, who seemed to be trying his best to entertain Sam, though Daphne could tell that he really wasn't interested in his old flame. Daphne looked at the bartender, thinking he was around thirty or so, his muscles flexing through his T-shirt each time he picked up a glass or a bottle of Jack Daniels. *This stud*, Daphne thought, *could have any man he wanted if one was around*. Sam was foolishly in lust, and the bartender seemed content to be patronized by Sam's flirtatious jokes and come-ons.

Sam agreed to finance the entire trip. Stella was the big star back in Birmingham, and Sam did everything she told him to do. Daphne didn't quite understand the relationship between Sam and Stella. She heard that years ago they were lovers but it hadn't work out, and she also heard that Stella had blackmailed Sam for some unknown reason and he was working off his debt to her. What Daphne did know for sure was that she was at the bottom of the pecking order in this small ménage, having to be complacent with every decision, even waiting for the next meal to be provided during the trip. The only time the group would eat was when Stella was hungry. Fortunately, Stella was famished most of the time, as all of her two hundred twenty-five pounds craved carbs, bacon, cheeses, and most anything that didn't include lettuce.

Daphne yawned, admiring the small trophy sitting in front of her, her prize, along with fifty dollars, for finishing third in the drag talent contest. It was her first trophy for anything. Winning for Daphne was never in question, nor was it a quest, because she never won anything and never expected to. But with only four entries in the contest, Daphne was proud to have not finished in last place with no trophy at all. However, when the contest was over, she felt so sorry for the weeping last place loser that she almost gave the local queen from Daytona her trophy. That's just how Daphne was. But Stella interfered with the transaction telling Daphne to "hold on to that piece of cheap gold plated shit, because when you get home, no one's gonna believe you were even here if you don't have evidence that says you were." Then she turned to the last place contestant, a crossed-eyed drunk who had too many shots of tequila during the night and thought she was Whitney Houston reincarnated, and told her if she took the trophy from Daphne she'd rip her a new asshole. She snapped her fingers and told the poor dear that it looked like somebody had already beat her to it, and then stuck it on her neck and called it a face.

Stella turned and added, "Girl, you are nothing but ugly! Is that a fart I smell coming out of your mouth? Come on, Daphne, we need to get away from here before we suffocate from all that methane oozing out of her pores." Of course, Daphne followed Stella out of the dressing room, embarrassed, but still obedient to her mentor.

The fifty dollars Daphne won for placing third wasn't as much or as impressive as the five-hundred dollars Stella received for winning first place with her two talent numbers. Stella had a way of wowing the crowd at any show, and this contest was no different. She had the audience in her hands the first time she walked on stage during the parade of contestants wearing a yellow costume consisting of tights and a rhinestone vest loaded with strobe lights on the front and back, with compact speakers on the shoulders, and a huge yellow feather collar that reached higher than most headdresses. When she hit the center of the stage and turned on the battery pack, the lights came on and then sirens blared. And if that wasn't enough, the old rock song, "Wipe Out", filled the stage as she broke into a short shimmy routine. Some people have said she was a cross between Big Bird and the Roadrunner when she wore that outfit. Stella made all her outfits, and working during the week at Radio Shack with her employee discount gave her so much access to the electronic gimmicks that she used in her acts. Though Stella was an old school drag, no other entertainer could compete with her.

But Stella's talent numbers for the evening were no less spectacular. The first was a rendition of "I Will Survive" as she brilliantly portrayed a kidney transplant patient in ICU, and of course, Stella always added flair to her acts. She would perform the operation on herself, pulling a donor kidney out of a cooler full of ice as she broke into the first lines of the song vowing that she could no longer live without the organ by her side. Stella had a way of taking a comedy concept that would normally be considered slightly entertaining or even offensive or in bad taste, and turn it around and deliver it in a dramatic fashion, totally serious, and get away with it. But it was her rendition of "God Bless America", that stole the show and secured the crown as she walked out on the stage with crutches portraying a battle-worn female soldier, her uniform torn by shrapnel, her right leg missing. And to top it off, she broke into "Boogie Woogie Bugle Boy of Company B", the whole time working the crowd into a frenzy with her energetic version of a combination of the Jitterbug and Quick Step, all on one leg.

Most people in attendance assumed Stella had her leg bent up behind her, her ankle taped up to her thigh, but Stella only had one leg. Stella was twelve when a group of middle-school bullies started to make fun of her during baton practice. Not being one to back down, not even at an early age, she returned the taunts until the preteens began to chase her around the football field. Stella was fast, but in this case, too fast. Unable to stop her momentum as she left the confines of the school grounds, she darted into the street, and was hit by a car. A blue Chevy Camaro, one witness said. It was a hit and run. She lay motionless in the street, her body mangled, the baton slightly bent, but still clutched in her left hand. An ambulance arrived and whisked her away. She would survive after weeks of recovery, and she was able to go back to school, her right leg replaced with a prosthesis. Stella's middle school dream of becoming a high school baton twirler in the marching band had come to an end. It was on that day, as Stella would testify, she decided to become a drag queen, but not just any guy wearing a dress in the weekend shows. Stella would become the drag avenger out to conquer any evil or hostility that would threaten the peaceful world of the domestic gay man. In other words, Stella was out to beat up any bully that got in her way. But in essence, Stella had become a bully in her own right, though the connotation took on a different meaning when it pertained to a fat man wearing a dress.

Daphne, like most people, was intimidated by Stella, yet she revered the way her mentor performed and even admired her outlook on life. By contrast, during the contest, Daphne walked out in the parade of contestants wearing a White Castle uniform because she thought it looked original and Daphne just happened to like White Castle sliders. Of course, the audience didn't get it, and her applause was light. And for both her talents, she performed two different Britney Spears medleys, quite simply because Daphne thought of herself as a dancer. Unfortunately, Daphne's impersonation of Britney was nothing more than a bad six-foot tall illusion of the pop star. Falling down at least three times during each act didn't help her score, but Daphne was of the mindset that regardless of her performance, with the help of her beautiful silver pumps and skimpy costume she would receive style points to make up for her slips that landed her on the floor. Each time she ended up on her ass in front of the confused audience, she just rolled over and spread her legs, pretending to be sexy. But she reasoned she probably lost a point or two when her left nut popped out a few times, exposing a bit of her chicken skin to the front row. From her perspective, her talent acts were no different from the real Ms. Spear's performances, except Britney had no scrotum.

Daphne was a bit demure, never overwhelmed with excitement, and in many ways, Stella's opposite. Perhaps that was the reason they got along so well. Daphne was the passive one, and Stella was the protector, the assertive one. In so many ways, she wanted to be like Stella, but she knew it would never happen. Stella was a doer, and Daphne was a dreamer. In fact, one of the reasons Daphne wanted to come to Daytona was to spend some time at the beach, to take a dip in the water early at sunrise, to walk out of the ocean with the sun at her back and onto the beach like Ursula Andress in the James Bond movie, *Dr. No.* Daphne had a yen to replicate certain cinematic moments, even if they weren't accurate. Stella had been so kind to recreate the famous white bikini that Ursula wore in the 1962 classic, and give it as a present to Daphne. That gesture was rare and only the people close to Stella would have the chance to appreciate her generosity.

Yes, the Ursula Andress ocean experience was the real reason Daphne agreed to come to Daytona. The pageant was just an afterthought, and Daphne knew she had been purposely invited so she could carry Stella's costumes in and out of the club, or at least the unimportant items. Only Sam was allowed to carry Stella's glamorous costumes and wigs. Apparently, he had earned that honor, or perhaps Stella only trusted him to take on that chore, but Daphne was okay with the situation. Back home in Birmingham, following Stella around was a real privilege for her protégés. She had mentored many drags, and the first requirement to be a "Stella's Girl" is to carry her things and do whatever she asks you to do.

The song on the jukebox changed. Some dejected woman was singing sadly about her divorce that became final that day. *Where do they come up with this stuff*, Daphne asked herself. Daphne heard the bar door open. She turned her head to see the bartender wave at a young man walking in the bar alone. She noticed by the way they greeted each other they must have known one another. Sam shook the man's hand and they engaged in conversation. Daphne took a sip of her drink, then leaned back, closing her eyes and resting her head on the wall behind her.

"Excuse me, can I join you?"

Daphne cautiously looked to her left, staring into the stranger's chest. He didn't look that low to the grown when he entered the bar, Daphne thought, but up close, he was really short. She paused, taking in the view by looking him up and down. Square jaw, black hair. He wasn't gorgeous, but he sure was cute. The cuddly kind of cute, she thought, and of course for Daphne, who was cursed with extreme height and an attraction to short men, she knew well the importance of judging a man for how tall he was laying down in bed as opposed to when he was standing up. For a moment, she got lost in the color of his eyes. They were a beautiful combination of Caribbean Ocean Blue and Bloody Mary Red.

"Hmmm?" she asked.

"Can I sit with you?"

"Sure," Daphne said, slowly coming out of her mental lapse. She moved closer to the inside of the booth allowing the young man to sit next to her. "Sorry," she said. "I was just thinking about some things."

"Like what?"

"Like, why do they play country music in places like this? It's such a downer."

"Yup, I agree."

"And like, why am I here when I should be out celebrating, partying where there are people, a lot of people?"

"Too bad, but I'm glad you're here."

"And like, what is your name?"

"Chuck. My real name is Charles, but people call me Chuck."

"You look like a Chuck. Let's see…Chuck, Chuck, bo buck, banana fana fo fuck. No offense, but that's the first thing that came to my mind."

"I guess you think that's the first time I've heard that one don't you?"

"Probably not. It just came out," she said as she took a sip from her glass.

"And what is your name?" he asked.

"Daphne," she replied in a soft voice.

"Daphne's a real nice name." He moved closer to her, the back of his hand touching the side of her smooth bare leg. Daphne normally didn't shave her legs, but Stella insisted if she were going to perform as Britney Spears and dance, she needed to do so without the restriction of dance tights.

She took another sip and said with a smile, "My real name is Buck." She put her hand on Chuck's thigh.

"Buck's not a very ladylike name," Chuck said, slurring his words.

"Who has to be ladylike?" Daphne asked in a playful way, realizing her lame attempt at humor wasn't being appreciated. "I'm kidding. My name's not Buck. Just call me Daphne." She glanced over to see Sam and the bartender watching the two nestled comfortably in the booth. The bartender gave a thumbs-up. Daphne took that gesture to mean that Chuck was okay.

Chuck leaned over, facing Daphne and asked, "So, why don't we blow this whole and go hang out together?"

"Honey, that's sweet, but I'm from out of town, and Sam over there is my ride, and unfortunately, I have to go where he goes, and whenever he decides to go."

"I got a place to go, and a ride outside as well."

"It's getting late, and I have to be at the beach at sunrise," she responded. She took another sip of her vodka and tonic. "You been drinking tonight?"

"Yeah, earlier." He moved his hand to the inside of Daphne's leg. "Been smokin' pot for the past few hours."

"Thought so. I could smell it."

"You want some?"

"Sorry, I don't do drugs. Just drag and alcohol. Hey, you keep touching me like that and something's gonna fall out of place." Chuck just grinned. Daphne could feel a sudden shift in her loosely compacted crotch. She had not anticipated being sexually aroused and suddenly became worried that some part of her package might pop out.

"Come on, come with me," Chuck pleaded, his lips pouting.

"You're so fucking high. I hope you're not driving."

"No, I'm not driving. I got my best friend and his friend outside in the car. We got the backseat all to ourselves, and then we'll go down the road to my place. Ten minutes at the most."

"And you'll get me back to the motel later, before sunrise?"

"Sure. I promise."

"Well…" she paused not wanting to seem in a hurry. "Okay." Daphne was about to give in to the fact that she would be in Florida and not have a tryst. She believed that ever since Connie Francis sang "Where the Boys Are", no one goes to Florida without searching for that special beach boy encounter, unless of course, you're bringing your family to Disney World. And even then, the thought of dumping the kids with the husband after the second day and driving to the closest shore just to get a glimpse of tanned masculine flesh keeps resurfacing as you wait endlessly in line for the next ride.

Daphne nudged Chuck to get up from the booth. "Let me check in with Sam, then we can go," she said. She gathered her purse and put on her silver pumps and stood up, standing next to Chuck, but looking down at him with a crooked grin on her face. She grabbed her trophy and drink, and wobbled over to the bar, her legs stiff from too much dancing in one night. Chuck followed closely behind.

She handed her trophy to Sam for safe keeping, and took the fifty dollar bill out of her purse and tucked it into Sam's pocket. Daphne had been around long enough to know a hustler when she met one, and Chuck was definitely hustler material which means anything of value should be put away. She assured Sam that Chuck would bring her back to the motel in a short time.

"I'll be there," Sam said. "And call me if you need me," he added reassuringly.

The bartender leaned over and whispered into Daphne's ear, "He's harmless. You'll be okay." He stepped back, then motioned for her to come near again. "He has a really big dick." Daphne arched her eyebrow, staring at the bartender.

"Is that all anyone thinks about?"

Sam jumped in and said, "Of course, we know that..." He paused, waiting for Daphne to put down her drink and set her pose, and together they completed the line from one of her favorite songs, "It ain't the meat, it's the motion," and then they both snapped their fingers in the air and laughed.

The bartender picked up his bar towel, grinned and sarcastically said, "Yeah, right."

"Come on Chuck, let's see what kind of chariot awaits us," Daphne commanded as she headed to the door. Chuck was right behind her, his hand holding the back of her dress as to not let her get away. Daphne stepped aside when she reached the door, and waited for Chuck to open it. He moved in front of her, his face even with her bosom, and looked straight up, his neck bent at a ninety degree angle.

"Daphne?" he said.

"Yeah, what?"

"When we get in the car, don't let them know you're not a woman."

"What?" she questioned.

"I said, when we..."

"I got that part." Her eyes darted from his face to the door, and then back. She suddenly had reservations about leaving with him. It was obvious that she was a drag, especially standing next to Chuck. Most drags who want to pass as real learn early on where to stand and who to stand next to when they're in public. Daphne never pretended to be a real woman, and was satisfied being considered a drag queen as she aspired to one day being an entertainer like her mentor, Stella.

"Sure. Whatever," she said as she nodded for Chuck to open the door. The timing was not right to train him in the ways of proper etiquette. *He's cheap trade*, she thought to herself as she sighed and then opened the door herself. She followed Chuck to a black Lexus parked a few feet down the street. She was surprised when he opened the back door, but shook her head as he crawled in first. Daphne followed Chuck into the backseat, and as soon as she shut the door, the car began to move.

"This is Daphne, and she's coming over to my place," Chuck announced, his face beaming with nervous pride. Daphne wanted to start a conversation, but realized her baritone voice would definitely be a dead giveaway to her not being a woman. The driver waved and said, "Hello, Daphne," as he made eye contact through the rearview mirror. Daphne was only twenty-two, but she was well aware her gaydar was on target about the driver. She also sensed the handsome man in his early forties behind the wheel had her figured out as well. But even so, she stayed mute. The burr cut young man sat facing forward in the passenger seat, never uttering a word. *Another hustler*, Daphne thought to herself, *but probably new to the game.*

The ride seemed short, just a few miles down from the beach. The car stopped in front of a stucco duplex with small palms in the front lining the sidewalk. The Daphne and Chuck got out, and the Lexus quickly sped off. The wind was blowing and Daphne could feel a few raindrops on her arms as they headed to the front door. She felt more and more apprehensive, not out of fear, but of not having control of the situation. Leaving the bar with a stranger was one thing, but walking into unchartered territory was another. As Chuck put his hand on the door to open it, he mumbled, "Don't forget, you're a woman."

"Now, how can I forget that?" Daphne playfully snapped back.

Chuck opened the door and led Daphne past the dimly lit living room, soft music playing, and then down a dark hall to the room on the left. As a precaution, Daphne scanned a bedroom lit only by the street lights shining through the window. No one was there. She walked in and sat on the bed as Chuck closed the door behind her.

"Why don't you get comfortable," he suggested.

"Here," she said as she turned aside, lifting her hair up over her shoulders. "Unzip my dress."

Chuck obliged her by pulling the zipper slowly down her back. She grabbed her falsies with her hands, stuffing them into her purse as though she were hiding them. The top of her dress fell down to her waist. She kicked off her shoes. She was ready for that Florida fun that Connie Francis had been advocating for so many years.

"Hey, I gotta go to the bathroom. I'll be back in a second," Chuck said as he backed away and moved toward the door."

"Hurry up. I'll be here waiting," Daphne said, her eyes batting flirtatiously as she fell back on the bed, her hair framing her face. The door closed and Daphne waited in anticipation for Chuck's return.

Fifteen minutes passed and no Chuck. In the meantime, Daphne heard cars pulling up to the duplex in the driveway, their lights illuminating the room through the window with each arrival. The volume of the music rose, and an array of voices seemed to fill the hallway outside the bedroom. Being the patient person, Daphne continued to wait for what seemed to be another fifteen minutes or so, becoming more and more annoyed with each passing minute. She heard rain hitting the window panes, and more and more car lights were coming and going. Apparently, a party was going on, and there was Daphne, flat on her back on a bed in a dark room in a stranger's house, in some faraway town, and she liked the situation less and less. All she needed was an image of Dracula peeking through the window to create that old Hollywood version of a vampire movie. That thought certainly killed the mood for fun.

"That's it," she said out loud as she sat up. She grabbed her purse and rummaged through it for her phone. She wanted to check the time, and perhaps give Sam a call to come to her rescue. She had a rude awakening when she realized her phone was dead. "Shit," she mumbled as she threw it back into her purse. She pulled her dress up and was attempting to zip it up, when the door opened and Chuck walked in.

"It's about time," Daphne said, glaring at him in the dark.

"Sorry, I got sidetracked." Daphne could smell the stench of pot on him. He climbed onto the bed and pulled his pants down to his ankles, and then fell on his back. Daphne sat next to him, gazing down at his semi-erect cock. She thought of touching it, but before she could even lift her hand, Chuck reached over and grabbed her by the back of the neck and shoved her head onto his crotch. "Suck my dick, you bitch!" he yelled.

Daphne's immediate concern was that he was flattening her eyelashes as he pushed her face into his pubes, and her second thought was that he had a lot of nerve, and for a moment she had a notion to bite off his cock.

"You suck your own goddamn dick," she quipped back as she stood up. She wanted to beat his ass right then and there, but Daphne was the passive type and stood there stewing instead. "I need to leave and I need to go right now," she demanded. Chuck lay motionless. "Chuck, I need to leave now, and I need you to zip up my dress." Daphne looked worried. She nudged his side and then tried to shake him.

"My god, I hope you haven't O.D.'d on me," she said to herself. "What have I gotten myself into?" She stepped back, collecting her thoughts, and then pleaded, "Chuck, please don't be dead."

There was silence, dead silence except for the noise in the other parts of the house and the sound of the storm outside. Suddenly, Chuck began to snore.

At this point, Daphne was far from being amused. "You son of a bitch. You cock suckin' son of a bitch!" She sat on the edge of the bed, trying to figure out what to do next, how to get to the motel and the beach by sunrise. Chuck kept snoring and the sound annoyed Daphne so much that she contemplated putting a pillow over his face and holding it there. She sat for what seemed an eternity when suddenly the door opened and the lights came on. It was Chuck's friend with the burr cut. Daphne looked up at him, squinting, as her eyes hurt from the bright lights. The guy was obviously disturbed, perhaps by a trick gone bad or the reality that his friend betrayed him.

"Chuck, get up," he ordered in a loud voice. He tried shaking Chuck, but to no avail. "Damn it, I said get the hell up!"

"He's passed out," Daphne said. The guy stood there, staring down at Daphne with rage in his face combined with a what-in-the-hell-are-you look in his eyes. Daphne suddenly realized she should have used a less masculine voice, especially under the circumstances.

"Would it be too much to ask you for a ride to my motel?" Daphne asked politely in a more feminine manner.

"Fuck no!" he said emphatically.

"Then perhaps you could help me zip up my..." and before Daphne could finish her sentence, the young stranger turned off the light and left the room, slamming the door behind him. There again she sat, troubled by feeling helpless, but more so about not being at the beach by sunrise.

Then another thought occurred to her, that she might have to walk down through Daytona in broad daylight, looking like last night's stranded hooker. The scenario gave her the urgency she needed to contort her body, enabling her to reach around and zip her dress. She took her falsies out of her purse and put them in place, spread her legs and readjusted her testicles, then lifted her hair with her fingertips, and took a deep sigh and opened the door to the hallway. If she was going to have to walk back to the motel, she would do it now. "Face your fears, Miss Daphne," she told herself.

She walked down the hall, holding her silver pumps in her hand, and went past the living room where two men sat on the couch watching television. She made no eye contact, hoping they wouldn't notice her. She went to open the door when a gust of wind and torrent rain slapped her in her face. She pulled the door shut and turned around, and remembering to act like a woman, she said, "Excuse me, can you tell me how to get to the Red Roof Inn?" Until now, she hadn't even thought about which direction to go.

The two men stared at her, probably trying to analyze what they were looking at. Daphne figured they got it that she was a drag, but on the other hand, she sensed they might think she was a hooker picked up by Chuck, and now he was done with her. Regardless, she could tell they were both high. The dark headed man raised his hand and pointed to the door, saying it was about five miles down the road.

Daphne took a deep breath and turned around facing the door, when the other fellow spoke up. "Can I give you a ride?" Daphne sighed, relieved that she wouldn't have to walk five miles in the rain in drag. It would be a horror movie in the making.

"That would be nice. Thanks," she said, a quick smile of relief coming over her face.

They hurried to his car, and within minutes, they neared the Red Roof Inn.

"I like your voice," the driver said as he slowed the car down to a crawl. "It's low and sexy."

"Thanks," Daphne replied back softly, her face hugging the window. She sensed he was about to make a move on her, and of course, she was in no mood, not to mention she was on a mission to make it back before sunrise. They entered the parking lot and he stopped the car.

"Why don't you ask me in?" he asked.

"I can't. There are other people in the room," Daphne replied. As she turned to quickly thank the man for the ride, he pulled her toward him, forcing his lips upon her mouth. Daphne grabbed the handle attempting to open the door. She pushed him away, again thanking him, and ran like hell in the rain to the oceanfront side of the motel, the surf a mere hundred feet away. She knocked on the door. No answer. The rain and wind pelted her, and she knocked harder. Apparently, Sam and Stella were inside, sound asleep, probably in a drunken stupor, and she was outside the door with no working phone and no key, and miserably wet. After about twenty minutes, the storm began to wane. Almost exhausted and defeated, she found a chair and pulled it next to the door, occasionally giving a knock in hopes that one of the two would hear her.

"Daphne, what the hell are you doing out here?" Stella was walking up to the door, still wearing her evening gown and tiara, the sound of her prosthesis slightly dragging on the concrete flooring.

"Please just let me in," Daphne pleaded. "And don't ask me any questions, just let me in." Stella was obviously drunk as she shuffled around in her black sequined purse to find her key. Once inside the room, Daphne looked at the clock and sighed with relief knowing she had about forty-five minutes before sunrise. Sam was not there, but he had the good sense to bring in the costumes and properly hang them up before going back out to spend the rest of the night with his boyfriend.

Daphne glanced at herself in the mirror. Her eye makeup was smudged and her eyelashes bent, her hair flat and wet from the rain. Simply put, she was a real mess. She pulled out a jar of Albolene from her makeup case on the counter, and began to remove the coat of last night's grease paint from her face.

Stella quietly helped Daphne by unzipping her dress. She limped across the room and stood at the open door and announced, "There's a hell of a party going on down on the other end. I just went by there and made an entrance. Straight guys, and they think I'm hot. I'm heading back down there."

"Stella, it's getting late, and well, you seem a little high right now, and…" Daphne looked up, her eyes barely open to keep the makeup remover out of her eyes. Stella was gone. "Crazy old woman," Daphne said out loud. A few moments later, she heard a commotion. She wiped her face with a towel and ran over to the door. Outside on the beach between the motel and the ocean, Stella was hollering at two men who seemed to be taunting her.

"You want some of this?" Stella screamed at the two. Daphne saw one of the men get physical with Stella, lightly hitting her with one hand as if he was trying to push her to the ground. Daphne had a flashback to a Nature Channel episode where two wolves singled out an old caribou cow, nipping at its hindquarters for hours until the poor dear was so weak it fell to the ground and the two carnivores began feasting on the carcass while it was still alive, no strength to fight back. Stella's voice was getting higher, and Daphne felt a sense of panic setting in with her mentor.

"Come on you cocksuckers, I'll show you who's more man than you are!" Stella yelled. One of the men lunged at her as she tried to kick him. He grabbed her leg, and she fell to the ground. The surprised bully found himself holding her prosthesis in his hands. Stella was helpless and the wolves approached. Daphne knew she had to do something, and quick.

"Give me my leg," Stella weakly demanded, sobbing in defeat. The old cow was down and the kill would come soon. She lifted her head and looked back at the motel to give one last call for help, when a blaring siren sound filled the air, and rays of strobe lights pierced through the early morning darkness. There stood Daphne wearing the Big Bird vest, her Ursula Andress white bikini, and she had a four-inch silver pump in each of her hands, her arms outstretched as she posed in the doorway. When "Wipe Out" began to play at full volume, Daphne's adrenaline and killer instinct kicked in like that of a mother bear protecting her cub, and she screamed like an attacking Apache as she ran to the beach, coming to Stella's rescue. Out of fear of the unknown, the two perpetrators ran like hell, one still holding onto Stella's fake leg. Daphne pursued the men down the beach until she overcame them, and after threatening the scared lugs with being beaten to death with her silver pumps, she retrieved the prosthesis and returned to find Stella alone sitting cowered on the beach.

"Stella, are you okay?" Daphne asked.

"You're wearing my costume," Stella responded, looking up like a wounded animal.

"Yeah, well the idea came to me, and…"

"You didn't ask my permission to wear my costume," she added, sounding a bit angry.

Daphne stared at the beaten down, but once almighty Stella. She took a sigh, and said, "Fuck you, Stella," and she tossed the plastic leg right at Stella's lap. She undid the straps of the vest and dropped it to the ground, standing there in nothing but her white bikini, her wet blond wig, and a face with no makeup. The sun was about to peak over the horizon, the purple haze from the east casting muted hues on her flesh.

"Good bye, Stella. I have to go now," Daphne said as she gave Stella a brief forgiving smile and headed to the surf, first walking and then breaking into a quick run as if the ocean were calling her in. Stella watched in horror as Daphne made it further and further into sea. Within moments, Daphne was under water.

Stella was more than concerned for her friend, who she'd always considered a bit delicate and suicidal. "Somebody help!" she screamed, still sitting in the sand. "Somebody's drowning out here!" she yelled over and over. No one came to the rescue, probably because of the crazy commotion a few minutes earlier, but a number of early morning joggers gathered around, curious about the creature in front of them who appeared to look like a beached whale in full Liz Taylor drag. As they circled Stella, phrases like "what the hell is that?" to "that poor dear thing" could be heard from the sparse group that did gather, when suddenly a woman said, "Look, over there!"

And just like in *Dr. No*, fifty years earlier, Daphne, reincarnated as a young movie sex goddess, rose out of the water, the sunlight at her back, in what seemed like slow motion. The small crowd clapped as the sultry silhouette moved forward, and Stella, just happy that Daphne was alive, reached into her bra and pulled out her phone to take pictures of her prized protégé coming out of the water.

"She's beautiful," one woman said in admiration.

"It's a man," another said. As Daphne approached Stella, the voyeurs dispersed, leaving the two of them alone. Daphne sat in front of Stella, the saltwater beading and running down her skin. They gazed at each other for a moment.

"Daphne, I'm so proud of you," Stella said, drunken tears of joy in her eyes.

"And why?" Daphne asked.

"I've never seen you more beautiful than now, but more importantly, I'm proud of you because, you see…" She paused, wiping her runny nose with her hand, leaving sand remnants on her upper lip. "Tonight, honey, you became a man. I know you don't want to hear that, but it's true. You stood up to those guys. You stood up to me. You saved my life and my leg. I will owe you forever. Here…" Stella took off her tiara and placed in on Daphne's head. "You deserve this more than I do."

Daphne blushed with pride, finally feeling the respect that she had always wanted from Stella. "Thank you, Stella," was all she could muster.

"Is that a nut I see hanging out there?" Stella said, pointing to Daphne's left testicle peaking out of the bikini bottom.

"Sorry," Daphne embarrassingly replied as she tucked it back. "I've had a problem with that all night long." The two laughed.

As Daphne helped Stella attach her leg, Sam appeared just as he always did, conveniently when all the drama was over. He helped walk Stella to their motel room and put her to bed.

The ride back to Birmingham that afternoon following a few hours of sleep was a quiet one, as no one really wanted to talk about what had happened the night before. Each of them would have a story to tell, to later embellish after a few drinks. But the dynamics between the three would be changed forever. Sam as usual, drove the sedan, while Stella, wearing a ball cap on her head, a red scarf around her neck and shades to conceal her swollen eyes, sat crunched up in the passenger side, shifting her weight around trying to find some semblance of comfort. Meanwhile, Daphne lay sprawled out in the back seat asleep, surrounded by feather boas and pillows, a tiara on her head, a trophy in one hand, and her silver pumps in the other.

STAINED GLASS
KARIS WALSH

Rory shut the door and slid the heavy bolt into place. She dropped her mail and grocery bags onto the kitchen table—sighing with relief as if she had just shed 100 pounds—and sank into a chair. She pulled a thick envelope out from under the stack of junk mail and bills, her fingers tapping a rhythmic beat against its smooth surface. A packet from Anne. A new story for their series of graphic novels that Rory would soon bring to life with sketches and ink. The words in the envelope were worth the struggle of going outside, but Rory didn't feel the slightest urge to open it yet. She would wait until her stilted breathing returned to normal, until her fidgeting eased, until she felt completely safe again in her home.

This day had been a particularly bad one. On the way into the market, she had been jostled by a woman who was chasing after her child. The woman apologized, but the damage had been done. Rory hadn't even started to shop, and already her skin was crawling and her startle reflex was on overdrive. She had stumbled through the store, wincing at the bright fluorescent lights and loud intercom, grabbing familiar labels of soup and milk and peanut butter. She had stood in front of the bread display for over 10 minutes trying to sort through the variety of choices since the store was sold out of her usual brand. She had finally just closed her eyes and grabbed a loaf off the shelf. She had no idea what she had bought. Then a few agonizing minutes making small talk with the checker who wore too much of a gardenia-scented perfume before she was able to maneuver past the other customers and out the sliding door.

Outside was better than the chaotic market. Natural lights, no need to sidle past people in the confined aisles, no protruding displays to trip her up. But outside still wasn't as safe as home. Rory had walked fast, her eyes on the pavement as it sped under her feet, ignoring the grating sounds of traffic on the street. She had finally pushed through the heavy door into the post office—relieved that no one was trying to leave at the same time so she'd have to decide how to move in order to avoid a collision. She had found her box in the sea of similar boxes. Fumbled to insert the tiny key and open the door. Pulled out a stack of mail. *Anne.* Rory sat at the kitchen table and sighed, echoing the sigh she had made in the post office when she had recognized Anne's handwriting, her familiar style of envelope. The trip out of her apartment had been worth it just for this, and Anne's letter was more vital to Rory than the food she had gone out to buy.

Rory braced her hands on the table and pushed herself into a standing position. She shoved the grocery bags into the near-empty fridge—not bothering to sort the items by what needed to be refrigerated and what did not—and she tapped the mail into a tidy pile and set it precisely in the corner of the table. She took Anne's envelope with her into the living room.

Narrow white boxes lined the walls, each neatly labeled and stacked. Rory selected one of the cardboard boxes and sat down in the center of an oval rug in the middle of the living room. She put the envelope next to her, the edge just grazing her thigh as she sat cross-legged on the floor. She would open it when her mind was clear enough to fully savor the contents. She took the lid off the box and carefully pulled the comic books out by the handful, surrounding herself with small stacks.

She knew what she'd find inside Anne's envelope. She didn't know the exact words of the story yet, of course, but she could picture the pages and pages—always handwritten, never typed—of Kristall's next adventure in the *Stained Glass* series. Rory loved the sway of Anne's cursive. The way some letters were hastily strung together as if Anne's ideas were coming too fast for her to legibly capture them on paper. And the way some sentences were marred by scratched out phrases and tiny inserted comments, as if Anne had to force a thought to be made manifest on the page. Rory started to count through her stacks of the first DC series of *Wonder Woman* comics. *One, two, three...* Every time she made a stack of 10, she gently replaced it in the box.

Sometimes Rory would copy Anne's text, unmindful of what she was writing as she mimicked the curve of the letters and imagined the movements of Anne's hand as she wrote. But not tonight. *98, 99, 100*...Rory felt a slight easing of tension with each block of 10 comics. Tonight she would start penciling the first panels of Anne's story. She'd draw Kristall, gathering strength from the familiar shape of her hero's body, finding courage as she outlined Kristall's ventures into the dark world of crime and evil.

Rory finished the first box in the series and replaced it before settling on the rug with the second box. She would finish counting, experience the release of completing a task, let order replace the chaos in her mind. And then she would be able to disappear, with Anne's help, into a better life.

"I need to see you. Please come meet me. I'll be at the Engine-house at nine."

Kristall dropped the note onto the floor of the abandoned church she called home. Then she dropped to her knees in front of the altar. She wasn't praying—she had long ago given up the right to pray. Instead she let the cold stone floor bite into her knees, let the glow of streetlights streaming through stained glass bathe her face and body in the red of flames. Reminding her of the past that had destroyed her hope, her future. Reminding her of the night she had stood outside her family's house as it burned—watching without helping.

Now Sage wanted her, wanted to talk, wanted Kristall to join her for a drink in a bar as if she had the right to be Sage's friend. But, no. Kristall could admire Sage, fumble through a conversation at the office where they spent their days. Love her. But at night? Kristall had obligations. Sins to atone. A calling that kept her in the shadows or in the weakened glimmer of light through shattered glass. Sage—beautiful and innocent Sage—would sit alone in the bar. Kristall would never join her there.

❖

Anne glanced over her shoulder again, searching for a familiar shape or face. Someone who might recognize her and share her whereabouts without realizing what damage the information would do. Nothing. A street filled with people who had no idea—no need to care—who she was or where she was going. The peace of invisibility overwhelmed her, but it didn't last—it never did—beyond the few footsteps until she was compelled to look behind her again.

She walked into the post office—the one as far from her home as she dared go—and got in line behind a man with several poorly wrapped packages. Her heart raced and her breathing grew so shallow she worried she might faint, but years of practice had taught her how to hide every tremble of fear. She didn't fidget, didn't move beyond the occasional step required to keep her place in line. Her gaze remained chest-level—not downcast enough to invite contempt, not direct enough to challenge.

Finally it was her turn to step up to the counter and pay—in cash—for the postage on the first installment of Kristall's latest adventure. She stared at Rory's address on the envelope while the clerk weighed and stamped it. Two women, two post office boxes, two cities only 50 miles apart. Such a tenuous connection to another person, but Anne treasured even the slim contact with Rory. She left the counter, scanning the people behind her in line out of habit, and hurried to check her box. She didn't expect any communication from Rory, but she always hoped. Theirs was a one-way conversation. Anne sent Rory her words, and Rory set them to the music of her drawings before mailing the completed novel to their publisher. The flow never reversed. Anne knew she should be relieved since a letter from Rory would be too precious to destroy, and much too dangerous to keep. But still, she hoped.

Her heartbeat quickened when she saw the slim white envelope in her box. Not a note from Rory, but a royalty check from her publisher. Anne's fingers trembled as she slid them under the flap of the envelope. She needed the money—money meant freedom—but now she faced the daunting addition to her trip. A walk to the bank, another wait in a long line, a grueling few moments with the teller before she had her cash in hand. *No, thank you, I don't want to open an account. Yes, I understand there's a fee for cashing the check. Please, please, just give me the money and let me go.* Anne paused in the empty post office vestibule before she took a deep breath and pushed open the door.

❖

In the space of an exhale, Rory was wide awake and sitting upright in bed. The feeling of someone hovering over her while she slept was tangible and slow to fade. She fumbled for the switch on her bedside lamp and turned it on. She had flung her pillow on the floor as she had struggled against the memory, struggled to break free from the nightmare.

She curled into herself, hugging her knees into her chest and using the pressure of them to force air in and out of her lungs. The light didn't help chase away the dark presence in the room. She never saw *his* face in the dream—but was it really a dream if it felt so real?—she only saw the bearded face of a wizard from the book she had been reading that first night. When she had been alone in her room. Thinking he was only there to yell at her for keeping the light on so late.

He had always left the light on, and Rory had learned to crave the darkness. In the shadows, she could pretend to be invisible and pretend to be strong. Her mother had tried to use a nightlight to chase away her daughter's nightmares, and she had never understood why Rory screamed herself hoarse whenever it was turned on.

But the light could help her now. Rory slowly released her legs, relieved to feel her breathing continue to flow. She grabbed her sketch pad off the bedside table and opened it to the panel she had been penciling before she had turned out the light. Kristall, bereft because she could never love Sage the way she wanted, was dressing for the night. Stripping off the suit she wore at work and stepping into the black outfit that would help her blend into the shadows. Pushing the wooden altar aside to reveal the hiding place for her amulet.

Rory carefully sketched the details of Kristall's amulet, the pain on Kristall's face as she placed the chain around her neck and the resolution that replaced her pain as Kristall slipped out of the abandoned church and into the dark night. Rory had been drawing Kristall since she was a child, but it wasn't until she was 28 that she had finally shown the sketches to her friend Mike. She had spent years hanging out in the relative safety of his comic book store using it as a way station, a transition point, between the ordeal of work and the sanctuary of home, before she had dared to ask his opinion of her pictures. He had been impressed, had encouraged her to turn the rough drawings into a novel, but she had only been able to create the shape of her hero. She needed someone else's words to create the shape of the story. So she had placed an ad in her favorite collector's magazine. And she had found Anne.

Rory had the story concept clear in her mind. Kristall found the amulet and, unaware of its power, used it to destroy her family as her anger was transformed into flames. She ran away from the inferno, trying to run away from her guilt, and took refuge in the old, rubble-filled brick church with its fragmented glass window. There, Kristall had learned to control the amulet's energy and use it for good. Always seeking atonement, always hiding her past. Loving the beautiful Sage, but never able to truly join with her in the light of day. Rory had hesitantly shared these details with Anne—details that felt as intensely personal as any story Rory could have told about her own childhood. And Anne had understood. Anne had sent the words that perfectly captured Kristall's anguish and courage. Written in her flowing script—sometimes smooth, sometimes marred by ink blots and scratched-out words.

She shouldn't have come, but she couldn't resist. Kristall hid in the alley across the street from the Enginehouse, staring at the window that framed Sage. She sat alone, cradling a beer in her steady hands. Eyes downcast, body so still she might have been carved in wax. Blond hair falling over one shoulder and filtering the light from the bar. How Kristall longed to run her fingers through Sage's hair, watch it shine with the light of the sun—not the glow of flames that had permanently transformed Kristall's own hair. How she longed to touch Sage's skin, feel Sage's heartbeat under her fingertips, under her lips, under her tongue.

Lost in her daydreams, her constant aching for Sage, Kristall failed to notice someone else who had eyes only for Sage until he stepped away from the bar and into the frame of the window. Until he stood next to Sage and Kristall finally focused on his scarred face. Until he grabbed Sage and flung himself against the glass in one smooth motion—shattering the window and running into the shadows with Sage screaming in his arms.

The Redeemer.

Anne hurried through her dinner preparations. Chicken pot pie baking in the oven, plates and silverware neatly arranged on TV trays, beer chilling in the fridge. She checked each step off on her mental list as she rushed to make up for her extra trip to the bank that morning.

Her tasks were further delayed by her constant need to open the closet and reach for her coat. Run her fingers along the satin lining until she felt the small tear. Briefly touch the comforting stack of bills. Tomorrow, when she worked in the garden, she would carefully bundle the money in a saved sheet of plastic wrap and bury it under the bird bath. She wanted to unearth all of her cash and count it—reveling in the increasing numbers and the feel of worn paper. But she couldn't risk the time, the mess, the possibility of being caught. Instead, she relied on the running total in her mind.

Almost enough. Almost.

The sound of the front door opening made her jump even though he was precisely on time. She smoothed her hands over her hair and down the front of her blouse, tidying up even though she was already tidy. She wished she could have one of the beers out of the fridge, just to ease her trembling nerves. Or have a whole case of them, just to numb her beyond any sensation.

"How was your day?" she asked politely as he opened the closet door and took out a hanger.

"Fine," he said. He spoke of his workday, told a story about a coworker, but she couldn't decipher his words through her fear. She felt a tingle in her palms and along the nape of her neck. Surely the bulge of money would be noticeable, as glaringly obvious as the light from a neon sign spilling out of the closet. But he hung up his coat and shut the door, and she willed her tense muscles to relax.

"What did you do today?" he asked.

"I went to the grocery store," she said. "The receipt's on the counter."

He walked into the kitchen and picked up the receipt, verifying—she knew—what she had bought and when she had checked out. He counted the change she had put next to the receipt.

"I tried to call at two," he said with no emotion in his voice. "But you weren't home yet."

She had gone through the check-out line at 1:45 p.m. before her 20-minute walk home. "The store was crowded," she said. She struggled to keep her voice as free from inflection as his. "And I had to wait for the woman at the meat counter to cut the right-sized roast."

"Ah, of course."

He walked over to where she stood, near the refrigerator. Everything seemed to freeze as he got closer. Her breath, her movements, her mind. Time was measured only by the beat of her heart. *One…two…three…*He reached past her, so close she could feel the brush of air from his movement, and opened the refrigerator door. He took out a beer and moved away and she felt her body explode into relief. He looked at her with an almost imperceptible lift of his eyebrows, a hint of a smile, before he went into the living room.

She was running out of time.

❖

Kristall raced down the street. Sage's screams had been silenced, and the Redeemer had vanished. Still, she ran. Seeking. Desperate. Her breath burning in her lungs.

Into alleys, through abandoned buildings, Kristall searched for Sage in the darkest corners of the city. Finally she looked toward the river and saw the black plume of smoke barely visible against the navy blue night sky. One of the old warehouses along the riverbank. She knew the Redeemer had set the purifying fire for her. Sage was the bait that would lure her there. Kristall ran toward the blaze without hesitating.

She didn't know the Redeemer's real name, only the false title he had given himself. But she knew the pain he caused, the harm he inflicted. While she fought to bring peace to her city, to bring evildoers to justice, he lived only to punish the people for their sins. He judged and found them guilty, offering no leniency.

He was her enemy, her nemesis, and he had taken her one true love.

Rory finished penciling the last panel, a view of Kristall's back as she ran toward the river and toward the rising column of smoke. She would have to go back to the post office tomorrow, back outside even though it wasn't a shopping day. Anne had only sent the first half of the story, and the second half usually arrived two or three days later.

Anne occasionally sent the novels in two installments, but not often. Rory found both options excruciating, each in its own way. To fight her way back to the post office a second time—or even a third, if she was mistaken when she estimated the arrival of Anne's second envelope—filled Rory with a sense of dread. It meant two, maybe three more nightmares. But the let-down of receiving the full story at once rivaled the week of poor sleep. If forced to choose, Rory would accept the nightmares as fair payment for the doubled pleasure of opening two packets and drawing out papers crammed with Anne's handwriting.

Normally Rory would move on to the inking process while she waited a suitably long interval before her next trip to the post office. She'd have the first half of the novel colored and completely finished before she came home with the second half and started the process again. But this time she anticipated a panel that hadn't been described yet by Anne. She started sketching Sage, lying unconscious in the riverfront warehouse while flames and smoke swirled around her.

Rory's pencil moved over Sage's waist, her cheekbones, her hair. Just as Rory felt a connection to Kristall—a sense of living more fully through her—she had always inextricably linked Anne and Sage in her mind. She traced the curve of Sage's body as if it were Anne's, like she traced the swooping letters of Anne's expressive cursive. Safer than the feel of skin on skin, but not as satisfying, Rory lived for the moments when she could draw Sage and bring Anne to life—bring her to life in the safety of Rory's living room. Like Kristall longing for Sage, Rory wanted to pull Anne through the paper wall they had between them and into her home. But, like Kristall, she knew she'd never be worthy of such a relationship. She felt some hope as she helped Kristall perform the heroic deeds that brought her closer to atonement and forgiveness, but the hope always flickered out at the end of the novel, when guilt and solitude once more flamed to life.

In Anne's last envelope, she had mentioned that she might attend the nearby Comic-Con. Would Rory be there? Wouldn't it be fun to finally meet? Anne's casual comment had been tempting. Rory could take a bus there…No, she couldn't. Spend an hour on such a dirty, seething boil of humanity? Cringing in horror as it erupted with departures and new arrivals at each stop? No, not even for the opportunity to meet Anne. To see the real curves and lines of her face and body.

Besides, Anne would be disappointed in the real Rory, just as Kristall knew Sage would be disgusted if she knew her real self, her past. Rory would stay home, safely sheltered, and continue to live with Anne through the fiction they created together.

Rory put aside her sketch of Sage in the burning building and got her ink kit out instead. She would complete the panels from the first half of the story instead of moving ahead to panels that hadn't been written yet.

❖

The following week, Anne hurried past the grocery store without even glancing at it. The one allowed stop on her one allowed day outside of the home. But she wouldn't be shopping today.

She crossed a side street, tempted to turn down it and visit the small comic book store one last time. She had first noticed the unobtrusive storefront almost two years ago, when she had circled around the grocery store in an attempt to pad the amount of time she was allowed to be out. A slow trip around the block added a precious 10 minutes to her trip, and if she followed the same routine every week, the extra time would be hers—unquestioned and unnoticed.

On the second week, she had stepped inside the world of comics and completely changed her life.

She hadn't realized the significance of her act on the first visit. She had simply been seeking a safe place to spend her time, safer than walking in full view on the streets. She had no doubt none of their friends—none of *his* friends—would ever come in the shop with its comics, graphic novels, and action figures. She had smiled vaguely in the direction of the clerk and had browsed through the shelves, ever mindful of the minutes ticking away. And then she had picked up a novel at random, drawn by the voluptuous woman on the cover, and she had been swept away into the world of fantasy.

Souls like her—hundreds of them—lost and scared and helpless. But for every one who cried out in the night, there was a hero who came to the rescue. Anne had consumed the stories, rushing through her walk to the store and her grocery shopping to give herself as many seconds as possible to read. Occasionally, when she could, she bought a comic or two even though she had to throw them away before she got home. Carrying them with her for even a short time seemed to give her strength.

And one day she had read a small want ad in a collector's magazine. Rory's ad. How easy it had been for Anne to scribble onto paper her fantasies and dreams. The stories she made up when she desperately needed to distract her mind and slip out of the world for a few hours. And the extra time she had managed to add to her shopping trip was put to good use as every few weeks she hurried to the post office or the bank instead of reading in the comic book store.

Today she wouldn't read comics in the dimly lit store. She wouldn't go to the bank because she had all of her cash, dug out of the earth and crammed in the lining of her coat. The weight of it gave her the strength she needed to make one final trip to the post office. No thick packet of handwriting this time. Just a small white envelope with a brief note inside.

She bought a stamp and mailed the letter before she hurried outside again. She turned to the right—away from home—and started to walk.

❖

Rory huddled in the weak beam of her bedside lamp as she hastily penciled in the final panels of the novel. She gasped for air along with Kristall as together they broke into the burning warehouse and struggled through the thick smoke. Rory felt panic seize control of her breathing and heartbeat as the Redeemer grabbed her from behind and struggled to bind her wrists. To leave her helpless and bound as she suffered the same fate as her family had, so many years before. And she felt her own muscles—so weak in comparison—bunch and gather as she fought him off, broke free and faced her attacker with the full power of her amulet swirling between them.

The Redeemer got away, of course—he always did—but both Rory and Kristall were prepared to let him go. More than the need for revenge or justice, they had to find Sage. To find Anne. To save them before the building collapsed and they were lost forever.

By the time Rory finished the final panel, she was sticky with sweat. She felt grimy as if she herself had been battling through the smoke, trying desperately to see even though everything was clouded and distorted. But she also felt elated. She had found Sage…or Anne…She wasn't even certain how to tell them apart anymore, but she knew the feeling would pass. It always did in the days after she completed a novel. The exhaustion would ease; the stress of coming so close to losing the woman she loved would dissipate. But the strength and courage she borrowed from Kristall would fade as well, leaving her as alone as before. As far from redemption as ever.

Rory tapped her sketches into a neat pile and set them on the bedside table. She needed a shower, and she needed to buy groceries again. She would stop by the post office, not because she was expecting a new story from Anne, but because she might have a royalty check waiting.

Rory went into the bathroom and turned on the shower before stepping into the hot stream of water and gently rocked back and forth as the spray beat against her shoulders. She squeezed her fingers against her temples as the pressure behind them increased.

Yes, Kristall's influence was starting to ebb. Soon Rory would be herself again. Alone. With no amulet to give her strength.

❖

Kristall carried the unconscious Sage into the abandoned church. She gently laid her down near the altar where the dawn's rays streamed through the stained glass window and tinged Sage with shades of green and blue.

Kristall knelt next to her love and pulled the amulet over her head, returning it to its hiding place under the altar. Once the amulet was away from her skin, hidden from view, Kristall felt the relief and the weariness of her night wash over her. So tired, so very tired. She wanted to lie down next to Sage, breathe in the cleansing scent of her skin where it had been enhanced by the heat of the fire. She wanted to touch Sage's face, her shoulders, her stomach. To gently wake her with a kiss, and to let the passion flare to life between them.

But she wouldn't. Or couldn't? Kristall got to her feet and went to the back of the church, washing away the soot and grime from the fire with a towel and a basin of water. She changed out of her nighttime black and into the muted colors she wore during the day. She would carry Sage back home. Leave her where her family would find her and tend to her.

Because Kristall hadn't yet earned the right to love her.

Rory hurried home, more agitated than normal after a trip outside. She had made it through the sensory onslaught at the store, and had gotten to the post office without incident. And there she had found—among the bills and junk mail and the hoped-for royalty check—a letter from Anne.

A letter in a plain white envelope. Not a folder full of story notes, not another adventure for Kristall and Sage. A letter.

Rory went through the usual motions of her routine. Bags in the fridge, mail tidied and sorted by size. She went into the living room, prepared to choose a box of comics to count while she sat on the floor with Anne's letter next to her, the edge barely touching her thigh. But Rory felt Anne's pull more strongly than she had before. She couldn't wait for the chaos in her mind to settle. She had to open the letter now.

Rory slit open the envelope and pulled out a single sheet of paper. She dropped to her knees in the center of the rug in the middle of her living room floor. She read Anne's note before she let the paper drop to the floor.

I need to see you. Please come meet me. I'll be at Comic-Con on the ninth.

Runner up

SKY BLUE
'NATHAN BURGOINE

The woman they dredged from the bottom of the falls is my brother. It was an easy mistake to make, and Sky had no doubt worked carefully for the result. Trapped a few steps beyond where the reality of two dead bodies lay, I take a moment to acknowledge Sky's efforts. Fell—Pushed? Thrown?—into the rapids, so swollen with the spring runoff, Sky would have been drowned, twisted and pummelled on rocks. Still, when found, the first message the cops had put out had been that they'd found the body of an unidentified woman.

I can almost smile. She would have approved.

It was the second message—and the second body—that had brought me here. Too big a story, too large a name for it to be quiet. Not in today's world. Not in such a political city.

Not with my father.

"James?" Ryan takes my shoulder with one hand. "You shouldn't be here." His voice is pitched low enough that no one will hear him but me. Not over the water. I've come to Hog's Back so many times in my life. As a kid I'd lived near here with Sky. Even this far down from the dam, the water is roaring, and I shiver. Has it ever looked so angry?

"James?" This time his voice is a bit louder. His fingers tighten on my shoulder. "Come on."

I'm struck again by how beautiful his eyes are. They're gray—no trace of blue to them at all, which I can't help but find amusing. They're almost pretty rather than handsome, which makes them all the more striking since the rest of him is so masculine and rough. A dull blue-green ache of a colour is leaking from his grip, but I can't decide what it means—there's a tangle of pity, and sadness, some duty and nostalgia. Maybe a little bit of compassion. It's all possible—they're all somewhere near that awful shade of washed out blue.

Just like Sky's lips.

"Okay." I nod, and the world tips a little sideways. Ryan saves me from a real stumble, and leads me away from the two bodies under the tarps and the awkward dance of men with stretchers moving over the trampled slush. I don't need to see any more of the bodies—and I don't want to know what else I might see.

I make it a few steps before I retch into the snow.

My father had forbidden alcohol in our home since he'd found Jesus. He'd filled his empty hands with his bible and cigarettes instead. The house near Hog's Back wasn't large, and always smelled of cigarette smoke and old newspapers. It was one of the nicest houses on the street and had been owned by my grandfather, a man I'd never met, who didn't love Jesus and drank. Our mother was a native woman who'd been born-again like my father had, but that hadn't saved her from my father's temper. Sky's birth when I was four had called a halt to his anger for the duration of her pregnancy, and I remember her taking me by the hand and telling me that Jesus had found my father a new path, and had sent the baby inside her to keep him on it.

Even at four I'd been skeptical. By five I'd learned that nothing had really changed at all, and once the baby—my brother Warren—was born, things had returned to the way they'd always been: quiet and angry and dangerous inside the house, quiet and polite in public.

My mother didn't leave him. There were times when his temper and anger would almost disappear, and it gave her a kind of sick hope—something I had started to see in the air like smoke. It was the same colour as the awful yellow nicotine stains that soaked their way into everything in our home over time.

I knew better than to ask either of them about the colours I could see, the ones behind my eyes that sometimes covered things or lit people from the inside. Sunday school teachers, my Catholic grade school teachers, the people at my father's annual company pic-nic, and even the other kids I sometimes played with—none of them felt safe to talk to.

I'd learned enough from my father's stories to know that different was wrong.

Then Sky—he was still Warren then—asked me about them one afternoon while I was looking after him and our parents were fighting upstairs. We were colouring—I was outlining stick figures in black marker, and Warren was gripping crayons in his slender fingers and colouring them in—and out of nowhere, he turned and looked at me, put down the red crayon, and sighed.

Upstairs, there was a soft thud. Warren flinched. I was more practiced at this game—the game of not noticing, not reacting, not saying anything.

"All done?" I asked him, picking up the crayon and handing it back. "His shirt's not coloured yet." I tapped the hollow black outline of the stick figure's body.

"It's a girl," Warren said. Then, his dark eyes looked up at the ceiling. "I don't like it when everything turns red." He put the crayon back down again. He never argued. Telling me he didn't like something was as close as Warren ever got to open rebellion.

"What do you mean?" I asked. I continued to ignore the red haze that was seeping through the air from upstairs. There was a second thud, and this time a soft cry—barely audible. I was ten years old. I knew what parents were supposed to sound like.

This wasn't it.

Warren frowned. "You see it, too. I know you do." He tilted his head, his incredibly dark hair sliding off his forehead. He brushed it behind one ear with his finger. He looked more like mom than I did. Our father would tell him to cut it soon. It was getting too long.

"Let's go to Hog's Back," I said. My voice came out uneven. Warren's gaze met mine, but he didn't argue. We put on our boots and left through the back door, careful not to let it squeak. We walked towards the river together in silence. I couldn't decide what it meant, that Warren could see the colours, too.

"It's just feelings," I said, after we'd gotten to the bridge that crossed over the man-made falls beneath the dam. Ducks swam around lazily in the water, which was low and vaguely green.

"What?" Warren asked. He wasn't quite tall enough to lean on the railing like I was.

"The colours," I said. "It's…it's just how people feel. It can't hurt you."

Warren frowned. "Yes it can."

❖

Ryan shows up at my door close to midnight. I open it before he knocks, catching him with his hand in the air, fist balled. It used to make him shake his head and smile in wonder when I answered the phone before it rang, or called people by their name before I'd been introduced.

He's not smiling now.

"I thought I'd check up on you," he says. He looks at the beer in my hand.

"I'm just having the one," I say. It's the truth. He regards me for a moment. Nods.

I step aside and he comes in.

"It'll hit the papers tomorrow," Ryan says. "Which means it probably hit the internet a few hours ago." He rubs his face with both hands. He hates the internet.

"I guess I should just Google it." I take a sip.

He smirks. "Got any more beer?"

I stick to one bottle, but he has three before we put aside the pretense and I pull him to the bedroom, desperate to feel the hair on his chest and to stop thinking for a while. We fuck the way only two former lovers can–angrily and tenderly. When the spit and sweat and spunk has dried, I stare at the ceiling, finally ready to hear it. Even in the dark, I can see the colours claiming the corners of the room.

"Go ahead," I say.

The room fills with Ryan's hesitant blue kindness. There's more than a trace of pity there, too, and I try not to hate him for it. I take his hand and squeeze, glad at least that if I have to hear this, he gets to be the one to tell me.

"It looks like your brother"

I don't correct him.

"Called your father late last night. They must have met near the dam. Coroner isn't one hundred percent sure, but it looks like there could be signs they fought. Physically, I mean. At some point, they went over the fence, and…well…"

I breathe in. Out. "Okay."

His hand squeezes back.

"What happens now?" I ask, but I don't listen to his answer. I know enough to guess. A media circus. My father was becoming a name. Local politics, sure, but local politics in a government town. Jesus mentioned with every other breath, and enough money from his business, support from his church, and votes in his riding to start his climb up.

Everybody loved the self-made man. But they'll love tearing him back down.

I close my eyes.

I was supposed to take care of Sky.

The only thing accidental about my mother's "accident" was her survival. High speed, no seatbelt, an impact she created with a twist of the steering wheel. A way out, I suppose, that she'd imagined would be quick and painless, unlike the life she'd been living.

The cloud of blacks and steel grays that had been leaking from her every time she moved had made me feel sick, and Warren could barely stand to be in the same room with her. When she'd told us she was going out for a drive, we'd both been relieved.

After—and our childhoods were divided by that moment, into before the "accident" and after—everything was different. It took months for my mother's bones to heal, for the surgeries and physiotherapy. My father prayed and dragged us with him to the church to pray as well. My mother became quiet and still, her colours almost never appearing, even to Warren, who could see them much better than I could.

"You help take care of your brother. But don't you worry, I was spared for a reason," she told me. Both of us pretended she believed it. I caught Warren crying almost every night, and tried to do as she asked. We tip-toed around the house, trying to avoid garnering any of our father's attention, only speaking to him when spoken to, or when he called on us to visit our mother in the hospital.

"I'll heal," my mother said. "I'll heal, and then the Lord will show us all the path."

But healing seemed to take forever, and no path was appearing for my mother.

Then her sister came.

Aunt Cheryl—who my father called a sinful pagan whore when my mother wasn't around—hadn't visited our house since Warren was born. I had only a vague memory of her. She didn't hide her native heritage like my mother did. No make-up, no perms and chic haircuts, no clothes that would look at home on a preacher's wife. Aunt Cheryl was like a force of nature.

"I'll look after the kids," she told my father, who had recoiled from her when he'd opened the door. "You have no idea what you're doing." Then, in the middle of the kitchen while my brother and I watched, she slapped him, hard.

The silence after that slap made me hold my breath.

"You'll never touch her again," she said. "I know enough. And I've got nothing to lose." Her anger pulsed like the last few moments of a sunset, and my father cringed away from her. Something had just changed, but I hadn't quite seen it happen. I didn't understand what power this woman could have over my father, and my stomach roiled with a slick feeling at the sight of him nodding and turning away from us, his cheek still red.

What was this woman? My aunt turned, nodded at us both, and said, "Pack up some clothes."

Warren fell in love with her on the spot.

"Can we stay here with Cheryl?" he'd ask me, after she had tucked us in and told us stories to help us go to sleep—stories we'd never heard before, with tricksters and cunning and a world that seemed more spirit than flesh. In my aunt's stories, the dead gave advice to the living, and nothing had to be the way it started. Her house was smaller than ours, but we'd both decided it was better. The colours here were almost always a mix of golds and oranges. When Cheryl glowed that way—like she did when she was telling stories to us—everything seemed possible. When she wasn't telling us stories, the blues that seemed to creep into every corner of the room were softer and as warm as a summer sky.

Love. She loved us.

"Maybe," I'd answer, because I didn't think we could, but I didn't want to be the one to tell him.

"I think she sees the colours," Warren had muttered, but he was almost asleep.

When our mother was finally released from the hospital, we had to go back. Warren was shaking, and threw up before breakfast. Cheryl knelt in front of him and hugged him.

"You're going to be fine," she said, and even though she was as bright as the sun to my other eyes, I knew neither of us believed her.

"I don't like my life. I want to make a new one," Warren said. He was crying. I was trying hard not to join him.

Cheryl took him by the shoulders, and waited for him to calm down. She just held him, watching his tears. Eventually, after he regained control and wasn't shaking so much, he smiled at her.

"It takes two lives to make a new one," she said, speaking slowly and clearly. "Your mom and dad made you yours. But what you do with it is up to you. Don't forget that." When she'd started speaking, the room had filled with a golden light so bright I'd had to look away. It made me nervous.

There were times I wondered if I should be afraid of my aunt.

"Do you see why you can't stay here?" she asked.

Warren just looked at her. His mouth opened. Slowly, he nodded.

"It's time to get your things," Cheryl said. When he left the room to obey, I managed to look at her.

There was a fist-sized darkness inside her that made me want to cry.

I leave Ryan still sleeping and dress quietly in the living room after picking up bits of clothing we shed along the way. I end up with his shirt, which is too big and smells of him and makes me remember too much when I pull it over my head. I'm just putting on my boots when he steps out of the bedroom.

"I'll drive," he says.

I close my eyes so I don't have to see the pity, the worry, or the hesitant love. Faded blues, pale greens. I will it all to go away.

"Thanks," I say.

We park behind Hog's Back, and walk in, heading for the glow of the portable police lights. Our breath is clouding in front of us, and the stars are out. There are still cops around, and now a small crowd has joined them. Reporters, I suppose, are mixed in with the gawkers. I pull my hood up around my head, and scan the path that leads back to the bridge and the dam. The water is still pounding through.

"Not up here," I say, willing myself to actually see the other way I can see the world. It's painful—the blur of colours is a riot behind my eyes.

Ryan touches my shoulder. "James…"

"It's further that way." I point.

He breathes. "Do you want me to go with you?"

Not the first time he's asked me that. But it's the first time I'm going to tell him the truth.

"Yes."

We walk.

❖

"I'm not right."

"Are you wrong?" I said.

My brother rolled his eyes and threw himself onto my bed. I put down my book. For all his drama—and turning 13 had dialed his drama *way* up—my brother was being serious. The pale green nervousness that was floating around him—and the ugly bruised purples welling from within—told me more than I wanted to know.

I decided to go first.

"I'm gay too," I said.

Warren burst into tears. Misery and fear and sadness bled out of him like liquid bruises—browns and pale greens and deep purples. I wrapped my arms around him, afraid our father would hear him. My father's dislike of Warren frightened me more than anything. That Warren was gay seemed to be the general consensus of anyone who'd met him for more than a minute. He was just so gentle and quiet, softer and delicate than a boy should be. I could hide—I did hide. But Warren…

I'd dreaded this, even as I'd hoped it wouldn't come.

"It's okay," I said. That made him cry more. I finally just held onto him until his tears died down. I had a sudden memory of my aunt holding him like this. She'd known better than to try and calm him down, and had just waited for him to get there on his own. That had been the year before she'd died of breast cancer, before our mother had come home with her cane and her quiet agony, before I'd realized the way I'd been feeling about the other guys at school wasn't like the way I was supposed to be feeling.

So I waited, holding my brother, and closing my eyes as the room filled too full of greens and purples.

Warren cried, then sniffled, then coughed a few times. Finally, he pulled back and wiped his eyes.

"I'm gay too," I said it again.

He just shook his head, miserable.

"I'm not gay," my brother said. "I'm a girl."

"I stayed as long as I could," I say. We've walked almost all the way up the path from where they found the bodies. Soon we'll hit the rise and then we'll be at the dam and bridge itself. "I tried to stick up for her."

Ryan's voice is even. "I know." He does know. I've told him more than I've ever told anyone. He knows how someone told my father about seeing me outside the wrong kind of bar. He knows how I was tossed to the street, how I almost didn't make it. He's seen the scars.

I'd been thrown out, but it still felt like I'd walked out. My father had forbidden my brother from seeing me, and our few covert meetings had been painful for both of us—me knowing he wasn't who he wanted to be, and him knowing I was doing things I didn't want to do.

Neither of us doing much more than surviving.

I clear my throat. "When our mother died, Sky told my father the truth. She was going to be herself. She moved out, got a place with friends…" I shake my head. "My father never wanted to hear from us again. Why would she have called him?"

Ryan doesn't answer.

I stop. My eyes are almost aching from the effort of looking, but this is the place. It's close to the edge, close enough to the main path–there's even a railing still.

"There," I say.

I can see Sky waiting, if I look just right. It's an effort, seeing these echoes. My eyes ache. The dress—long and white and too thin for the weather, but beautiful nonetheless. Her hair, always her pride and joy, long and loose over her shoulders. The omnipresent scarf—one of many that Sky had, each a different blue silk—tied around her throat.

She's beautiful.

Then she turns, and I know what it means a moment before the memory of this place replays itself for my eyes.

My father appears.

"Do you think so?" My brother let his ponytail free, and brushed his hair carefully with a thick brush. "I don't know. Yours was so pretty."

I watch him for a while from the hallway, unsure if I should interrupt. He seemed happy—bright yellows flickered from him with every sweep of the brush. He'd put a wide black belt, our mother's, around the red collared shirt that he was wearing. The shirt was our father's and he'd left it un-tucked.

It looked a little like a dress that way.

"Who are you talking to?"

Warren jumped. "I don't like it when you scare me," he said.

"Sorry," I said. I waited, but he didn't stop brushing his hair.

"So who were you talking to?" I asked.

He sighed. "Aunt Cheryl."

I bit my lip. "Don't let mom hear you say that." I caught a glimmer of something out of the corner of my eyes, and willfully refused to look at it. The dead sometimes seemed to echo for me. I didn't like seeing them.

He nodded. "I know." He looked up at me. His eyelashes were very long, and as much as he was trying hard not to let it show,

I could feel the femininity of him. My stomach clenched. I'd be sixteen soon. Surely we could make it that long. I could drop out, get a job…something.

I'd take care of him.

"What…what did she say?" I asked. I didn't really want to know.

Warren shook his head. "Doesn't matter. All her stories are just stories." He shrugged. "We'll get out of here, right?"

I didn't answer. Instead, I said "They'll be home soon." Some fundraiser or another had been keeping our parents busy for weeks now. Her cane and her story, coupled with his beliefs and his willingness to speak of the man he'd been—and the man he'd become thanks to Jesus—had propelled our father into local politics. He was planning on running for our riding in the next election.

Warren nodded again. He looked in the mirror for a long time, then pulled his hair back into a ponytail.

"What do you think of the name Sky?" he asked.

I thought of the way our aunt's house was full of that lovely blue.

"I like it."

"What do you see?" Ryan asks. I hold up my hand, and he falls silent. He's seen me do this before.

Hello, Sky says. *Thanks for coming.* She even smiles.

The gesture isn't reciprocated. *What do you want?* My father moves close to her, a little too close, towering over her and crossing his arms. Even this echo of him makes me feel uncertain. *What the hell is wrong with you? Look at you. You're wearing a dress.*

Sky's smile fades, but she stands her ground. I want to tell her to run. *I want your help*, she says.

He laughs. It's an unpleasant sound. For the first time, I notice that I cannot see the colours of either of them—this is what it's like to be everyone else. I can't see how they feel. Not that I need the colours to see the fury in this echo of my father. I shiver.

You're watching the past, I remind myself. My eyes are burning from the effort.

You're sick, he says. *If you really want help, you'll pray. You'll pray, and then you'll go to the hospital.*

That's what I meant. Sky's smile takes him aback this time. *Not the church, the hospital. I want to go to a hospital. I want surgery. I'd like you to help me with some of the money.*

Every word she speaks is polite and gentle. It takes him a moment to realize what she's asking him. The anger is immediate. His fists clench, and I almost forget–again–that it's too late. They are both dead. Nothing I say or do can change that.

No son of mine is going to have his dick cut off! My father's voice is a roar.

I shouldn't be your son, Sky says. She's still so calm. I don't understand. Surely she knew this wouldn't work–our father would never help either one of us. *And if you do this one thing for me, I'll go away. I won't tell a soul anything about you.* She pauses. Smiles. *Especially during the election.*

Ah. Now I understand. The urge to close my eyes is overwhelming, but I don't.

Never, my father's voice is iron. *Never. You think you can threaten me? Blackmail me? Who do you think you are?*

Sky looks at him. Really looks at him. *I'm your daughter. You and my mother, you made me. It takes two lives to make a new one.* Her smile is thin and tight. *You and me, we're going to make me a new one.*

I jerk. Ryan takes my hand.

"James?"

I shake my head, but he doesn't let go.

My father reaches for Sky, gripping her by the shoulders. She flinches, but the calm look never leaves her face. Fear is slick in my stomach.

*Listen to me, you little bitch…*My father says, and then stops, mouth still open. Too late, I think, he realizes what he just said. What he just admitted.

Sky's smile is triumphant. She shifts her stance, and her whole body agrees with him. Every motion she makes blends into a thing of beauty. She nods.

Yes, she says. *A bitch.* Then she reaches up and grabs his heavy coat and throws herself back at the railing.

"Sky!" I cry out. She doesn't react, of course. She and my father struggle a few moments more. It's over so quickly—one moment my father is trying to push her away and the next she is falling, and her hands never let go of his jacket. He tips after her.

I close my eyes. There is no splash. The echo is done. Ryan squeezes my hand. I'd forgotten how rough his fingers felt, and how great they feel.

"Okay," I say. "We can go."

❖

I was at home reading when I reached for my phone. When it finally rang, the display read Ryan Stoler. I shook my head and went back to the book. I didn't need another run through Ryan's list of reasons I couldn't open myself to being with him the way he wanted me to. It took a second longer for me to realize the screen had said it was his work number calling, and I looked back at the phone, frowning.

Ryan Stoler was many things. My ex-boyfriend, a little controlling, and a cop. If he was calling from work, I didn't want to answer it. Delaying bad news was probably on his list of my many failings, right after refusing to ask when I needed help.

I put the phone down, and waited for the ringing to stop. When it did, I looked up, and saw my Aunt Cheryl standing by the window of my small home. She was a figure in golds, as though she'd been woven from the sunlight itself. When she turned to look at me, I felt tears in my eyes.

"Aunt Cheryl?" I said.

She didn't reply. My aunt held up her hand, then raised two fingers. There was a smile on her face, but it wasn't entirely kind. Vengeful, perhaps. Righteous.

I picked up my phone and waited for it to ring again.

This time I answered it.

I turned my back on my aunt when I put on my coat and boots. I knew she'd be gone before I came back.

❖

"I can drive you home," Ryan says. "If you want."

I smile at him. I have never been so tired in my life. "I would. Thanks."

He nods. At the top of the rise, the bridge and dam come into view. The water is a dull roar. There is a bigger crowd now, and the sun is starting to rise. I can't equate everything happening in a single night, but the morning is here. These people are on their way to work, but have stopped just long enough to glance down at some death. I look up, angry at them, and I spot a flash of pale blue.

Ryan walks on ahead, not noticing that I've stopped.

The woman on the bridge is watching me. Her dress, long and white, is not warm enough for the cold spring day and it whips in the wind, pressing against the lean muscles of her thighs and the curves of her breasts. Her hair is black and free, and she smiles at me as she unties a pale blue scarf from around her neck.

Her throat is smooth, and as lovely as the rest of her.

The scarf trails from her fingers, and catches on the wind. I watch it fly, snatched up among the treetops on the other side of the water and then out of my line of sight. When I look back, she has already left the bridge, and is walking away.

"James?"

Two fingers. Two lives. My aunt's smile. *It takes two lives to make another.*

I look at Ryan. The blue that surrounds him is warm, and caring and—yes—there's some pity.

I decide not to care about that.

"Let's get breakfast," I say. His smile is hesitant, but he nods. "And then…" I pause. And then? My father is dead. And my sister… my sister *is*. My life?

What you do with it is up to you.

Ryan waits. "And then?"

"We'll figure something out." I clear my throat. "If you'd like." He smiles.

In the corner of my eye, I catch something golden.

Contributor Bios

Born and raised in Chicago, **N.S. Beranek** received a Bachelor of Arts degree in Technical Theater and Design from Southern Illinois University. From 1990 until 2009 she was the Assistant Propmaster for Stage One: The Louisville Children's Theatre. In 2006 she was admitted into the Faculty Mentor Program of the Green River Writers Novels-in-Progress Workshop, where she benefited from one-on-one discussions with four-time novelist Keith Snyder.

'Nathan Burgoine lives in Ottawa with his husband Daniel. His short fiction appears in *Fool for Love, I Do Two, Saints + Sinners 2011: New Fiction from the Festival*, Men of the Mean Streets, *Boys of Summer, Night Shadows*, and *Mortis Operandi*, among others. His first novel, *Light*, is forthcoming from Bold Strokes Books. You can find him online at http://redroom.com/member/nathan-burgoine.

George E. Jordan, art historian, was born in Kentucky, and lived in New Orleans for 20 years before moving to Connecticut in 1988. A free-lance writer and authority on Louisiana art, he wrote the art column for the *Times Picayune* in the 1970s. He has authored two books, and numerous articles for museum and art publications. Writing about gay life before the AIDS epidemic has been a parallel pursuit.

J.R. Greenwell resides in Louisville, Kentucky, and relies on his queer past for creative inspirations. His literary accomplishments include a number of full length plays, short stories, and his memoir, The Quest for Tiaras, available on his website. His acknowledgements include being a finalist and published in the anthologies *Saints + Sinners: New Fiction from the Festival* in 2011 and 2012.

SANDRA GAIL LAMBERT writes both fiction and memoir and lives in Gainesville. Sandra's work has been accepted into the journals *New Letters*, *The North American Review*, *Arts & Letters*, and *The Alaska Quarterly Review* as well as the anthologies *Something to Declare: Good Lesbian Travel Writing* and *First Person Queer*. She blogs about her writing life, with diversions, at http://www.sandragaillambert.com/.

JOE LANDRUM is a retired public library consultant. He recently began writing short stories set in his hometown of Natchitoches, LA. His work, "Elinor's Coup", was included in the anthology *Something in the Water: Twenty Louisiana Stories*, (Portals Press, 2011). Joe's ambition is to craft his stories into a short novel or into a collection of short stories.

ANNE LAUGHLIN is the author of four novels: *Sometimes Quickly, Veritas, The Collectors (under a pen name),* and *Runaway.* Her short fiction has appeared in a number of anthologies. *Veritas* won a Goldie award for lesbian mystery in 2010, and *The Collectors* was shortlisted for a Lammy Award in lesbian erotica in 2011, as well as winning a Goldie award and a Rainbow Readers award.

JEFF LINDEMANN is a graduate of Stephen F. Austin University located in the heart of East Texas, the setting for his short stories. He received his M.A. in English in 1976 and has been teaching composition and literature for the last thirty-four years at Houston Community College. After a long career of teaching stories, he has now—at last—started writing them!

JAMES RUSSELL writes, teaches, and blogs in New Jersey. His work appears in *Penduline Press*, *The Quotable*, and *Blipmagazine.net*. His debut novel *Jesse Rules* is about the fall from grace of a homo-repressed, grunge age Holden Caulfield. His debut short story collection, *Men in Strange Arrangements*, features Saints and Sinners finalists "Mountainview" and "Divine Hand", and other stories that wrestle with male issues.

VINCE SGAMBATI's short fiction appears or is forthcoming in *Nimrod International Journal of Prose and Poetry*, *North American Review*, *Gertrude Press*, and *Off The Rocks* (New Town Writers, Chicago). His creative nonfiction has appeared in the anthology *Queer and Catholic* (Routledge) and the *Journal of GLBT Family Studies*, and his essays regarding LGBT parenting have appeared online and in print, including *Lavender Magazine* where Vince was a regular columnist.

After twenty years at the Chicago Public Library's history department, JIM STEWART retired and started writing. Stewart authored the award winning *Folsom Street Blues: A Memoir of 1970s SoMa and Leatherfolk in Gay San Francisco*. His work is included in *Among the Leaves: Queer Male Poets on the Midwestern Experience*; Chicago NewTown Writers' *A Gay and Gray Anthology*; and other publications.

KARIS WALSH is the author of lesbian romances, including the novels *Harmony*, *Sea Glass Inn*, and *Improvisation* that have been published by Bold Strokes Books. Her paranormal short fiction can be found in the Cleis Press anthologies *Girls Who Bite* and *She-Shifters*, as well as *Women of the Dark Streets* from Bold Strokes Books. She can be found on Facebook and at www.kariswalsh.com<http://www.kariswalsh.com>.

ABOUT THE EDITORS

AMIE M. EVANS has published over 55 short stories and essays as well as one novella. She is a creative-nonfiction and literary erotica writer. Evans is the co-editor of four volumes of *Saints + Sinners: New Fiction from the Festival* with Paul J. Willis and the anthology *Queer and Catholic* with Trebor Healey. She also writes gay male erotica under a pen name. Evans is on the board of directors of Saints and Sinners LGBT Literary Festival. She recently enrolled in the Fashion Design Program at MassArt and has worked at Harvard University for 15 years. She is currently working on a memoir about food, religion and mothers as well as a satirical novel about saving lesbian sex.

PAUL J. WILLIS has over 18 years of experience in non-profit management. He earned a B.S. degree in Psychology and an M.S. degree in Communication. He started his administrative work in 1992 as the co-director for the Holos Foundation in Minneapolis. The Foundation operated an alternative high school program for at-risk youth. Willis has been the executive director for the Tennessee Williams/New Orleans Literary Festival since 2004. He is the founder of the Saints and Sinners Literary Festival (established in 2003), and has edited various anthologies including the award-winning *Love Bourbon Street* with his partner Greg Herren.

Saints and Sinners Literary Festival

The first Saints and Sinners Literary Festival took place in May of 2003. The event started as a new initiative designed as an innovative way to reach the community with information about HIV/AIDS. It was also formed to bring the LGBT community together to celebrate the literary arts. Literature has long nurtured hope and inspiration, and has provided an avenue of understanding. A steady stream of LGBT novels, short stories, poems, plays, and non-fiction works has served to awaken lesbians, gay men, bisexuals, and transgendered persons to the existence of others like them; to trace the outlines of a shared culture; and to bring the outside world into the emotional passages of LGBT life.

After the Stonewall Riots in New York City, gay literature finally came "out of the closet." In time, noted authors such as Dorothy Allison, Michael Cunningham, and Mark Doty (all past *Saints'* participants) were receiving mainstream award recognition for their works. But there are still few opportunities for media attention of gay-themed books, and decreasing publishing options. This Festival helps to ensure that written work from the LGBT community will continue to have an outlet, and that people will have access to books that will help dispel stereotypes, alleviate isolation, and provide resources for personal wellness.

The event has since evolved into a collaborative effort between the Tennessee Williams/New Orleans Literary Festival and the NO/AIDS Task Force. The Saints and Sinners Literary Festival works to achieve the following goals:

1. to create an environment for productive networking to ensure increased knowledge and dissemination of LGBT literature;

2. to provide an atmosphere for discussion, brainstorming, and the emergence of new ideas;

3. to recognize and honor writers, editors, and publishers who broke new ground and made it possible for LGBT books to reach an audience; and

4. to provide a forum for authors, editors, and publishers to talk about their work for the benefit of emerging writers, and for the enjoyment of readers of LGBT literature.

Saints and Sinners is an annual celebration that takes place in the heart of the French Quarter of New Orleans in the month of May. The Festival includes writing workshops, readings, panel discussions, literary walking tours, and a variety of special events. We also aim to inspire the written word through our short fiction contest. Each year we induct individuals to our Saints and Sinners Hall of Fame. The Hall of Fame is intended to recognize people for their dedication to LGBT literature. Selected members have shown their passion for our literary community through various avenues including writing, promotion, publishing, editing, teaching, bookselling, and volunteerism.

Past year's inductees into the Saints and Sinners Literary Hall of Fame include: Dorothy Allison, Ann Bannon, Lucy Jane Bledsoe, Maureen Brady, Patrick Califia, Bernard Cooper, Jameson Currier, Mark Doty, Jim Duggins, Otis Fennell, Michael Thomas Ford, Katherine V. Forrest, Nancy Garden, Jewelle Gomez, Jim Grimsley, Tara Hardy, Ellen Hart, Kenneth Holditch, G. Winston James, Michele Karlsberg, Joan Larkin, Lee Lynch, William J. Mann, Stephen McCauley, Val McDermid, Tim Miller, Michael Nava, Achy Obejas, Felice Picano, Radclyffe, J.M. Redmann, David Rosen, Steven Saylor, Carol Seajay, Kelly Smith, Cecilia Tan, Patricia Nell Warren, Jess Wells, and Paul J. Willis.

For more information about the Saints and Sinners Literary Festival including sponsorship opportunities and our Archangel Membership Program, visit: www.sasfest.org. Be sure to sign up for our e-newsletter for updates for future programs. We hope you will join other writers and bibliophiles for a weekend of literary revelry not to be missed!

"Saints & Sinners is hands down one of the best places to go to revive a writer's spirit. Imagine a gathering in which you can lean into conversations with some of the best writers and editors and agents in the country, all of them speaking frankly and passionately about the books, stories and people they love and hate and want most to record in some indelible way. Imagine a community that tells you truthfully what is happening with writing and publishing in the world you most want to reach. Imagine the flirting, the arguing, the teasing and praising and exchanging of not just vital information, but the whole spirit of queer arts and creating. Then imagine it all taking place on the sultry streets of New Orleans' French Quarter. That's Saints & Sinners—the best wellspring of inspiration and enthusiasm you are going to find. Go there."

—Dorothy Allison, National Book Award finalist
for *Bastard Out of Carolina*, and author
of the critically acclaimed novel *Cavedweller*.